Prelude

Müller was twelve years old when his life changed irrevocably; although he could not have known that at the time. He could not have realized how this would traumatize and scar him. Permanently. He remembered a tearful Aunt Isolde telling him about the air crash that had killed his parents in their private jet; but he could not have known at the time that this was not true. He remembered her telling him that with his father gone, he was now the Graf von Röhnen, and that he had inherited everything.

Aunt Isolde had herself not known the truth behind the crash, and Müller would not find out until decades later. Married to an Englishman at the time, his Aunt had cared for him, bringing him up as her own. His education had followed the path set down by his parents and the boy from Berlin had eventually become a student at Oxford.

Then he had chosen to go into the profession he had long decided upon as a boy. He had become a policeman. Freshly out of training, he had met the chain-smoking Pappenheim. The two could not have had more different backgrounds. Born on a farm, Pappenheim's family had little wealth; but the apparently rough farmboy had been impressed by Müller's almost deliberate attempts to play down his own heritage. He had also quickly realized that Müller tended to go his own way. It was something that had pleased Pappenheim's own rebellious soul.

They had progressed as a team, moving up through the ranks, an almost unseen friendship creeping up upon them. They grew to trust each other implicitly.

When someone, somewhere, had decreed that a new special unit would be formed and headquartered on the Friedrichstrasse in Berlin, they had been selected, with Müller – by now a *hauptkommissar* – being subordinate only to the man in overall charge: the political animal Kaltendorf, whom they had irreverently dubbed the Great White Shark. Pappenheim, now known for his formidable networking skills, had become Müller's deputy.

Life had seemed normal, with Müller completely oblivious of the existence of the Semper – until a supposed black man, apparently fleeing from three racists intending to do him some serious harm, had suddenly turned and shot them dead. Thus had begun a nightmare; but one that Müller had not realized had actually started on the day that Aunt Isolde had told him of the death of his parents.

With each contact with the Semper the true nature of the inimically ruthless, shadowy organization whose genesis stemmed from the ashes of the Second World War, began to slither into the light of day. The battle had become more vicious with each contact; and as his knowledge of what he was fighting grew, Müller gradually began to understand how invidiously the Semper had fed itself into society at first nationally, and then internationally, while remaining hidden from view. To maintain this invisibility, the Semper's determination to stop him knew no limits.

Killers had been sent after him, and those close to him; and though there had been casualties among his colleagues, the Semper had so far failed to get him and the core members of his team. They had even tried to get Aunt Isolde, and had also failed.

So far.

One of their most accomplished assassins, Sharon Wilson, was now on the loose, and hunting.

The core members of Müller's team were Pappenheim, the hawk-eyed and tough Lene Berger, the diffident but highly competent Reimer, and the ethereal electronic genius Hedi Meyer, whom everyone called the goth. What she did not know about computers would feel lonely on the head of a pin.

And there was Carey Bloomfield. She had appeared right

at the beginning, ostensibly a journalist authorized to shadow Müller for an article. Kaltendorf had approved. But Carey Bloomfield had turned out to be someone with her own very personal reasons for hunting out the Semper. She was no journalist. A United States Air Force officer with a desk job at the Pentagon, she had shown herself to possess skills that were strongly at odds with someone who, supposedly, spent her time organizing the papers on her desk. She forcefully continued to insist she was *not* CIA.

Despite his initial reservations, she had become a semi-official member of the team who could be relied upon. Both he and Pappenheim had taken her into their confidence and she had reciprocated, sometimes hunting out valuable information for them.

The trail of the Semper had now led Müller – accompanied by Carey Bloomfield – to Western Australia's Outback region. The Hargreaves, Müller had been informed, possessed information of such dangerous quality that they had, with good reason, secreted themselves in the isolated, red heart of the Kimberley. If the Semper got to know of the Hargreaves, or of the existence of the information, they would go to any lengths to prevent its ever falling into Müller's hands. This information, he'd been told, was of a magnitude that was sufficient to eventually destroy the Semper. Müller could only hope this would turn out to be true.

But he was not prepared for the biggest shock that awaited him: the Hargreaves themselves.

One

He tipped his palm, and let the shell fall to the ground; the little blue shell that he had found on a beach – a long way from here – when he was six. He had given it to her then, nearly thirty years ago.

He turned away from her, and began walking along the white beach, a heat behind his eyes. He thought he heard Carey Bloomfield shout his name, but he took no notice.

He kept walking until, at last, he came to a stop a long way from the group. He stared out across the darkening of the ocean, and the blaze of the sun on the horizon.

'A million miles away,' he said bitterly.

Some time later, he sensed a presence behind him. He did not turn round.

There was a long silence.

'I can understand how you feel,' Jack Hargreaves said at last.

'You have *no* idea how I feel. I was *twelve*. Why did you do it?'

A heavy sigh followed. 'I would like to think that we had the courage to betray neither our son, nor our country. There are many things you do not know. Come to Woonnalla tomorrow. There's a cellar which holds many of the answers you're looking for. Perhaps you will understand then. We are not asking for your forgiveness . . . just for your under-standing. It would matter a lot to Mina. Her heart has been broken for all these years, because of what we had to do.'

Müller said nothing, and still did not turn round. After a while, he sensed he was once more alone.

He continued to stare at the ocean.

Some time later, he heard the Cessna 337 start up. He did not turn round to look.

He heard it accelerate into its take-off run, then it was airborne. It passed right above him, seemingly heading into the setting sun, before it began to curve back towards the land, on course for Woonnalla.

That was when it exploded in a ball of fire that rivalled the blaze of the sunset.

He stared at the falling pieces of wreckage, shock distorting his features. Then he heard a strange, unhuman screaming that went on and on, and seemed to reach far into the darkening red of the sky.

'*No-no-no-no-nooo . . . !*'

As the sun appeared to wink out beneath the horizon, it took him a while to realize he was listening to his own voice.

He knew he had been crying.

Müller had no idea how long he had been standing in the dark, at the edge of the Indian Ocean. The heat was still behind his eyes, and a ribboned tightness to his cheeks where the tears had run down them and had dried.

The darkness of the night was stabbed at twenty-second intervals by three bright flashes from the lonely automated lighthouse. It was a little distance over to his right and slightly behind him near the airstrip, and close to the wilderness resort at Kooljaman.

He knew he had been standing there since just before the sun had blinked out beneath the horizon; since the flaming pieces of the aircraft had splashed and winked out in the ocean. He had not moved from the spot since then.

He was aware of hushed voices away to his left; and of the single glowing Tilley lamp at the centre of the loose gathering on the beach. Just beyond them was the amorphous mass that was to have been the beach fire; and beyond that, the barely visible shapes of the four-wheel-drive vehicles neatly parked side-by-side, noses towards the water. After what had happened, no one felt like having a beach party. He did not turn to look.

He remembered the flurry of shocked activity when the plane had exploded. It had fallen too far out for anyone to have been able to do anything in time. There had been no boat – even on the horizon – which would have been far too

5

late in any case; no small boat close enough to push out, and swimming out to the fast-sinking pieces of wreckage would have been pointless, and recklessly dangerous.

The darkness was deceptive. It was not pitch black. In the clear air and cloudless sky of the wild emptiness of Cape Leveque the stars were bright, seemingly mirrored upon the ocean. But the 'stars' on the water was the glow of plankton.

He sensed someone coming towards him. He still did not turn to look when a while later, Carey Bloomfield stood close. She did not speak but simply remained there, looking out upon the darkened ocean.

'Aren't you afraid?' he finally said to her. 'Saltwater crocodiles probably patrol around here at night, as do the snakes.'

'Sure I'm scared. I try to see those damned things in the dark every time I put a foot down. The snakes I mean. Probably be way too late by the time I spot one. Why the hell do the ten worst snakes on the planet have to live in this country? The Garden of Eden had just one. This is overkill.'

He said nothing to that.

'I'm so sorry, Müller,' she said after another pause. 'I feel so . . . helpless.'

'There was nothing you could have done. Nothing anyone could have done to prevent it.'

'Your parents . . .'

'My parents died when I was twelve.'

He said this in a voice that was so cold and lacking in all emotion, she felt chilled.

'Müller. That plane . . .'

'You've heard what I've said.' He began to walk away from her.

'*Müller . . . !* Sure,' she went on to herself, 'heard, but I don't buy it.'

She hurried after him at once scared of being left alone to the imagined snakes and crocodiles waiting for her in the gloom, and intensely worried about him. She followed in a strange, zigzag movement as she tried to spot any lurking snakes, or monster salties.

'I'll either get bitten by one of those crawling toxic

bastards,' she again muttered to herself, 'or be a croc's dinner. Some choice.'

She kept as close to the water's edge as she dared, deciding a crocodile would be harder to miss than a snake. In the dark, the surreal beauty that was Cape Leveque had, to her, suddenly become sinister, hiding all manner of possible nightmares. To her, the alien-world daylight canvas of deep red rockface, pristine white beach, green ocean and blue sky was cloaked by a gloom full of unseen menace.

They continued in this fashion, Müller striding on ahead, Carey Bloomfield trailing close behind, watching out for her snakes and crocodiles.

Behind them, the lighthouse continued to pierce the night with its beam, every twenty seconds.

As Müller reached the little group of ten, everyone fanned out slightly, faces medieval in the glow of the Tilley. They all watched him with an uncertainty and a wariness reserved for something untamed.

Paul Lysert looked beyond him. 'What's she doing?'

'Dodging snakes and crocodiles,' Müller replied.

'More'n likely frighten one into attacking,' Lysert remarked with a straight face. 'They're more scared of you than you are of them,' he added as she joined the group.

'Think they've read that book?' she countered, not believing him for a second. 'Your snakes are wild animals with enough venom to kill an army. I respect them so much, I'll leave them alone if they leave me alone. Being bitten as a kid by a Florida cottonmouth does that to you.'

Lysert grinned at her. ''sides, if anything's out there, it'll probably be a lonely python.'

'Great. Not only fanged, or chomped to death, but strangled as well.'

'Or maybe a brown,' he added for good measure.

'You're enjoying this, aren't you? What's a brown? One of the top ten nasties?'

'Oh yeah. High up the list. You met two, once. Speckled mulgas. One killed that sniper.'

'Thank you, Paul. You just made my night. As for the sniper, he deserved all he got. He killed Jamie Mackay in cold blood.'

'We'll never forget,' Graeme Wishart said. 'I've been out here many times . . .' he continued, '. . . during the night, during the day . . . Never seen a snake, or a croc.'

'I'm happy for you,' Carey Bloomfield said. 'But you just heard Paul. And this *is* saltie territory, isn't it?' she added with an almost feverish insistence.

'It's within their range, yes . . .'

'There you go. Night-time . . . feeding time.'

'Anytime's feeding time,' Lysert put in with a sly look at the others.

'Thanks again, Paul. I really needed that.'

Despite the badinage, everyone continued to cast surreptitious glances in Müller's direction, as if anxious about what he might do next.

The Tilley lamp cast its eerie glow upon their cautious faces as they studied him.

Wishart made a tentative start. 'Anyone at Kooljaman will have seen what happened,' he said to Müller.

He had already alerted his distant colleagues in Broome and closer stations by radio, at the moment of the crash. He had also sent two off-duty officers who had come to Mackay's beach party, to the general area of the coast near where the aircraft had gone in.

'Every phone with a connection,' Wishart continued, 'will have been in action. Can't keep this one out of the media.'

'I would not expect you to. Jack and Maggie Hargreaves, well-known and well-liked owners of Woonnalla Station, successful ecological farmers, going down in their plane, in full view of witnesses. No. You can't keep it secret.'

Müller spoke without emotion.

They stared at him, clearly wondering what was going on in his mind.

Wishart tried again. 'Jens . . . Jack and Maggie were . . .'

'People I just met.' Müller turned again to the dark ocean.

Wishart glanced helplessly at Carey Bloomfield, then said to Müller, 'Get a night's rest. Nothing you can do for now. In the morning . . .'

'In the morning I'll have a swim, then head back to Broome.'

'We're all going to leave. I've got to organize a search for whatever's been left of the . . . bodies and . . .'

'Do you seriously believe there will be anything left to find?'

'I'm a policeman . . . just as you are. You know this has to be done.'

Müller nodded, kept his gaze upon the ocean, but remained silent.

Again, Wishart looked helpless. 'Can I at least give you two a lift back to your car?'

They had left their own 4WD, an Explorer, a ten-minute walk away, near the airstrip.

Müller shook his head. 'Thank you, no. I'll remain here for a while . . .'

'I'll leave the Tilley . . .'

Again, Müller shook his head. 'Take it with you. I'll be fine . . .'

'Do I have a say in this?' Carey Bloomfield asked.

'And take Miss Bloomfield with you. She . . .'

'*Miss Bloomfield?*' she interrupted. 'We're back to that? What happened to Carey, Müller?'

Before the explosion, before they had left Broome for Cape Leveque in order to surprise the Hargreaves, Müller had at last begun to call her Carey.

'You don't have to wait here,' Müller said, ignoring her remark. 'It would not be fair to you . . .'

'Who's talking about "fair", Müller?'

He said nothing.

'You should not blame yourself . . .' Wishart started to say.

But Müller turned round to interrupt him. 'And who else is to blame? I came to this country, looking for the Hargreaves,' Müller went on in a voice that was so unnaturally quiet, it unexpectedly gave his words greater impact. 'The sniper followed, hoping to find them. Jamie Mackay got in his way, and paid the price—'

'Jamie was a copper. He knew the risks.'

'Jamie had been a copper for *twenty* years or more,' Müller said harshly. 'He lived through all of them. I turned up, towing a professional hitman. Now Jamie is dead. That's why you're all here isn't it? A beach party in his memory.

9

But I came here, hoping to surprise the Hargreaves, who had flown away – literally – when I tried to see them before. I discover they were people I had thought dead since I was twelve. They fly away again, and their plane explodes. Who else is to blame? You tell me.'

In the eerie glow of the Tilley, Müller's eyes were pools of unfathomable darkness. They fastened upon Wishart, until the policeman began to feel he was the prey of some unmentionable predator.

It made him feel strangely uneasy; but it was Müller who turned away once more.

Wishart looked at Carey Bloomfield as he slowly picked up the Tilley. 'I'll take you to your car.'

She paused, glancing uncertainly at Müller, who continued to look towards the ocean.

'OK,' she said at last.

The little group had begun to disperse, heading towards their vehicles as Wishart and Carey Bloomfield walked towards the policeman's own 4WD.

'He's in a state of shock,' Wishart said. 'He'll be all right. No worries.'

'Is that to convince me? Or you?'

'Tell you the truth . . . I don't know.'

The sound of engines broke upon the night as the other cars were started.

'Later, Graeme!' someone shouted. 'Watch how you go, Carey . . .'

'See ya, mate!' came another. 'I'd watch Graeme!' the person added to her with a definite grin in the voice.

But it was an enforced cheerfulness, masking the sadness and the sense of horror they all felt.

One by one, the others called out as they left.

'See you, guys,' she called.

'You coming over to the station after the search?' Pete Lysert, twin brother of Paul, called. There seemed to be a hidden meaning in the question.

'That to both of us?' Wishart demanded.

'Reckon.'

Wishart glanced at Carey Bloomfield. 'Reckon we all will,' he answered.

'Yeah.'

The Lyserts' 4WD headed off the beach, leaving just the one belonging to Wishart.

'What am I going to do, Graeme?' she asked into the sudden silence that had descended. The soft hiss of the Tilley seemed unbelievably loud; louder than the gentle lap of the ocean.

'About him? I'd leave him be for a while. Plenty for him to come to terms with. As for yourself . . . spend the night at the Kooljaman resort. It's still Cape Leveque. Kooljaman is the People's name for it. I'll talk to someone over there . . . see what can be done. A safari tent would do you. Well equipped, and with a balcony. Then you can go find him in the morning. He's a big boy. He can look after himself.'

Wishart never called the indigenous people Aborigines. It was always the People. He began to turn off the Tilley. 'Get in while I put this away.'

A very few knew that the green-eyed, white-blond Wishart, with a Finnish mother and a German father of part Irish descent, had a smidgen of Aborigine blood in him. To him, they were the People; and he said this with respect.

The Tilley died suddenly, giving the impression of the darkness dropping like a curtain as she took her seat. She looked back, but even as her eyes became accustomed, could not see Müller's shape.

'Don't worry,' Wishart said as he stowed the Tilley. 'He'll be OK.' He got in behind the wheel, and looked towards her in the gloom. 'You're not going to Kooljaman, are you?'

'No. I'll pick up the car, and come back here.'

'He might not like that.'

'I'll keep out of his way.'

'OK,' Wishart said, sounding uncertain as he started the car.

'What are you doing?'

They were at the airstrip, and Carey Bloomfield was in the driver's seat of the Explorer. She peered out at Wishart who had a bright torch, and was walking round the vehicle, now and then pausing to sweep the beam beneath it.

'Snakes love a warm axle,' Wishart replied calmly.

11

'*What?*' She looked poised to jump off the seat. Then she gave a weary sigh, remembering. 'Müller told me about this before. So it's true?'

'It is true. They tend to wrap themselves—'

'Are you *telling* me, one of these things could be . . . could be under *this* car . . . right now . . . under my butt . . . with me sitting up here?'

'You're all right,' Wishart said, straightening. 'She's clear. Not a snake in sight.'

He sounded as if he'd said that with a smile. He came round to stand next to the driver's door, pointing the torch away from them. It shone upon the red dirt of the airstrip, some metres away. The backglow gave plenty of light.

'I still can't believe that Jack and Maggie are gone,' he said in a quiet, thoughtful voice as he looked at the airstrip. 'They took off from here just a short while . . .'

He stopped, turning back to face her, torch still pointing away. Night insects darted in and out of the beam.

'Still going back out there?' he said to her.

'Yes. I'll park on the beach, and keep out of the way. When he's ready, he'll come over.'

'You know the man. I don't.'

'I'm not sure I do . . . but . . .'

'But you'll go over there to wait for him.'

'Yes.'

'Then you might as well give him this.' Wishart took something out of a pocket, and handed it to her. It was a small envelope, unusually heavy.

'What is it?'

'No idea. I haven't looked. Jack was insistent. He said Jens would find what he was looking for in there. Remember when he went down to the shore to talk to Jens?'

'I remember. Not much response there.'

Wishart nodded. 'Well, after that, you remember Jack and Maggie going off to the plane?'

'Then Jack came back. I saw him give you something, before he left again. This envelope?'

Again, Wishart nodded.

Carey Bloomfield ran exploratory fingers over the envelope. 'Feels like some kind of key . . . Inside a note, perhaps.'

'Whatever it is, it's his now. They were his parents.' Wishart paused. 'Imagine that. All those years . . .' He paused again. 'I can't even begin to understand how he feels.'

'And I'm not going to try,' Carey Bloomfield said. 'I saw Maggie pick up that little blue shell he'd dropped at her feet,' she went on, 'and take it with her. He'd found it as a kid, and had given it to her then . . .'

'I was wondering about its significance.'

'He saw it again, after all these years, at Woonnalla. That's how he knew for sure who they were.'

'Well . . .' Wishart paused a third time, '. . . it's gone back to the sea . . .' He paused again. 'Jesus. What a mess.' He gave the vehicle a pat. 'You'd better get back. I've got a search to organize. Bruce Laker and Rina James will have warned the forensic people by now – who will not fly in till tomorrow – and arranged for divers to help with the search and keep the site clear of the well-meaning. And . . . I'll have the usual reports to make. Won't be much sleep for me tonight.'

'The people at the resort will be up all night wondering what happened.'

'I reckon.' Wishart sighed. 'And I'll be dodging media questions tomorrow.'

'You know you won't find anything, Graeme. That explosion was huge. It wiped out the plane. I've seen enough in my career to tell the difference between a plane going wrong and a bomb. That was not just a plane going wrong. That was a bomb of some kind on there.'

'I reckon,' Wishart repeated, admitting this with marked reluctance. 'The question is . . . who placed it? And when? I'm a lowly police inspector. My superiors will be looking to me for answers.' Wishart glanced up at the night sky. 'Which I don't have. It went down in deep water, but something might be washed ashore.' He paused. 'Eventually. They had that plane equipped like a private jet. Perhaps the flight recorders – when they're found – might help.' He paused again. 'And the media, as I said, will be sniffing around. Things like this just don't happen up here. Snake bites, bad-tempered crocs, drunks, tourists getting lost, that's what passes for excitement.'

'But since we came—'

'I didn't say that,' Wishart began with more than a touch of guilt.

'I know you didn't.' She started the Explorer, and switched on the lights. 'Later.'

'Yeah.'

She drove carefully away, leaving Wishart staring after her, torch still pointing downwards.

When she got back to the beach, she could not see Müller in the lights of the vehicle. She parked nose-on to the ocean, but a good distance from the shore and away from the tide line.

She killed the engine, and turned off the lights. As her eyes grew accustomed, shapes began to take on definition in the gloom. The intermittent beam from the lighthouse helped.

There was still no sign of Müller.

'Where the hell are you, Müller?' she enquired softly. 'I'm not getting out to wander around looking for you . . . not with snakes on patrol, I'm not. Even if Pete and Graeme say there aren't any.'

Wherever he was on the beach, she told herself, he would have seen the Explorer arrive. With the doors and windows firmly shut despite the night heat, she decided to doze off until Müller came looking.

She awoke to the sound of one of the externally mounted, spouted freshwater cans being removed from the left side of the Explorer.

She had 'dozed off' for much longer than she had expected. It was daylight, and the back of the Explorer was open.

The vehicle was comprehensively equipped for Outback travel, including GPS navigation, and a satellite phone, in addition to radio. It was fully air-conditioned, and sported expensive in-car entertainment.

From the driver's seat, she slowly turned her head round to look. A bare-chested Müller, unbound hair just reaching his shoulders, was sparingly using the water to soak a small towel, which he then used to wipe himself down.

Carey Bloomfield said nothing, admiring the fitness of his body as he worked. He resoaked the towel, and began to wipe at his hair. Throughout, he appeared not to have noticed her scrutiny. When he was finished, he replaced the can, then secured his hair in its customary ponytail. His single earring gleamed briefly as he moved. He put on his lightweight cotton shirt, then jammed his bush hat upon his head.

Only then did he look at her. 'Good morning,' he greeted, unsmiling. 'I thought spies could wake at the drop of a pin.'

'I wouldn't hear it in this sand,' she retorted. 'And as I keep saying since we first met, I'm not a spy. I'm an air force lieutenant colonel who just happens to work in a small office at the Pentagon.'

He secured the back of the Explorer without comment, then came round to the front. There was stubble on his chin.

'Where the hell have you been, Müller?' she demanded. 'And you need a shave.'

'I don't need a shave.'

There was a look in his eye that was at once haunted and frightening. He seemed a very different person to the one she thought she knew, and to the one he was the night before.

'I was worried about you,' she said.

'Why?'

The question was so unexpected, and delivered with such lack of emotion, it checked her for some moments.

'Well . . . I . . .'

'I found a nice rock to sit on,' he said into her hesitant response, 'to think about many things, and watch the dawn come up. Mainly, I thought about betrayal. Then I went for a swim. Very refreshing, but I needed to wash some of the salt off, as you saw.'

'You haven't *slept*?'

'I'm fine. You should try the swim. You'll enjoy it.'

'You're avoiding my question, Müller.'

'I answered you. Try the swim. Then we head back to Broome, to catch a flight home.'

'Müller . . .'

'Try that swim.'

She began to get out of the vehicle. '*Müller* . . . *!*'

'Careful,' he said. 'Snakes.'

'*What?*' She hopped back in.

15

But Müller was walking away, heading for a red cluster of rocks. Furious, she peered down at the ground. There were no snakes.

'Müller!' she said again in a strangled voice.

She remained where she was for some moments, watching as he strode away from her.

'Damn you, Müller!' she seethed.

It was not until he had again disappeared behind the wild red of the rocks that she decided to move.

'Might as well have that swim,' she muttered. 'Nothing much else to do till his majesty gets back.' She reached behind the front seats for a small beach bag, unzipped it, and took out a minimal bikini in dark blue. 'I've been to this country twice, but it's the first time I'm going into the ocean . . . and on my own. Not what I expected.'

She put the bag down, then pulled out another, this time in bush canvas. She opened it. Two Beretta 92Rs – with plenty of spare magazines – nestled there. Satisfied, she returned the bag to its hiding place.

'No one around to steal those while I'm in the water.'

She changed into the bikini, placing the keys to the vehicle in the beach bag, climbed out and shut the door.

She looked down at her legs critically, gave her upper thigh a brief pinch, and made a *pftt*ing sound.

'A skeleton, I'm not.' She did not sound displeased. The bikini did justice to her curves. She glanced about her, but there was no sign of Müller. 'Might as well go say hello to a shark, or a saltie, or a goddamned snake.'

She began to make her way towards the water, her footprints mirroring the slight toe-in of her walk. It gave her the natural wiggle that Müller liked to see, but had never allowed her to know of. She was the epitome of what he liked in a woman; but that, too, he had kept to himself.

From the cluster of rocks where he sat, Müller spotted distant movement, and turned to look.

'Well,' he said to himself. 'So you decided on the swim.'

He watched as she first hesitantly tested the water with a probing foot, then went all the way in. He felt a smile within him, but it did not make it to his lips. He looked at her for some moments, small with the distance, before returning his scrutiny to the vastness of the ocean.

His vantage point completely screened him from her, even if she turned to look directly towards him. From where he sat, pillars of rock formed an effective wall; but there was a wide crack between two of them, which gave him an uninterrupted view of her position.

This was where he had spent the night. In the darkness, he had seen two pinpricks of light slowly moving towards where the aircraft had gone down. He had assumed that Wishart had probably attempted to see what could be done. The small boats had gone quite far out. He wondered if they had found anything.

As he remembered this, he spotted tiny shapes on the water. He counted five boats of different sizes, making their way towards the crash site. Above them, the dragonfly silhouette of a helicopter appeared to hover.

'You still won't find much, Graeme,' Müller said in a quiet voice. 'Not after an explosion like that.'

He made no move to leave his position.

Carey Bloomfield finished her solitary swim and made her way back to the Explorer. Taking a leaf out of Müller's book, she washed off the salt with water from the can.

She was in the process of wiping at her hair when a voice behind her said, 'Enjoyed the swim?'

She jumped. 'Damn it, Müller! Don't *do* that!' She turned round to face him, continuing to wipe at her hair.

'Did you enjoy the swim?' he repeated.

'I spent a lot of time watching out for swimming teeth, but apart from that . . .' She gave her hair a final wipe. 'So? Where were you this time?'

'Where I was last night.'

'Have you seen the boats out there? And that chopper?'

'Can't miss the helicopter and yes, I've seen the boats.'

'Think they'll find anything?'

'I doubt it.'

'Perhaps we should go over. You never know . . .'

'The only place we're going,' Müller said, 'is back to Broome, to catch a flight home. Nothing for me here.'

She finished attending to her hair, and replaced the can with deliberate movements.

'So that's it? You're giving up?'

'On what, precisely?' he countered.

She turned from the can to stare at him. 'On *what*? On *everything*, Müller!'

He said nothing to that. If anything, he seemed indifferent.

'Look,' she continued, 'I'm not even going to pretend to understand what's going on inside of you right now. Hell . . . I don't know how *I* would behave in a situation like this. Your parents, you believed, died in an airplane crash when you were twelve. At first, you were told it was an accident. Then the stories came out about a bad marriage, father cheating, mother deliberately crashes the plane. Years later, you find out they were actually murdered . . . by an organization we now know as the Semper, that your father had infiltrated. You'd never heard of them, until they dragged you in by trying to destroy your career, and when that failed, tried to have you killed.

'You get pointed to the Hargreaves by Grogan, who knows a lot more than he is telling. You find that the Hargreaves have been living in their own little haven in the middle of nowhere in Western Australia, for over twenty years. The Hargreaves turn out to be—'

'Not my parents. My parents died when I was twelve.'

'Damn it, Müller! You called her mother! And that howl of pain when the plane exploded—'

'If you're quite finished, get dressed and let's be going.'

'Not yet, mister! I'm not done!'

Carey Bloomfield stomped round to the front of the Explorer, opened a door, and reached for the envelope Wishart had given her. She grabbed it, stomped back to Müller, and thrust it at him.

'What's that?' he demanded.

'An envelope.'

'I can see it's an envelope. What is in it?'

'I don't know. It's not my envelope. Graeme Wishart gave it to me. It's from your fa . . . from Jack Hargreaves. You should take it. I'm certain it's important.'

Müller stared coldly at the envelope. Then he took it, and dropped it to the ground.

'Now you've given it to me. Time to leave.'

Her mouth opened and closed in astonishment. 'Damn it, Müller!' she shouted. 'You're a *cop*! Behave like one!'

'Are you quite finished?'

'*No, dammit!*' she yelled. 'I am *not* quite finished! These people have tried many times to kill you, me, Pappi, Aunt Isolde, and have succeeded in killing some of your own colleagues. They won't stop. They kidnapped, raped, and murdered the wife of US Army Colonel Bill Jackson, who sees you as a friend, just to get to you. They kidnapped Kaltendorf's teenaged daughter and tried to blow her to pieces. They will probably kill, or try to kill, anyone in your unit. They tried it with Pappi right outside your police building, for pete's sake. You once told me you would take a bullet for Pappi, because he once took one for you. They are hunting Greville, so that they can take a sample of that DNA poison he is carrying, to perfect it into an even more efficient weapon.

'You told me you spent the night thinking of betrayal. Well, Müller, if you back off now, you're betraying a hell of a lot of people: Pappi, Greville, your aunt, Berger, the goth, your parents – yes, dammit! Your parents. But most of all, you're betraying yourself.'

'Are you now quite finished?' he asked coldly.

'*Yes, dammit!*' she repeated furiously.

'And I suppose your interest in all this is quite altruistic, and nothing at all to do with the Pentagon?'

She stared at him in a kind of shock. 'That was a cheap shot, Müller.'

The emotion in her voice, and the pain in her eyes, seemed to take him aback.

'Yes,' he admitted after a long silence. 'It was. Sorry.'

She looked at him for long moments, as if deciding whether to accept his apology.

'Loo . . . look,' she said. She paused. 'Look . . . at least see what's in the envelope, and . . .' She began to stoop, to pick it up.

'*Freeze!*' he commanded in a sharp but low voice.

The way he spoke made her stop moving as if turned to stone.

She swivelled her eyes towards him. There was a sudden anxiety in them. 'What?' she asked in a squeaky whisper.

'Just . . . don't . . . move.'

'Jesus, Müller . . . !'

'If you can turn your eyes without moving the rest of your body,' he said very quietly, 'and if you won't react whatsoever . . . look to your right, on the ground. If you are afraid you might react violently, then stay exactly as you are until I tell you to move.'

'I can hack it.'

'Are you sure?' He sounded very uncertain.

'I . . . I . . . I'm sure.'

'You don't sound it.'

'Gawd, Müller!'

'And don't . . . shout. In your own time . . . look.'

She calmed herself down, taking her time about it. Then she slowly turned her eyes to look in the direction he had told her.

'Oh . . . my . . . Lord . . .' she said in a faint whisper.

'Don't bloody move!'

'I'm not . . . I'm . . . I'm not . . .'

She was looking at a small snake, perhaps just over half a metre long. It was not far from her right leg, and was poised to strike.

'It . . . it looks like a midget-sized version of those big monsters we saw near Woonnalla.'

'It's the same type. Mulga.'

'Jesus! This small . . . is . . . is it dangerous?' She stared at the snake with macabre fascination.

'As Graeme Wishart might have said, it comes fully kitted. It can kill you just as quickly. I'm no herpetologist, but I would err on the side of caution.'

'So now what?' she asked, not taking her eyes off the reptile.

'You remain absolutely still until it senses there is no danger. You're too big to eat.'

'Oh thanks! You're saying I'm fat?'

'Only a woman would make a remark like that in such a situation.'

'Same to you, Müller.'

'If you don't move,' Müller went on, ignoring the retort, 'it will simply avoid you, and move on.'

'So it thinks I'm a tree?'

'Or something.'

'They bite trees. I've seen them do it in those nature broadcasts . . .'

'*Trees?*'

'Well . . . bits of wood . . .'

'If you pin a snake down with something, of course it will bite whatever you're using.' Müller saw that the snake was swaying slightly. 'Better stop talking. Snakes can't hear, but their sense of vibration is acute.'

They fell silent.

For what seemed like hours, the snake remained in its reared position, then it relaxed, lowered itself to the ground, and moved away, heading towards the ocean.

Carey Bloomfield let out a long, slow breath. 'God! That seemed like hours.'

'Probably just a minute.'

'Müller! There are snakes on this damned beach! There are!'

'Calm down. As you've seen, you leave it alone, it leaves you alone. Animals are like that . . . unlike some humans . . .'

'And like some humans, some animals are plain mean. You're not going to convince me about snakes, Müller, so forget it.' She stared at the snake, now tiny at the water's edge. 'It's not a sea snake. What the hell is it doing?'

'Snakes can swim . . .'

'Land snakes in the *sea*?'

'Salties can handle dual environments, as can some sharks. Why not snakes?'

'Anyway, shouldn't we get away from here? Where are its big parents?'

Müller stared at the snake. 'He's a loner. He's got none.' It sounded as if he had discovered a fleeting affinity with the lonely snake.

Suddenly, he stooped to pick up the envelope.

She stared at him, but said nothing.

21

He looked back at her, focussing on her eyes.

'I've noticed something, Müller.'

'What?'

'Ever since we've been talking, you've been looking at my eyes. Either you're really stuck on them, or you're trying hard not to look at other parts of me. I'm in a bikini. My body that horrible?'

'Your body is many things. Horrible is not one of them.'

'That sounds like the old Müller. Welcome back.'

She went round the vehicle to change, then came back with ham rolls from their coolpack. 'We should eat,' she said, handing him one. 'So where to? Broome?'

'Woonnalla,' he said.

She smiled briefly. 'The old Müller is definitely back.'

'Thank that snake.'

'I'll thank anything.'

Two

The goth was about to turn her Beetle to enter the police garage, when the woman suddenly walked into her path.

She had no choice but to stop, doing so with plenty of distance to spare. She frowned in annoyance; then the frown deepened. Something did not feel right.

Feeling slightly foolish, she called Berger on her personal radio, doing so surreptitiously. The highly sensitive unit was clipped to the dashboard of the Beetle, and she spoke into it without the need to hold it closer. She would be able to hear just as easily.

'Lene?'

'Why are you whispering, Hedi?' Berger asked, giving Reimer one of the few tolerant smiles he tended to receive from her. The goth, she said to him silently.

Reimer gave an amused grimace.

'And where are you?' Berger asked.

'Just outside.'

'Just *outside*?' Berger rolled her eyes.

Reimer pointed a finger at his temple and described a windmilling motion.

'What's wrong, Hedi?' Berger asked patiently.

'A . . . a woman just walked in front of my car. She doesn't seem the type who would be so careless. It's all a bit weird. I thought that perhaps . . .'

Berger's manner changed immediately. 'We'll be right down.' She ended the transmission, and quickly called Pappenheim. 'Chief, we may have trouble. A strange woman's just walked in front of Hedi's car . . . right outside. It could be nothing . . .'

'But you feel you should check it out.'

'Yes. Just in case. I know we sometimes think the goth's in a world of her own but she has good instincts. I'm taking Reimer.'

Reimer stared at her, and pointed to his chest questioningly.

She narrowed her eyes at him. He got the message.

'I warned her to be on the alert,' Pappenheim said. 'She may be overreacting, but better that than the other. I'll warn Klaus at the desk to be ready to let you through the protective door so you're not delayed. Keep me posted.'

'Thanks, Chief. We're just leaving.'

Berger drew her weapon, double-checked it, and kept it in her hand. 'On your feet, Reimer.'

Reimer sighed, and drew his own weapon. 'It's probably just her bad karma phase. She's seeing portents of doom everywhere . . .'

'*Shut* it, Reimer! Come *on!*'

They hurried out of the sergeants' office.

Down in the street, after her quick call to Berger, the goth spoke pleasantly through her open window to the woman. 'Are you OK?'

'I'm fine,' the blonde woman replied in perfect German as she approached. 'Do you work in there?'

For all her air of a distracted computer geek, the goth was not – as she was frequently and mistakenly seen – as vulnerably helpless as she appeared. Something about the woman had put her senses on high alert and the unexpected question had increased her misgivings even further. Out of sight of the supposedly inattentive pedestrian, she had reached for the gun in her bag.

'I do,' she replied.

'Police officer?' The woman had stopped, hands behind her back.

'Yes,' the goth answered.

'And you have a gun, which you've probably now got in your hand.'

So much for being an absent-minded, accident-prone pedestrian.

'Yes,' the goth repeated, though this was not quite true.

Her fingers were on the weapon, but she had not yet fully grasped it.

The woman smiled. 'Lucky for me I'm also a police officer then. *Kommissarin* Lotte Ellermann, *BKA*. I'm here to see *Hauptkommissar* Müller.'

The goth did not introduce herself. 'Go through to the entrance. The *hauptmeister* at the desk will attend to you.' The goth now had her gun. She brought it up, and trained it unerringly on the person who had said she was Ellermann. 'If you are not who you say you are, you've got a problem. If you are, I'm certain you understand . . .'

The blonde smiled again. 'I certainly do. They've trained you well,' she said with approval. 'Take no chances.' She gave a little nod. 'I'll go to the *hauptmeister*.'

But the blonde woman did something else entirely. She had begun to turn, as if to comply with the goth's intruc-tions, but the movement became a swiftly flowing action that ended with the goth realizing she was herself staring at a gun. Her heightened alertness made her shift position, but she was not quick enough.

'This is just a *fucking* warning to Müller!' she heard the woman snarl.

There was a sharp report, something hot seared into her. She thought she heard herself scream.

Then the world went dark.

At that moment, Berger and Reimer burst out of the building. They focussed instantly upon what was happening.

'*She's shooting at the goth!*' Reimer shouted in horror, gun rising. '*Hey! You!*'

Sharon Wilson spun round to face the new threat. 'Shit!' she snarled to herself. 'The *fucking* bitch sent a warning.'

Berger was darting to one side, Reimer the other, splitting attention.

Cars were screeching to untidy halts, their drivers and passengers getting out as quickly as they possibly could.

But Sharon Wilson was no amateur. She had pulled out another gun and began a rapid-fire assault on Berger and Reimer. The seemingly gigantic automatics roared like big-bore shotguns. They seemed too huge for her hands; yet she held them in a steady grip as she fired.

Reimer ducked behind a recently vacated car. 'Jesus!' he hissed. 'She's fucking crazy!' He had not got off a single shot.

Sharon Wilson was darting in a rapid sideways movement, keeping up the firing from the two big automatics. Their combined roar could be heard the entire length of Friedrichstrasse, it seemed.

'Got to get the hell out of here before the hornets come out of their *fucking* hive,' she told herself, almost casually.

Berger was racing to cut her off. Like Reimer, she had not yet used her gun. She intended to choose the right moment for the precise, killing shots she intended to fire.

'*See to Hedi!*' she yelled at Reimer.

'*OK!*'

Sharon heard the exchange, and understood what was happening. 'Trying your luck with *me*, bitch?' she uttered softly. 'That should be interesting.'

She ducked behind an illegally parked car to reload. She did so swiftly, with an economy of movement that spoke of much practice. Her direction was taking her towards where her own falsely licensed car was parked down a side street.

'Are you Berger?' she shouted abruptly.

Berger could not hide her astonishment. 'You *know* me?'

'I know *of* you. You're on my list.'

'What list?'

'Let's not be so *fucking* naïve, shall we? Do you think I'm talking about Christmas cards?'

Berger thought about that for a fleeting moment. 'You don't have a chance!' she shouted back. 'You do know that, don't you?'

'Ah. You mean your colleagues will be swamping this place any second. Bad calculation. I'm not staying for the party. I plan to meet up with you, Müller, Pappenheim, Reimer and, of course, *fucking* Colonel Bloomfield, at another time. One down, today. I still have a lot of hunting to do. Sorry I can't oblige you for now. I'd run from behind that car, if I were you.'

Within the reload of one of the big automatics, were two incendiary rounds which would be first off.

'I'm never predictable,' she muttered softly.

Then she fired the incendiaries into the parked car where her deliberately planned conversation had located Berger.

It took Berger fleeting nanoseconds to understand that what was about to happen would take her by unpleasant surprise. She was smart enough to yield to discretion, and so limit the effects of that surprise, whatever it would be. She thus began moving immediately after Sharon Wilson's last words to her.

'Shit,' she said, annoyed with herself. 'I let her sucker me. She used the conversation to zero on my location. You're supposed to be a professional, Berger.'

Even so, she did not expect what happened next.

She was well on her way when the rounds slammed into the car behind which she had previously taken refuge but she was still close enough to feel the heat of the double explosion when it erupted in a violent burst of flame, as she rushed into a narrow passage between two buildings.

The blast flung a smoking, twisted lump of metal into the passage, missing her by scant centimetres. She saw it was one of the doors.

'*Shit!*' she exclaimed, startled by the narrowness of her escape, and even more annoyed with herself.

She knew that the unknown woman would now be long gone. Though it had seemed much longer, bare minutes had passed from the moment she and Reimer had left the building.

'*Shit!*' she said again, in mounting frustration.

She left the passage to be greeted by the smouldering wreck of the shattered car, and a crowd of gawpers being kept at bay by more of her colleagues.

The unit had its own fully equipped emergency medical team, complete with vehicle. Two of them were already moving the goth into the vehicle, its lights flashing. A sheepish Reimer stood by.

She hurried over to the medical vehicle, but was stopped by Rüdi Burgstein, the civilian doctor, and leader of the team.

'Is she . . . ?' Berger began.

'Very lucky,' Burgstein interrupted. 'She's unconscious. Shock of the bullet. She's a lot stronger than she looks. It's touch and go. Now if you all really care about her, get out of my way. She's lost plenty of blood. She needs surgery.'

'Bad karma?' Berger said to Reimer as the vehicle streaked away, sirens yelping.

'It was a stupid thing to say,' he said.

'It was,' she agreed without mercy.

A grim-looking Pappenheim arrived. He looked at them. 'A problem with you two?'

'Is there a problem?' Berger said to the hapless Reimer.

'No problem.'

'No problem, Chief,' Berger said to Pappenheim. 'Are we going after the cow who did this?' she added.

'No need,' he replied, staring after the medical vehicle. His eyes burned with a cold fire. 'She knows where to find us.'

'She said we were on her list.'

'I'm honoured.'

Western Australia.

At about the same time, Müller and Carey Bloomfield were on the red dirt of the unsealed road that led to Woonnalla. It was 15.00 local.

Taking turns to drive, first along the swathe of red, undulating vehicle killer of an unsealed road from Cape Leveque, to turn left more than 200 kilometres later on to the sealed Great Northern Highway, they had not hurried. They had again turned left off the highway, and on to the unsignposted road which ended at Woonnalla, twenty or so kilometres further on. Bordered by stunted clumps of bush, the road was a red artery that fed itself towards a straight that was at least three kilometres long.

It had taken them close on six hours to get there. They had listened to CDs most of the way, but not to the radio. From time to time, Müller had retreated into long, thoughtful silences.

Carey Bloomfield turned down the volume. 'They must have been searching for a while now,' she began. 'Should we see if there's anything about the crash on the radio?'

Müller was driving. He shook his head. 'I'd rather not.'

'OK.'

She left the volume low, as Handel's Largo in F major

from *Xerxes* swelled gently out of the speakers. Neither spoke until the piece had ended.

She stopped the player with a faint sigh. 'I love that piece of music.'

'What do you see in your mind when you hear it? The king? Or Handel's comic opera?'

She gave him a longish glance. Eyes on the road, he missed it.

'The king,' she said, her own eyes now studying the landscape.

'Well,' Müller said after a while. 'He certainly burned his boats . . . in a manner of speaking.'

Another silence fell.

'How does it feel,' she said, breaking it, 'being back on this road?'

'Strange,' he admitted.

Müller once more retreated into his thoughts.

Again, it was Carey Bloomfield who broke the silence a while later, as the vegetation on either side of the road began to change. The road entered the now familiar wide, shallow cultivated valley that had so unexpectedly greeted them the very first time they had come here. The neat segments that formed a patchwork of riotous colour; the small trees dotted within the patchwork; and the breathtakingly beautiful, low white house in the middle of it all.

'If I come here a thousand times,' she said, 'I'd still be knocked out every time I see it. This place is so beautiful. I can understand wanting to live here.'

'What about the snakes?' Müller broke his silence to ask.

'This is an Eden. Snakes go with Eden.'

Müller shook his head slowly. 'Sometimes, you truly amaze me.'

'Hey. I'm a woman. We've been amazing you guys since when.'

The 'patchwork' had turned into the now familiar neat fields of flowers, vegetables, and fruit, stretching as far as the eye could see.

The road came to its natural end in the sealed section that went right up to the house. As with their previous visits, distance had deceived. The house had gone through its strange metamorphosis of being far bigger than it had at first seemed from a distance, and was surrounded by its own vast, flourishing garden of unparalleled beauty.

'An oasis,' Carey Bloomfield said as Müller brought the Explorer to a stop and switched off the engine. 'I've said that before, haven't I?'

'You have.'

'I know. But what the hell.' She glanced at the tower with the vaned wheel at the top. It was not turning. 'The water pump's off. No one's home. Guess the Lyserts must still be at the search.'

Müller was looking at the tell-tale strip that looked like a road in the wrong place, his face unnaturally still.

She noticed his scrutiny, and knew what he was thinking. The aircraft that used it would never be landing again; and Jack and Maggie Hargreaves would never be coming home alive.

He seemed to tear himself away from looking at the airstrip, and turned on the radio, already tuned to the local station.

'Might as well hear what they have to say.'

She watched him with a cautious uncertainty, unsure of how he would react to any news about the crash.

'. . . and to those of you just joining us,' the presenter was saying, 'I'm afraid I have some terrible news. Jack and Maggie Hargreaves, well liked – I would even go so far as to say well loved – famous throughout the state and indeed nationally for their ecologically sound produce, are no longer with us. Many of us know that beautiful, eccentric little plane of theirs. Unfortunately, last evening, they made their last flight.

'Investigators are at the crash site, which is in deep water. So far, no bodies have been found. It is anyone's guess at this time what actually happened. There are confused eyewitness reports, but the police ask that wild speculations should be avoided until the investigation is over, and the truth of the matter known. They have also asked that while it is perfectly understandable that people will rightly wish to express their sorrow for Jack and Maggie – as they were known to so many – that they do not go to their home at Woonnalla to leave flowers, either by road or by air. The *entire Woonnalla area is to be considered totally restricted until investigations are complete. I am sure you will all understand why this has to be. We have been assured that as soon as is possible, any restrictions will be lifted.*

'*However, the police have also agreed that we at this station can offer a little service. We have a number for you to call to express your thoughts about Maggie and Jack, and somewhere to leave your flowers. Call us, and we'll give you directions.*' The presenter gave out a Broome phone number.

'*We have someone here to whom the restrictions do not apply, and who has kindly agreed to take some of your calls: Paul Lysert, one of the Lysert twin brothers, who have been with Maggie and Jack since their early teens. Welcome, Paul.*'

'*How do,*' came Lysert's voice.

Carey Bloomfield darted an enquiring glance at Müller. But Müller's attention was fixed upon the radio.

'*Paul,*' the presenter said, '*we appreciate your taking some time out from the search up there at the Cape, to talk to us.*'

'*No worries, mate.*'

'*You saw what happened, didn't you?*'

'*Yeah. We were on the beach to have a party for Jamie . . .*'

'*That's Senior Constable Jamie Mackay – another well-known person – who was killed in the line of duty only about two weeks ago.*'

'*Yeah. S'right. It was a send-off. He always told us if anything ever happened to him, we shouldn't look like the sky fell in but go to the beach instead, and he'd join us for some nectar.*'

'*Pure Jamie.*'

'*Too right. Jack and Maggie were there too. They knew Jamie well.*'

'*For many years.*'

'*Yeah.*'

'*Can you tell us what happened?*'

Müller seemed to sit up at this, waiting to hear what Lysert would say.

'*Not much to tell,*' Lysert began. '*It was getting dark . . .*'

'*Excuse me,*' the presenter interrupted, scenting fresh meat.

31

'Getting *dark? They were leaving* before *the party had started?*'

But Lysert was not caught out. '*They had to leave early. Business to attend to. They are . . . were very busy people.*'

'*I'm sure they were. Many of us have enjoyed the fruits of their labours, and yours and Pete's, of course. Sorry I interrupted. You were saying . . .*'

'*Well . . . the plane went out to sea, then turned to head inland. That's when it happened. It seemed to fall . . .*'

'*Excuse me, Paul. You're saying it just* fell? *Some people said there was an explosion.*'

'*Yeah. There was. But I'm not sure whether that happened* before *or* after *it hit.*'

'Oh ho,' Carey Bloomfield remarked. 'Who's a clever boy, then? Think Graeme Wishart had a hand in this?'

'I'm certain Graeme had a word, but this sounds like pure Paul.'

'He's protecting us, Müller. Nothing about our presence. What about the others who were there?'

'They were all friends of Jamie Mackay, and the . . . Hargreaves. They won't talk out of turn.'

'*. . . and the plane simply broke into many pieces,*' the presenter was continuing. '*Must have hit very hard.*'

'*Oh it did.*'

'*Your brother is a fully qualified pilot, and he has flown the plane often. And anyone who knew that plane will tell you it was the most well-maintained aircraft flying. Has he expressed any opinion about what he thinks may have happened?*'

'*Not to me. But he's talked to Graeme Wishart about it, I reckon.*'

'*That's Inspector Wishart.*'

'*Yeah.*'

'*Well, thank you for talking to us at this terrible time, Paul.*'

'*No worries.*'

'*Are you OK to take a few calls?*'

'*Sure.*'

'*Thanks again, Paul. Now if you'll stand by, we'll connect you to the callers. Before we go to Paul again, I'd like to pass on some information to any media colleagues out there.*

I know some of you will be hunting out a story on this, but the police have expressly said that the restrictions currently existing at Woonnalla also apply to the media. So no sneaking out there, guys. You'll get into trouble. And in any case, think of Jack and Maggie. Respect their home. And now, our first caller . . .'

Müller turned off the radio. 'Wishart is keeping a tight lid on it.'

'Nice touch about the media. It means we won't be surprised by some reporter sneaking around, turning up here, and wondering who we are.'

'There is that.' Müller took out the envelope that Wishart had passed on. 'Might as well see what's in it,' he continued, climbing out.

'I'll wait in here till you're done,' she said.

He turned to look at her. 'No need.'

'I'll wait.'

'If you insist.'

'I do. Go read whatever's in there, Müller.'

He gave her a brief, speculative look, then turned away to move a short distance from the vehicle. He stopped, and slowly tore the envelope open. There was a longish note inside, and a key.

He took out the key, and put it in his pocket. Then he removed the note, and spread it open with great care. The familiar writing seemed to leap at him. It was in German.

He began to read.

We hope you will come to Woonnalla. It is your home too. If you do not want us to be there, we understand. Just call before you decide to come – if you do decide – and we'll make sure we're absent. But of course, we hope you will want to see us. It has been many years, son, and we want to tell you why we have kept ourselves from the one person we love beyond anything else.

The key is to the main door of the house. There is an alarm control just inside. The first set of numbers will disarm it. The second set is for a keypad in the cellar. The cellar door is not locked, but there is another section which is protected by the keypad. Go to the wine rack. Go to the port storage, and in a section with 1968-vintage bottles, remove

33

four bottles from the middle. You will see a small panel. Open it. Behind that is the keypad. Tap in the code written below, close the panel, replace the bottles, and step back. The pressure of the bottles against the panel acts as a trigger. A section of the wine rack will swing open. Go into the room. The rack will swing shut once you're inside. There is a second keypad. The code operates it – to open or to close. There is a filtration unit which comes on automatically, as do the lights.

What you will find in there will explain everything to you. You will have entered a Pandora's Box. You will have information that will put you at even greater risk, but it will help you understand why we have hidden ourselves out here for all these years, and why we did what we have done, separating ourselves from the one person in our lives who means so much to us. Among other things, it was to protect you.

We have never stopped loving you.

It was signed with the real names of the people he once called Mother and Father.

Müller slowly folded the note and put it back into the envelope. He felt more heat behind his eyes, and remained standing with his back towards the Explorer.

'I'm not going to cry again,' he said to himself.

Carey Bloomfield had watched Müller move away before turning back to the radio to switch it on.

'. . . *and the calls have certainly been coming!*' the presenter was saying. '*Sure you want to continue, Paul?*'

'*No worries. Jack and Maggie had a lot of friends.*'

'*And we're certainly finding that out. Here's the next caller.*'

'*Paul?*' a male voice began, slightly hesitant. '*Jacko Meehan here . . .*'

'*Hey, Jacko. How's that old rust bucket you call a plane?*'

Meehan gave a short, nervous laugh. '*Still chugging along. Paul . . . we're in shock, mate. Just can't believe it. Jack and Maggie . . . great, great people. It's always the good who go first . . .*'

'*Yeah, mate. It's going to take us a long time, Jacko, to get over it.*'

'*They were like parents to you.*'

'*Not like, Jacko. We lost our natural parents when we were kids. Jack and Maggie were our parents.*'

'*Anything you need,*' Meehan said, '*don't hesitate.*'

'*Good on ya, Jacko. Thanks, mate.*'

'*Anytime.*'

'*Another good soul,*' the presenter said as the call ended. '*So many good people around . . . and the next . . .*'

'*Paul?*' a woman's voice came on. '*My name's Angie Haslam. I'm with Helstrup and Jones. Many years ago, our firm – I was not with them then – sold Woonnalla to the Hargreaves. If you have any plans to sell . . .*'

'Jesus!' Carey Bloomfield exclaimed in disgust. 'The vultures are already circling.'

'*Do I have to talk to this . . . person?*' Paul Lysert was saying in a hard voice to the presenter. It was clear he had wanted to say something other than 'person'.

Clearly extremely annoyed with the caller, the presenter said, '*No. You don't.*'

There was a sharp click as, without further ceremony, he cut off the call.

'*I want to say this,*' he announced to his audience at large. '*Any further calls like that will be cut off immediately. Have some respect. Who's next?*'

'*Good on you, Paul,*' the new caller began. '*This is Helen Reston . . .*'

Carey Bloomfield turned the radio off and looked towards where Müller was standing. Something about his stance made a slight frown crease her forehead.

She decided to get out of the 4WD.

Müller heard, and composed himself. He was ready when he heard her come to a stop behind him.

'Hey, Müller. You OK?'

'I'm fine.' He turned, eyes dry, and took out the key. 'Key to the house.'

'So we're going in?'

'We're going in.'

'Something you're not telling me, Müller?'

'Wait and see.'

'I'll get the guns out of the car.'

35

'We shouldn't need them,' Müller said. 'But you're right. One never knows. Besides, good idea not to leave them unattended out here . . . in case someone comes sneaking, despite the police restrictions.'

Müller looked about him as she went back for the gun bag.

The big outhouse, some distance away from the main building, was not visible from the vantage point of the approach road. Partially encircled by low trees, some of the machinery used on the station was at the front. A wide, attached open garage housed two big trucks, with space for a third.

Müller decided he would park the Explorer next to them.

There was a top floor to the outhouse, with wide windows at which venetian blinds could be seen. He assumed that was where the Lyserts stayed when they were at Woonnalla.

The main house, a low-lying building in cool white, had more than a hint of Colonial style to it. He remembered the spacious interior, also a cool white, with terracotta flooring; the vast living space segregated by low walls, and columns reaching to the high ceiling, serving as portals to the different areas; the huge windows with white Roman blinds that let in floods of natural light. Only the dining area and the bedrooms were carpeted, in neutral colours. All the furnishings had been carefully chosen. Many were classic antiques.

It was this that had jogged at his memories, the first time he had seen the place. Something indefinably familiar had tugged at him. The apparent impossibility of what he had been thinking had led him to initially doubt his own instincts; but events had soon proved him right.

At the back of the house was a large, roofed terrace that was accessed from the big kitchen via wide French windows. Bordering the terrace was a neat flower-bed and at one end was a small plant pot. In it, he had seen the little blue shell, mirroring the spot where in another time and place as a child of six, he had put that same shell. Then the faint scent of her perfume had confirmed the impossible.

Carey Bloomfield's return broke into his reminiscence.

'Let's do it,' she said.

He pointed to the garage. 'I'm going to park the Explorer in there, where it won't be seen from the road. If anyone comes this far, with a bit of luck they'll think it belongs here. Anyone breaking the restrictions is not going to know the difference.'

'Meaning?'

'A journalist looking for a scoop.'

'Or?'

'I think you know that part.'

'The part where we might need the guns.'

'Something like that. Wait here while I move the car.'

Carey Bloomfield looked pointedly about her. 'I'm going somewhere?'

'You know what I mean.'

'Sir, yes, sir.'

'Behave,' he said.

Job completed, they entered the house.

'Now I've seen this place more than once,' she said, 'I'm beginning to understand why it rang some bells for you when we first got here. It's not like that palace you call an apartment in Berlin, but something about it links the two, even for me. That's what you recognized that first time.'

'If you say so.'

Unabashed, she continued, 'Want to look around?'

'I would first like to check the cellar . . .'

'He would first like to check the cellar,' she mimicked. 'Müller, have you any idea how Brit you sound when you speak English?'

'You've told me before. Blame it on the English part of my education.'

'I know I've told you before, but I guess it sounds more so out here in Aussie land. They all say you sound like a Pom.'

'They mean it nicely.'

She made a sound that was suspiciously like a snicker.

Their arrival at a tall, closed door of dark wood at the end of a short hallway beyond two columns killed whatever riposte he had intended. A light switch was close to it.

'The door to the cellar, I believe,' he said. 'It's supposed to be unlocked.'

He tried it, and it came open. He flicked the switch. Bright light flooded below, showing a solid staircase of dark wood, built into a wall on one side, and balustraded on the other. The staircase went further down than expected.

Müller pulled the door shut behind him as they went down. When they got to the bottom and into the cellar proper, they both stared.

'Wow!' Carey Bloomfield said, looking about her and up at the high ceiling. '*This* is a cellar? It's an apartment.'

The cellar did indeed look like a huge apartment. It was virtually spotless, and not at all like the average cellar, clogged with the detritus of everyday life. This was no untidy storage room.

'Müller,' she said, 'I could eat off this floor. And Gawd. Look at that wine rack!'

The wine rack went from floor to ceiling, and wall to wall.

'How many bottles?' she asked. 'A hundred? Two? Three hundred?'

'Nearer four hundred.'

'*Four* hundred? This is not a vineyard, Müller. I've seen less at a wine store. Will your Aunt Isolde have as many at the Schlosshotel?'

'Oh yes.'

'She's got a hotel to run,' Carey Bloomfield said. 'She's got an excuse.'

'It's not all wine,' Müller said as they approached the rack.

'It matters? Four hundred bottles are four hundred bottles.'

'In this instance, it matters.'

The way he said that made her look at him closely. 'One of the things you haven't told me yet?'

Instead of replying, he said, 'Look at the rack. What do you see?'

She glanced at him as if he had taken leave of his senses. 'Wall-to-wall bottles.'

'Anything else?'

'What are you talking about, Müller? A wine rack is a wine rack is a wine rack. That's it.'

'Good.'

She gave him a sideways glance. '*Good?* You're starting to worry me.'

'Again?'

He went close to the wall of bottles, and began to study them.

'Funny man. What are you looking for?'

'Port,' he replied. '1968 vintage.'

'I won't ask the question.'

'That's a relief.' He found the bottles he was looking for, and began to remove them.

'Hey . . . what are you doing, Müller? You can't . . .' She paused. 'What am I saying? This belongs to you now.'

He said nothing to that, attention focussed upon the small panel mentioned in the note.

'So what have you hidden behind this, Jack?' he said to himself.

Carey Bloomfield heard. 'Don't bite my head off, Müller,' she said, 'but why do you keep calling him Jack? He's your . . .'

Müller turned round, eyes betraying nothing. 'Allow me to cope with this in my own way, if that's all right with you.'

He turned back to the panel, without waiting for her response.

Chastened, she said, 'Sure.'

He gave a low sigh. 'Sorry.' He did not look round. 'Just let me come to terms as I have said, in my own way . . . and leave it at that.'

'OK.' She stared as he opened the panel, and the keypad was displayed. 'You've got to be kidding me. A *secret* passage?'

'Let's see.'

He tapped in the eight letter and digit code, closed the panel, replaced the bottles, then stepped back as the note had instructed.

Nothing happened.

'Now what?' Carey Bloomfield said.

'Wait.'

As soon as Müller had spoken there was a soft hiss, and a section of the wine rack, roughly the size of a tall double door, began to pivot through ninety degrees. Beyond it lights, softer than in the main cellar, came on, and another vast room stretched before them. The back of the opened section was reinforced by a thick slab of what looked like armoured steel.

'I'll be damned,' Carey Bloomfield said in astonishment.

'Let's see what's in there,' Müller said, going through.

She hesitated.

He looked back at her. 'If you're coming, better hurry. It will close in a few moments.'

'And how do we get back out?'

'There's another keypad in here. I've got the code to reopen that panel. Are you coming?'

After another fleeting, hesitant pause, she followed him in. A bare second later, the wine rack pivoted itself shut.

'If we're trapped in here, Müller, I swear I'll kill you before I die of starvation, asphyxiation, or whatever.'

'No need for such a drastic measure. I am certain they thought of everything.'

He pointed to the massive steel rectangle that was so flush to the brick wall it seemed to be a fixed part of it. A keypad was recessed into the steel.

'There,' he said. 'The way out.'

'And if that doesn't work?'

'I'm certain there will be another way. The people who created this would not have depended on one exit. There will be another one.'

'You should know,' she said.

He ignored the comment.

They had entered what looked like a small antechamber of what would prove to be an apartment almost as big as the wine cellar. The flooring was terracotta, as was the long hallway which led from it along the right wall.

Carey Bloomfield began to remove her boots and socks.

Müller stared at her. 'What are you doing?'

'What does it look like? Müller, this place is *clean*. It's cleaner than your place in Wilmersdorf, and that's saying something. It's cleaner than the wine shop outside. We've got boots and socks with sand and dirt. I don't think they came in here with dirty boots after working outside. Keeping this place clean is your job now. I'm trying to help.'

He continued staring at her, amazed. 'You're serious.'

'You bet. Now off with yours.'

'*What?*'

'Off with them, mister! Or I don't move from here.'

'This is ludicrous.'

She stared back at him, and did not move.

He sighed. 'We have a lot to do, so I'll humour you.' He removed his boots and socks. 'Happy?'

'I'll bet they've got shoes that they use in here . . .'

'If they have, I'm not going to put them on.'

'Nor I. But you'll have to get a pair when you take over.'

'Who says I'm taking over? Can we continue now?' Carrying his boots, Müller went over to look along the hall. 'The next exit,' he said as she joined him.

At the far end of the hall was another steel door, this time with a wheeled locking system, reminiscent of a bank vault.

'OK, Müller. I'll give you that one.'

Along the left side of the hall were several doorways; but only two had doors.

'This place is big,' Carey Bloomfield said. 'It's either a five-star panic room or a five-star nuke bunker. Combine it with the wine store, and you've got yourself a whole basement floor.'

'I think it is rather more than a panic room, and not a nuclear shelter. Let's see.'

What they discovered was a large, well-furnished two-bedroomed apartment. In the main bedroom, they discovered many photographs of Müller from a baby up to the age of twelve. They also discovered two pairs of soft house shoes.

Carey Bloomfield was in two minds. She wanted to smirk because the shoes had proved her right but instead she looked at Müller with concern as he stared at each of the photographs in turn, his face expressionless.

'You OK, Müller?'

'I'm fine. I'll give you the point about the shoes. Let's see the rest.'

She gave him an uncertain look, but followed him out.

'Two bedrooms,' she said later as they stood by one of the doors, 'beds fully made up . . . two bathrooms, a kitchen that reminds me of yours, with a huge fridge full of food; a living room the size of a small apartment and . . . do we see what's behind those doors? If they're not locked.'

They were not.

The first one turned out to be an office/study, complete with a powerful computer, and a communications system that would have made a normal outback radio unit look as if it belonged to the steam age. There was also a huge wall-mounted monitor.

'Now what do you think that's for?' she asked.

'Time enough to find out,' Müller said. 'Let's check the next.'

The next was a treasure trove; books and files in neat rows on built-in shelves that covered two walls. There were also plenty of guns, and ammunition. The guns were not ordinary ones for use in shooting dingoes. One was a Dragunov SVD.

'A *sniper* rifle?' Carey Bloomfield exclaimed, staring at it. 'And a Dragunov? What the hell, Müller?'

'We'll find out soon enough.'

'Keep saying that.'

There was a large desk, with a high-backed leather chair pushed against it. On the desk was a large, creamy yellow envelope with one name upon it: *Jens*.

Staring at it, Carey Bloomfield said, 'Looks like you were expected, after all.'

Müller looked at it for long moments, before finally picking it up. He opened the flap slowly, then pulled out the contents. He put the envelope back down, then began to read the first sheet of a thick sheaf of paper. Surprisingly, unlike the first note, this was written in English.

'Jens: if you are reading this and we are not here, this means just two things – you did not wish us to be here, or we won't be seeing Woonnalla again.'

Müller paused, swallowed, then continued to read.

In here, you will find all that you are looking for about the Semper and, perhaps, rather more. I have itemized the documents in this room, to help make things easier to find. The guns will be explained. This is a Pandora's Box, as I've said in the note we gave to Graeme Wishart. We are passing on to you, our son, a terrible inheritance. Do with it the best you can. The existence of this 'Pandora's Box' is unknown to the Lysert brothers, for their own protection. It was constructed before they first came to us and was improved and updated over the years, whenever they were away on Woonnalla business. Apart from your mother and I, only one other knows of it; and now, so do you and Miss Bloomfield.

The deeds to Woonnalla are already in your name, and have been for years. Woonnalla is yours. Do with it as you wish.

Always remember, we love you.

Again, the note was signed with the names he knew as a child. Wordlessly, he handed it to Carey Bloomfield.

'Müller,' she began, 'you don't have to . . .'

'Please.'

She took it, and began to read.

'Jesus,' she said when she had finished. 'You've inherited this place. Just as I thought, Müller . . . and all that wine too. You keep inheriting places . . . like the Lavalieres' house in Grenoble . . .' She paused. 'What do they mean by "Pandora's Box"?' She handed the note back to him.

'We're *in* Pandora's Box,' he said. He looked at the shelves with all the carefully gathered bound files and box files, full of documents that would incriminate people he probably knew of, and those he did not. He waved an indicating hand briefly. 'And these are its contents.' He took out the first note, and passed that to her. 'This one goes a little further.'

She had excellent German. She read it, and was very quiet when she had finished.

She handed the note back to him. 'I'm so sorry about them, Müller.'

Not as sorry as I am, he said in his mind.

'What's done,' he said to her, 'is done. I can't bring the Hargreaves back.' He turned from her, to study one of the other sheets of paper.

She looked at him, sensing his pain, yet helpless to do anything about it. To hide what was in her eyes, she looked about her, and went towards a shelf.

She touched a file. 'Your Pandora's Box.'

He did not look up from the paper. 'For my sins.'

'I'm not sure I would like to have custody of something like this.'

'That makes two of us,' he said. 'But I do not have a choice. I never did.' He began to put all the papers back into the envelope.

'Two bedrooms,' Carey Bloomfield said.

'And?'

'Why would they need *two* bedrooms in a place like this? This is a bolt hole, a secret storage for explosive documents, a bunker . . . whatever. The Lyserts don't know of it and to the outside world, they had no children – assuming they would even have brought children down here. So they had only themselves to think of. From what little I know of them – from you, from Aunt Isolde, from those notes – I don't think they were the type of people to sleep apart . . . especially not down here. Perhaps it's because they expected to be with you, in here, one day.'

'Or they had a visitor from time to time – someone they could trust completely – who probably brought them up to date with new information and documents.'

'The "one other"?'

He nodded. 'It seems far more likely than waiting for me to turn up, even if they expected me to find them one day.'

'Ever thought they could have arranged the sequence of events that brought you here?'

'It has crossed my mind. But that would have to mean they knew Grogan . . . or someone like him. But it was he who pointed me. It is also possible that they don't know Grogan at all. Grogan has his own agenda.'

'Tell me about it,' she said. 'For all his help, Grogan is not Santa Claus. He has his reasons for what he does. So who else could be "the other"?'

Müller glanced at the shelved files. 'Perhaps these will tell us. It is ironic,' he went on. 'I toyed with the idea that, one day, I would perhaps be offered this place as an inheritance . . . but I saw that possibility a long way into the future. If that ever did happen, I decided I would do one of two things: refuse, or accept and turn it over to the Lyserts. They have worked this place. If it belongs to anyone, it is to them.'

'And now?'

'And now, I can't. At least, not the house . . . not with the Pandora's Box hidden down here. It can't be sold, either . . . for the same reason. I think my . . . the Hargreaves knew that.'

'So what will you do?'

'I think I might still turn the land over to the brothers, but I'll have to retain ownership of the house and its garden. That way, no one will find out about Pandora's Box.'

'What if they refuse?'

'*Refuse* Woonnalla? Is this a serious suggestion? This place is worth . . .'

'Millions.'

'Exactly. How could they possibly refuse? They belong to this place. They built it with the Hargreaves. It is rightfully theirs. I have more than enough for my needs. And . . . I am a Berlin policeman . . .'

'That won't help you if they refuse.'

'They won't.'

'I think you'll be surprised. They are proud people, Müller . . .'

'I'm not buying them off, if that is what you're about to say.'

'I did think about it,' Carey Bloomfield admitted. 'But you're forgetting one thing.'

'Which is?'

'Their respect and love for the Hargreaves. They saw them as their surrogate parents.'

'All the more reason for them to—'

'Respect the real son. Taking Woonnalla from you, even if you offered it to them, would seem like an act of disrespect.'

'Now that is stretching it.'

She gave him a fleeting smile that said she understood something he did not. 'Wait and see.'

'Woman's intuition?'

'Wait and see,' she repeated. She waved at the shelves. 'So all this stuff will remain here?'

'What better place to keep it hidden? It's been like this for decades. It would be foolish of me to move anything. This will be a very secure extension of the rogues' gallery in Berlin.'

'So when do you tell Pappi . . . about the Hargreaves, and about this?'

'Not by telephone. I am not prepared to risk that. Even with the goth's secure magic system, I would not risk talking

45

about this from here. It will all have to wait until I see Pappi back in Berlin. Besides, I am still thinking about betrayal.'

'By whom?'

'When I'm certain, I'll tell you. A suggestion,' Müller went on.

'Shoot.'

'It will take months, perhaps years, to get through all of this material. But we might glean enough for now, if we spend some time while we're here, doing a quick scan.'

'Fine with me. How long do you think we'll need for this "quick scan"?'

'A day or two. We can remain down here. It also keeps us out of sight of the curious. There is plenty of fresh food in the fridge, as you saw.'

'I saw. They were definitely well prepared.'

'And there are the two bedrooms . . .'

'Shame.'

'What?'

'Nothing.'

'But you said . . .'

'I know what I said. You were saying . . . ?'

He gave her a warily uncertain glance, then went on, 'But before we do that, I would like to check that exit at the end of the hall. See where it comes out. Might be useful.'

'OK. We take the guns?'

Müller thought about it for brief moments. 'Just in case.'

She opened the bag and took out the Beretta 92Rs, already in shoulder harnesses, spare magazines in attached pouches.

They each put on a harness.

'Not your own shooter,' she said, checking the one she had chosen, 'but as we're not here "officially" like the last time . . . my "diplomatic bag" will have to do.' Satisfied, she placed the weapon back in its holster.

'I'm sure I'll be able to manage. I hope we won't need them while we're here. All right. Let's go.'

'Wait a second,' Carey Bloomfield said. She had been idly staring at a box file, and thought she had seen something protruding behind it. She went up for a closer look. 'Now what do we have here?'

She reached behind the box while Müller looked on with an air of mild expectancy.

'Will you look at this? Wow! Are these binoculars? Or are these binoculars?'

It was a solid-looking piece of equipment, weighty, yet not overly heavy. It was finished in a mottled camouflage that would be effective in many different terrains, and looked very high-tech. It did not have the customary twin lenses sticking out beyond the main body. It was a one-piece curving unit with a single oval glass section at the front behind which twin lenses were hidden, and coated to cut down unwanted reflections. A padded eyepiece was at the other end. There was a plethora of control buttons, and two sunken, knurled wheels. A mottled sling was attached.

'This looks like it's a nightscope, infrared scope, and daylight scope all in one,' she said, studying it critically. 'No markings on it anywhere. No way of saying where it's from.' She passed it to Müller. 'From his days in the Stasi?'

'He could have got it from anywhere,' Müller replied. He put it to his eyes and pressed a button at random. A uniform darkness suddenly became a bright, sharp image of the room. 'Light enhancer, even in this lighting.' He passed it back. 'Let's take it with us. Give it a test run. Find out which buttons do what.'

'Sir, yessir!'

'Behave.'

The exit at the end of the hall was, like the entrance, plated with armoured steel. An indented red button about the size of a two-euro coin was positioned into it, near the jamb.

They put their boots back on, then Müller pressed the button once. There was the soft hiss of solid bolts sliding back; then the door, a hefty twenty centimetres thick, swung outwards silently. A tunnel, softly illuminated by fibre optics, stretched before them. The roof was high enough to allow Müller to stand upright. The tunnel had concrete sides and roof, and a sealed floor. Ducting pipes ran along the roof. A neat line of grilled slits on both sides, at head level, went on as far as could be seen. Filtered air, at a comfortable temperature, came out of them.

Müller looked up at the pipes. 'Inlet and exhaust. Wonder where they come out.' He looked closely, studying the workmanship. 'This was very professionally done.'

'How did they manage to build all of this without people getting curious about it? The guys who actually built the house must have wondered.'

'Not necessarily. My fa . . . Jack Hargreaves knew a thing or two about construction engineering. It was he who converted the house in Wilmersdorf into apartments. So he will have picked his people well, and would have been on site thoughout its construction. Don't forget the Cold War was in full swing. It would have been easy for him to tell a convincing tale about building what they would have seen as a luxury nuclear bunker. They would have thought him a little paranoid, and given it no further thought. By the time Maggie and Jack became famous for their eco produce, no one would have been remotely interested in what was put down here when the house was being built all those years ago. The electronic wizardry will have been done by him. Let's not forget his own history as a successful spy, and infiltrator of both the Stasi *and* the Semper.'

'Very brave man, Müller. You should be proud.'

'Brave . . .' Müller said, as if in passing; and left it at that. 'Come on.'

As they moved, the door shut behind them.

Carey Bloomfield whirled. 'Oh great. Now we've got to start from up top all over again.'

'No need,' Müller said, pointing to the recessed keypad.

'He did not mention this one in the note.'

'No need,' Müller repeated. He went up to the door and tapped in the entry code.

The routine with the bolts sounded, and the door came open.

'Smartass,' she said.

'For my sins.'

The door swung shut again as they moved on. The tunnel ran straight for about fifty or so metres, before turning right.

'If I am gauging this correctly,' Müller said, 'we're under the rear garden, and heading in the direction of the outhouses.'

When they came to the turning, he stopped suddenly, peering at one of the grilled outlets.

'What is it?' Carey Bloomfield asked.

'I've been seeing something in there at irregular intervals, on both sides of this tunnel. At first, I was not sure what it was.'

'And now?'

'Cameras.'

'You're kidding.'

'See for yourself.'

She peered at the one he was looking at, and could just make out the small curvature of the lens, no bigger than the ones usually found in camera-equipped mobile phones.

'I'll be damned. Micro cameras. They thought of everything.'

'Not everything,' Müller said with quiet meaning.

She understood, and said nothing, turning instead to scrutinize the opposite side. She was barely able to spot another hidden camera.

'How many of these do you think there are?'

'Several . . . and perhaps not only here.'

As they walked, she kept fiddling with the binoculars, now and then raising the unit to her eyes. Every so often, soft exclamations would come from her as she discovered a function that impressed.

'You sound like a child with a new toy,' Müller remarked at one point.

'This is some toy.'

After a while, the tunnel began to rise gently. Soon, they came to a dead end. The only way was straight up. The ducting had vanished into the side of the tunnel.

A cylindrical shaft, roomy enough to allow one person an unrestricted climb, rose perpendicularly. A wide and solid ladder was permanently fixed to it.

'That's at least two, maybe three floors up,' Carey Bloomfield remarked, peering upwards. 'Who's first?'

'Beauty before age. You go.'

'No chance. If you fall, I can duck.'

'And if you fall, I'll catch you.'

'With a promise like that, how can a girl resist?'

Slinging the binoculars across her body from a shoulder, she began to climb.

Soon, she was calling down, 'Hey. There's a door up here.'

'Do what is normally done with doors. Open it.'

'Smartass,' came the retort. She opened the door, and natural light flooded in. She stepped off the ladder. 'Well. What do you know!'

Müller followed. When he got to the top, he discovered that stepping off the ladder took him through sliding doors and into a large, almost bare room that was arranged like a study, with two desks and a chair each. There was nothing on the desks. The room was on the top floor of one of the outhouses. A single door led off to the right. There were two big windows, with partially open venetian blinds. As he walked away from the doors, they slid shut.

Carey Bloomfield was looking at him with an expectant little smile.

He turned to look at the doors. They seemed to belong to what appeared to be a large built-in cupboard. A keypad was sunk into the left door.

'*Another* keypad?'

'Smart idea,' she said. 'As soon as I stepped through, they shut. I thought you'd be stuck, as I don't have the code to open them. But then they came open when you arrived. So you only need the code if you want to go *in* this way. Can you open it?'

'I can try,' Müller said. He tapped in the same code he had used below.

The doors slid open.

'There you go,' she said. 'Access.'

Müller stepped back, and the doors slid shut once more. 'The Hargreaves were certainly thorough. But that was to be expected.' He went towards one of the big windows, and peered out. 'Perfect view across the valley, and of the road and the airstrip. From here, they would have plenty of warning of unwelcome visitors, if they felt at all threatened. When I first saw these windows, I thought the Lyserts lived up here.'

'Maybe they use the other outhouse.'

'Possibly,' Müller admitted.

She passed him the binoculars. 'Try this. You'll be a little surprised. Its power supply is solar, just like the house and everything here that needs power. This has a long power durability.' She began to itemize. 'This button gives you power state. This one is for the floating target marker . . .'

'*Target* marker?'

'Wait, Müller! The marker,' she continued, 'is a fat red-gold circle with protruding cross-hairs. Transparent. This button locks the target, and the binoculars will always keep it in sight, automatically adjusting close up as you follow. This button changes mode to manual. This one switches day, night, and infrared mode. This is for zoom. This wheel is for distance . . . you've got a readout for all modes, distances, power state . . .'

She continued to show him all the controls, bringing her head close enough for him to catch the scent of her hair.

She looked up suddenly. 'What?'

'Nothing,' he said. 'I think I've got it all now.'

He turned back to the window and forced two slats of the blind apart with the binoculars. The valley was vividly defined. The airstrip looked as if he were actually standing on it. He activated the floating target marker and locked it on a bird. The marker stayed on the bird, automatically zooming, giving a precise distance readout.

He took the binoculars away from his eyes, and stood back from the blind. 'Very impressive.'

'This must have been their observation platform,' Carey Bloomfield said. 'Wonder how many times they came up here to check out the area, over the years.'

'Probably every day, once this place was built. They had to. They could never have been absolutely certain that their tracks had been well covered. They would have spent all those years on the alert . . . even though creating Woonnalla kept them in plain sight, so to speak. Best way to hide.'

'You sound like an old spymaster, Müller.'

'I had a good example to learn from,' he said, thinking of his father. He passed the binoculars back to her. 'Let's see what's behind that door.'

The door opened into another virtually empty room, with a wide balcony that faced the rear of the property, accessed via wide French doors. There were two white, adjustable loungers, upholstered in white. A small, round-topped low table, also in white, stood between them. There was nothing else on the balcony.

'Another observation platform?' Carey Bloomfield suggested.

'Possibly. But it looks more like a place to watch the sunsets. This faces west.'

They went out on to the balcony.

'It's beautiful,' she said, staring across the vast landscape of red earth, pockmarked with hardy clumps of bush, and boulders that looked like small hills. Lines of low dunes rose in the distance. 'As far as the eye can see.'

'Yes. It is.'

She turned to look behind, and upwards. 'Well, will you look at that.'

He followed her gaze. 'That' was an impressive array of aerials. Some distance from these, at the far end of the outhouse, were two large structures that looked like chimneys, with their ends turned downwards. Horizontal vanes topped by concave covers were fitted like stoppers. The vanes turned silently, in opposite directions.

'This almost puts our own array on the police building in Berlin to shame,' Müller said, staring at it. 'The way they have positioned these and the pipes, you can't see anything of them from the front. That monitor we saw in the Pandora's Box should show us some interesting things.'

'More smart work. They weren't exactly cut off from the outside world.'

'Not really,' he agreed.

'Müller?'

'Yes.'

'I need to eat.'

Three

Berlin, 12.01 local.

Klemp stood guard by the door of the hospital room where the goth was recovering from emergency treatment. The heavy-calibre bullet had gone right through, mercifully without hitting anything vital. Meant to have been a killing shot, it had still been a ferocious wound.

Despite being taken by complete surprise when the killer had appeared in front of her car, her alertness in ducking had definitely saved her life. Instead of ploughing through her heart, the round had struck her a 'glancing' blow that had been painful enough to cause her to lose consciousness; and severe enough to cost her a lot of blood.

Klemp was enjoying his perusal of one of his favourite fitness magazines. This issue was full of strong-looking women. Only illustrated tabloids came close.

He therefore looked up partly guiltily, and partly with pleasant surprise, when the female doctor came up to him. She looked like someone who enjoyed a good round of exercise. The close-fitting scrubs outfit betrayed enough to give that impression.

Her opening remark proved it to Klemp.

'Good magazine,' she said, glancing at it as Klemp hurriedly began to roll it up. 'Don't do that on my account,' she went on, giving him a radiant smile. Her green eyes were captivating and appraising. 'Good to see a man taking his health seriously. You look like someone who goes to the gym,' she finished with approval.

Klemp, flattered beyond his dreams, said, 'When . . . whenever I can . . . Frau . . .' He glanced at her name tag. '. . . Frau *Doktor* Klammert.'

The doctor stood close, within his personal space. He took the slightest of steps backwards, involuntarily making room.

But he was blocked by the corridor wall. He stood there, feeling himself getting excited by the doctor, and at once pleased and embarrassed by it.

'Terrible thing about your colleague,' she said. 'We're all shocked that something so horrible could happen to such a lovely young woman. Terrible to happen to anyone, of course . . . but she's such a frail-looking . . .'

'Oh don't let that fool you, Frau *Doktor*,' Klemp said in a superheated rush. 'She looks frail, but she's as strong as an ox.' Enough of his common sense remained for him to add, 'But it's touch and go if she'll make it.'

The doctor looked sad. 'I know. Amazing she survived this long . . .'

'Yes . . .'

'*Klemp!*' a female voice yelled. '*What the hell are you doing?*'

A remarkable change had come over the doctor.

Her face hardened in sudden fury. '*Shit!*' she snarled at the astonished Klemp. 'That *fucking* bitch!' She gave Klemp a quick pat on the cheek. 'Pity. You might have been an interesting specimen to fuck.'

Then she set off at a run, removing the doctor's outfit as she did so.

Berger and Reimer, guns out of their shoulder harnesses, were themselves on the run as they arrived.

'Get after her, Reimer!' Berger ordered. 'I'll not be long. And watch yourself!'

Reimer barely paused as he set off.

Berger glared at Klemp. 'What the hell did you think you were doing?'

'Don't talk to me like that!' Klemp began in an aggrieved tone. 'Just because they just promoted you to *Kommissarin* . . .'

Berger's eyes, likened to those of a hawk by Carey Bloomfield, were blazing. '*I'm in no mood for your whining shit about my promotion, Klemp!* Just do your job!'

Klemp would not give in gracefully. 'The doctor . . .'

'*That was no doctor, you moron! Can't you see that even now? Wake up!*' She tapped his head with the barrel of her gun, none too gently.

Klemp flinched. 'That's an assault on a colleague . . . !' he began to bluster.

'Don't try me, Klemp. Your brains are supposed to be up there . . .'

She pointed the gun at his crotch, and Klemp swiftly placed his hands there in an instinctive act of protection. He could not have helped it.

'. . . and *not* down there!' Berger went on. 'If you had got what you were after – which I doubt – you'd be dead as soon as you were done! You should change your reading material. Read about the sex life of spiders. The male has a very bad time afterwards if he's not fast enough on his feet. Now guard that door as you're supposed to! I'll talk to you later.'

She hurried on after Reimer, ignoring the curious stares of the hospital staff who had come out from every corner, it seemed, to have a look.

Klemp stared after her with outraged, injured pride.

Berger was speaking into her mobile to Pappenheim as she ran. 'Someone just tried to get into the room, Chief. A woman. I think it's the same one.'

'Sharon Wilson,' Pappenheim said, voice tight.

'Has to be. This time she was a doctor, and giving Klemp the great come-on. The idiot was falling for it. I gave him a roasting. He might complain to you.'

'He'd better not,' Pappenheim said ominously. 'Our killer's a very smart chameleon. First a biking tourist in Australia, then a *Kommissarin* when she shot the goth, now a doctor.'

'Reimer's chasing her, and I'm following.'

'Your voice tells me you already think you've lost her.'

'I'll be very surprised if Reimer catches her. Not doubting his ability. I doubt if *I'll* catch her . . .'

'I understand . . .'

'. . . this time,' Berger finished.

'I understand that too. But remember there's a queue, and it starts with Jens, then me . . . then perhaps even Colonel Bloomfield . . .'

'I won't stand back for *her*!'

'I know you won't,' Pappenheim told her in soothing tones. 'Keep looking all the same,' he went on, 'just in case she has decided to hide in the hospital.'

'I'd be surprised, but we'll check.'

'Keep me posted.'

'Yes, Chief.'

In the end, it was Reimer who spotted Sharon Wilson, but only because she wanted him to see her; and he had no idea at the time.

He had rushed into one of the hospital car parks, and saw an attractive redhead just about to get into her car. Expecting a fugitive brunette, Reimer was caught completely off-guard, especially as the redhead seemed to be smiling at him.

He instinctively smiled back, and when the redhead gave him a goodbye wave with fluttering fingers, responded with a brief hand movement. It was only when the car began to race away that it dawned upon him that he might have been taken.

He was still quick enough to get a licence number, and immediately called the unit's vehicle tracking section.

'Klaus,' he said when he got a reply. 'I have a number for you. It's very urgent. Berlin plate. Call me as soon as you have it.' He gave the number.

'Done. I'll call you right back.'

'OK.'

Berger arrived just as he ended the call. 'I saw you from upstairs. That was her, wasn't it, in that car?' Berger's stare was challenging.

'Look . . .' Reimer began awkwardly. 'I was expecting someone with dark hair . . . not, not bright red.'

'Ever heard of *wigs*, Reimer?' Berger sighed. 'What *is* it with you men? A woman simpers and you're jelly . . .'

'That's not fair, Lene . . .'

'The world's not fair, Reimer.' Berger stared in the direction that the car, a dark BMW, had gone. 'Shit.'

Reimer's phone temporarily saved his bacon.

He lifted it to his ear with relief. 'Yes, Klaus.'

'Dark blue BMW 525 with all the trimmings?'

'I wasn't close enough to check its equipment but yes . . . a dark blue 525 . . .'

Klaus Zerny gave a low chuckle. 'No criminals to chase? You're after bankers now? Mark you, some bankers can be . . .'

'A *banker*?'

'Says it right here on my monitor. Heinrich Höhntaler, investment banker, clean as ten whistles. You're way off target, Reimer. Pillar of the community . . .'

'It doesn't make sense.'

'What doesn't?'

'A woman was driving it . . .'

Zerny gave a short laugh. 'Perhaps he lets the girlfriend borrow it . . .'

'Not that one,' Reimer said, looking depressed. 'Look . . . see if you can find out a little more about this Heinrich Höhntaler. If he gave this woman his car . . .'

Reimer was cut off by Berger's taking the phone away. He stared at her, wide-eyed. 'What . . .'

She spoke into it. 'It's OK, Klaus. We'll take it from here.' She switched off on a startled Zerny, and returned the phone to Reimer.

'What was that all about?' Reimer demanded.

Instead of replying, Berger called Pappenheim on her own mobile. 'Heinrich Höhntaler, Chief. A name that's just come up. Sharon Wilson's driving his car.'

'I'll call you back,' Pappenheim said quickly. 'Might as well stay with Klemp, in case our friend tries again. Not likely for now . . . but you never know. You tell Klemp I'll have words with him later.'

'A pleasure,' Berger said.

'You've got me,' Pappenheim said into his phone when his contact rang back.

'No one ever gets you, Pappi,' the female voice said. 'Too slippery by half.'

'Talking dirty again; I see . . . So you've found the man?'

'I've found him. As your colleague at your vehicle tracking section has said, he seems clean . . .'

'"*Seems*"?'

'You know us, Pappi. No one's that clean . . .'

'Suspicious lot.'

'Look who's talking! Well, a contact made contact,' the voice continued, 'and left me in the loop. The car's stolen. Höhntaler had no idea it had gone, if his yell of outrage was anything to

57

go by. I heard it. He looked out of his office window, and saw a space where his car should have been. The company car park is supposed to be secure. He was very shocked . . .'

'Or a very good actor. See if you can dig deeper.'

'Now who's being suspicious?'

'You know me.'

'Oh yes,' the voice said with a sigh, then the call ended.

Pappenheim leaned back in his chair, took a Gauloise *Blonde* from an already opened pack, and lit up. It was one of many since morning. The full ashtray, ringed by a generous overspill on the crowded, untidy desk, was proof of that. He was blowing a neat set of smoke rings at the tobacco-stained ceiling, when a peremptory knocking spoiled his enjoyment.

Pappenheim sighed as the familiar, unwelcome knock came again.

'We haven't seen you for . . . oh days,' he muttered, '. . . weeks, and here I was hoping you'd been kidnapped. Peace has just ended.'

He did not respond, and kept on smoking.

The knocking came again, louder this time. '*Pappenheim!* I know you're in there! I can smell the stink of your cigarette!'

'Normally,' Pappenheim said to himself, 'you just barge in. What's keeping you?'

The door slammed open as *Polizeidirektor* (probationary) Heinz Kaltendorf barged in.

'My God!' Kaltendorf exclaimed, coughing loudly. 'How can you breathe in this smokepit you call an office?'

'You say that every time . . . sir,' Pappenheim said. 'So you've not been kidnapped. Nice to have you back.'

Kaltendorf peered through the smoke. 'What?'

'A weak joke, sir. Sorry.' Pappenheim did not move. He had taken the cigarette out just long enough to speak.

Kaltendorf stood there in the doorway, almost a silhouette in the veil of smoke, and glared at him, blinking, then frowned as if checking Pappenheim's words for hidden barbs.

'It is true that *Meisterin* Meyer has been shot?' Kaltendorf challenged.

'It is true . . . sir. This morning, as she arrived for work. Professional hit.' Again, the cigarette came out just long enough to facilitate speech.

58

'Is she . . .'

'It's touch and go.' Pappenheim gave up the struggle and reluctantly killed the cigarette. 'She has already undergone emergency surgery. Berger, Reimer, and Klemp are at her door . . .'

'You detailed *three* colleagues to guard her door?'

'The least I could do,' Pappenheim said, baby-blue eyes sending out a challenge of their own. 'The doctors are not allowing any visitors,' he added, lying.

'Why?'

'She's close to the edge. The doctors insist that, for now, she should be left strictly alone. They're not laying any bets.'

'I . . . see . . .' Kaltendorf stood there for irresolute seconds. 'And I was at a conference,' he said, strangely defensive, 'if it's any business of yours. I want a full report on this!' He slammed out.

The force of the shutting door caused a slipstream that briefly disturbed the apparent permanence of the veil of smoke.

'Ah . . . those exits of his,' Pappenheim said. 'I was almost beginning to miss them. Which should worry me.'

Pappenheim sighed, gave the half-finished cigarette a wistful stare, then lit up afresh.

'"And I was at a conference, if it's any business of yours",' he mimicked. 'He wants a report.' He blew four smoke rings upwards. 'Pisser.'

At the hospital, Berger was favouring Klemp with one of her coldest stares.

Klemp's returning look was at once defiant and sheepish. 'Look. I thought she was a doctor. OK? How was I supposed to know she was a fake?'

'You were not supposed to know,' Berger admitted. Her eyes, however, remained distinctly unfriendly. 'But, you're also not supposed to let anyone you don't know – even among the hospital staff – anywhere near that door. She does a job on you, and you forget why you're standing here. The chief will not be pleased.'

Before Klemp could respond, she turned to Reimer. 'You

stay here with him, Johann. I'm going in to have a look at Hedi.'

Reimer nodded. 'OK.'

Berger carefully turned the doorknob and entered.

Klemp shot a sour glance at her back, before looking at Reimer as the door shut behind her.

'The chief, the chief,' Klemp remarked bitterly. 'Pappenheim's pet . . .'

'Don't say it,' Reimer warned. He stared at Klemp in a manner that was no friendlier than Berger's. 'You're in enough trouble as it is. Cut your losses.'

'She's throwing her rank around,' Klemp insisted.

'She isn't . . . and you know it. And she's right. You know that too. Now shut up. And I don't want to hear any shit from you about how you outrank me, and I can't talk to you like that, *Hauptmeister* Klemp. Got that?'

Klemp looked outraged, but he finally shut up.

Gun back in its harness, Berger entered on silent feet. She moved towards the only bed in the room where the goth was lying, eyes closed, as pale as the sheet itself.

A single chair was near the foot of the bed on the left; and a low chest of drawers was near the goth's head, on the right. A huge bunch of flowers had been placed upon it.

The goth was in the usual post-surgery attire. The white cotton sheet was halfway down her body, baring the sling which held her left arm across her chest. Her right hand was beneath the sheet. She was connected to a drip, but there was no monitoring equipment. Hedi Meyer was as far from death as it was possible to be, after being shot.

'I know you're awake,' Berger said quietly as she stood by the bed. 'You can open them now.'

The goth was sublimely unique among the police officers of the unit. A supreme electronics genius, she had turned down lucrative work offers in commerce, and in a shadowy Intelligence group Pappenheim called the Blue Folder Boys. Her colleagues – Müller and Pappenheim among them – continued to be curious about her motivations. Müller had once asked, and she had retorted by asking why did he, titled and wealthy, choose to become a policeman. Unable and unwilling to answer, he had retired defeated.

The goth tended to appear at work in attire that was magnificently unconventional. The shock of her appearance on her first day at the Friedrichstrasse unit had long since dissipated; but the air of amused wonder had not. Even Kaltendorf, a stickler for the book, had given up trying to get her to be more conventional in dress. It also helped that the imagined coterie of Müller and Pappenheim – in Kaltendorf's heated brain – steadfastly defended her independence.

She had arrived for work that morning in her original black VW Beetle, a pristine example that was older than she was. For the occasion, she had been wearing a short-sleeved, ankle-length dress in what looked like black gossamer. On her feet had been black, elegant trainers that were more like ballet shoes, with white side stripes. Her fingernails were painted black, and blue eye-shadow had adorned her eyelids.

Her long, gleaming dark hair was now spread about her head. The colour accentuated the ethereal paleness of her face. Despite the emergency surgery, her eye-shadow was still in place.

She opened startling eyes that seemed at once blue and green. One appeared to shift colour infinitesimally.

She gave Berger a weak smile. 'I wasn't sure who would be coming in. I heard shouting . . .'

'I don't shout,' Berger said, pulling the chair close and taking a seat. 'I was talking firmly.'

'All right . . . you were talking firmly. To whom?'

'Klemp. Who else? Klemp is a tough policeman. Unfortunately, he is also soft in the head. He nearly got conned into letting the woman who shot you in here.'

The goth's eyes widened; but she controlled the surge of fear that came to her. 'Checking on her work?'

Berger nodded. 'She wants to make sure you're dead.'

'I would have been ready for her.' The goth pulled her hand out from under the sheet. In it was a big automatic. A Beretta 92R.

Berger stared at it. 'Now you're an official member of the Ninety-two Club. The chief gave that to you? He and the boss are the non-issue boys. They've got more than one each. I think *Direktor* Kaltendorf has one as well, from the days when he was a real policeman . . . so I've heard.'

The goth nodded. 'It must have been the *Oberkommissar*. He came to visit just after surgery. I was groggy, and I think I passed out on him. When I woke up, it was next to the flowers, with two spare magazines. There was a little note. Just in case, it said.'

'If Klemp had had his way, you would have needed it.'

'But you stopped him in time.'

'Yes, but not our killer lady. She ran. Reimer went after her, but she had planned her escape well. She got to her car, actually waved at Reimer, then took off. Brazen cow.'

'She'll try again,' the goth said, eyes wide, but in a calm voice.

'She definitely will.' Berger sounded hopeful. 'But you won't be here for her to find. After what has happened, the chief will have you moved somewhere safe.'

'The safest place for me is at Friedrichstrasse. I have work to do. They need me there.'

'They need you healthy,' Berger countered. 'That wound was not a pinprick. You've lost a lot of blood.'

'I'll be fine. I can . . .' The goth began to move, as if to get out of bed.

Berger just looked at her.

'You're not going to stop me?' the goth asked.

'Why should I? Perhaps you like hitting the floor with your head.'

'I'm stronger than you think.'

'Then be my guest,' Berger said, not believing it. 'Don't forget the drip on your way down. I'm not going to be a party to this.'

Ignoring her comment, the goth slowly pulled her legs up and swung them over the side of the bed.

Berger was as good as her word, and did not help.

She stared in disbelief as the goth then began to force herself into an upright sitting position.

The goth made it. 'You see?' she said to Berger in triumph. 'And there's no bleeding.'

Berger continued to stare at her. 'You've got alien DNA.'

'Then I've got it off you, Johann Reimer, and the chief. The doctor told me you all gave blood. Thank you . . . and thank Johann. I'll thank the chief when I see him.'

She glanced round at the flowers. 'And for the flowers.'

Berger did not tell her that Pappenheim had been pacing the hospital corridor in severe need of a smoke, but had stuck it out till he knew she was safely out of danger; that he had sat next to the bed while she had been still unconscious after surgery, now and then taking her hand as he would a much-loved daughter.

Pappenheim had forcefully forbidden Berger to mention it.

'Everyone wanted to do something,' Berger said, feeling awkward. 'The blood . . . the flowers . . .'

'I thought you all thought of me as crazy . . .'

Berger grinned at her. 'You *are* crazy. But then, *Direktor* Kaltendorf thinks the boss and the chief are crazy. Klemp thinks I'm crazy. It's all a matter of degree. And now that you've proved how tough you are, get back in that bed. That's not Lene talking to you, but the *Kommissarin*, *Meisterin* Meyer.'

The goth gave the barest of smiles. 'Yes, sir.'

This time, Berger got up to help.

'He needs me,' the goth said, as she gratefully lay back.

'Who needs you? As if I didn't know . . .' Berger added.

The changeling eyes of the goth looked at her steadily. 'If you mean *Hauptkommissar* Müller . . . perhaps I can ask you about *Oberkommissar* Pappenheim . . .'

Despite her best efforts, Berger could not stop the slight pink that briefly stained her cheeks. High on her cheekbones.

'I don't know what you mean.' There was just a hint of defensiveness in her voice.

'You must be the only one, then. Woman to woman,' the goth went on before Berger could protest. 'I know I've got to compete with that . . . colonel.' A sharp edge graced the word 'colonel' . . . 'and you've got to deal with the memory of someone you'll never see.' This was said gently, and without malice. 'Which is worse?'

Berger ducked that one, and studied the goth for long moments. 'How can someone so thin be so strong? You've just popped out of surgery.'

'Not "just" . . . and I am not thin. I'm slim. Many women would think I'm fat.'

'Sick ones,' Berger said. She got to her feet. 'You'll be OK?'

'I'm fine. Really.'

'Reimer will stay with Klemp,' Berger said, 'to make sure his brains don't soften at the sight of the next woman he sees in medical uniform. You won't be staying here for much longer. Don't worry.'

The goth nodded. 'Have my parents been told?'

'Not yet . . .'

'Good.'

'*Good?*'

'Let me handle it. They'll panic. They already think I'm crazy for joining the police.'

'Imagine that. Now get some rest,' Berger went on quickly. 'You need it. Your little show didn't exactly fool me.'

'I *am* fine.'

'I'm sure you are.'

With a tiny smile, Berger left the room.

The goth sank back gratefully. Then with her right hand, she shifted her left arm very slightly, just enough to allow her to peer beneath her hospital gown at the bandaged wound. A tiny spot of blood had appeared.

She relaxed, and shut her eyes, biting her lower lip to stifle the pain as the anaesthetic began to lose its potency.

It had been worth it.

A knock sounded on Pappenheim's door. He knew, with relief, it was not Kaltendorf.

'*In!*' Pappenheim called, recognizing it as Berger's.

He took a long drag on his Gauloise, and squinted through its smoke as she entered.

'So?' he began to her. 'How's the Ethereal One?'

'Better than she has a right to be after being hit by that cannon, and after surgery. How can someone who looks so frail take a shot that would probably have sent Klemp to a fitness heaven filled with strong-looking women, and still look as if she only stubbed a toe?'

Pappenheim briefly tapped at his temple.

'Oh she's crazy all right,' Berger said.

'I didn't mean crazy,' Pappenheim said. 'I meant she's very strong up there. Don't be fooled.'

'I'm not,' Berger said with feeling. 'I told her she had alien DNA.'

'She might enjoy the concept. Don't encourage her.'

'If Klemp would have had anything to do with it, she could well be on her way to goth heaven by now, tank gun or no tank gun.'

'Tank gun? Ah. You mean the little Beretta . . .'

'*Little!*'

'She would have surprised Miss Wilson and who knows? She might have won. Don't underestimate our goth.'

'I don't. When do we tell her parents? And the media are sniffing. Exploding cars and shot colleagues get them excited.'

'Another reason to get the goth out of that hospital. Despite our embargo, a staff member will talk eventually. Nothing like a camera to get some mouths blabbing. As for the parents . . . I'm not sure whether to leave them in the dark for now. She's supposed to be at death's door. Sharon Wilson, and the Semper, must be convinced that the attempt succeeded. The question is whether the Meyers could act out the grieving parents convincingly enough, knowing their daughter was really alive and while not exactly well, as close as it is possible to be after being shot by that woman.'

'The goth herself said not to.'

'She did? Why?'

'First, they already think she's crazy for joining the police . . .'

'When she could have been making so much more money working for some high-tech and *safe* company . . . or in Intelligence. Don't know about the money for that lot though. They're as badly paid as we are.'

'They get better expenses. Extra salaries, almost.'

'Now that is quite true.'

'She didn't say that about the jobs,' Berger said, 'but that's probably part of it.'

'And the other part?'

'They will panic.'

'Ah,' Pappenheim said. 'Well, that kills letting them in on the secret.'

'Which should please the goth.'

Pappenheim thought about the way she had replied, and gave her another squint. 'Something on your mind? There's an edge in there somewhere.'

'Oh . . . it's nothing.'

'I like nothings. They interest me. They are sometimes much more interesting than somethings.' He paused, looking at her.

'I'd . . . I'd better be going.'

'Don't duck, Lene. What is it?'

'She wants to be back at work,' Berger answered, after some hesitation.

'Not a chance.'

'That's what I said.'

'Good.'

'She thinks this would be the safest place for her.'

'In a way, she's right,' Pappenheim said. 'But out of the question. I have a very safe place in mind . . .'

'I think you'll have a tough time convincing her, Chief. She said . . . he needs her here.'

Pappenheim was silent for long moments. Then he gave a loud sigh.

'I thought that too,' Berger said. 'Whatever's feeding that torch . . .'

'. . . is not going to fade anytime soon, as Miss Bloomfield would probably say.'

It was Berger's turn to take refuge in an eloquent silence.

Pappenheim's baby-blue eyes peered at her through his permanent smokescreen. 'There's more.'

'She thinks of Colonel Bloomfield as a rival,' Berger began tentatively.

Pappenheim waited. Even his cigarette seemed to have run out of smoke, and was waiting as well.

'She . . . thinks that I would understand . . . as I have my own rival . . . a memory I can't see.'

Pappenheim looked away, expression betraying nothing. Then he turned to look at her once more.

'Lene,' he began gently. 'I'm too old . . . too fa— large, untidy, a chain-smoker . . .'

'Tell me something I don't know.'

'You need a young . . .'

'*Don't tell me what kind of man I need! You're not my father, and . . . and I wouldn't let him tell me!*'

Berger walked out, slamming the door.

Pappenheim stared at the door. 'Something I said? Something I said,' he added after a while.

The cigarette had died. He gave another sigh, but did not light up.

The phone rang.

He grabbed it. '*What!* Oh. It's you.'

'Somebody just bit you on the backside?' his female contact said.

'Don't get personal.'

'So somebody did.'

'As long as you don't say there's plenty to go round.'

'You just did . . . so I won't. Still interested in your banker?'

'I'm all ears,' Pappenheim said, interest sharpened, pushing the small confrontation with Berger out of the way.

'The car, as you know, was really stolen. But the strange thing is this: he does have a connection to the people you're interested in.'

Pappenheim sat upright. 'Tell me more.'

'It's all in something you will receive.'

'Why would they deliberately surface someone we knew nothing about?'

'You're the detective. Perhaps he was skimming off some of their money, and it pissed them off.' The contact hung up with a short laugh.

'Or perhaps they're trying to deflect our attention from something,' Pappenheim said quietly as he put the phone down. 'Or someone.'

He lit a fresh cigarette, taking his time about it. 'From Sharon Wilson?'

At the hospital, a pleasant-looking man in his mid twenties, wearing jeans, a baggy white T-shirt with a logo on the front, and trainers, walked to the reception desk. He carried a black leather backpack slung from a shoulder.

A young nurse was on duty. Over to one side, a private security guard looked at him interestedly.

'Good day,' he said to the nurse, smiling.

'Good day,' she responded. She smiled in return. 'Can I help you, sir?'

'My name is Max Erling, I work for *Berlin Hours* . . .' He pointed to the logo on his shirt.

'Ah yes. That new magazine about Berlin life.'

He beamed. 'So you know of us?'

'Oh yes. My friends and I all take it. Regularly.'

He grinned at her. 'That's good for us.'

'We like what you've got in there. A great mix of serious and fun. So? How can I help you? Doing a piece on us? We could do with some nice publicity . . .'

'Well, now that you mention it, I am here for the serious stuff.' He lowered his voice, as if taking her into his confidence. 'I'm after a scoop. My colleagues from the rest of the media don't know what I know. I want to get my piece before they find out.'

She liked the sound of that. 'And what is it that you know?'

'There was an incident this morning. An officer got shot . . . very badly, I believe.'

'Oh yes,' the nurse said without hesitation. 'Poor thing . . .'

'Poor thing?'

'Yes. A policewoman. I haven't seen her myself, but they say she was young. Pretty too . . .'

'Was? She's *dead*?'

'We-ell . . . I'm not sure, but . . .'

It was then that Max Erling noticed that the security guard was no longer there. He frowned, then unobtrusively began to search out the location of the security cameras.

The security guard was in a small room, talking quietly into his radio.

'Someone at the desk asking about that police officer who got shot. Warn her colleagues. Right. I'll just watch him and do nothing. I'll have to search his pack . . . OK. Not even that.'

Max Erling saw the guard return, looking sheepish.

The guard walked up to the desk. 'Just needed to . . . erm . . . go,' he said to the nurse. He glanced at Erling with a slight nod, then walked back to where he had been standing.

Erling gave another slight frown, before smiling at the nurse. 'So . . . will you give me an interview?'

'*Me?* I can't tell you much.' But she was flattered.

'You'd be surprised . . .'

That was when he saw someone approaching; a man who had policeman written all over him.

Max Erling, supposed journalist for *Berlin Hours*, suddenly said, 'Forgot something in the car. Be right back.'

He went out before Klemp arrived.

Klemp stared at the back of the rapidly moving Max Erling. 'That the man you were talking to?' he asked the nurse, still staring in the direction Erling had gone.

'Yes. He's just gone to get something from his car.'

'Then I'll wait here.'

'Is he in trouble?' she sounded disappointed.

'Not yet.' Klemp sounded ominous.

'He never came back,' Klemp said when he had rejoined Reimer. 'He told the nurse his name was Max Erling, journalist with *Berlin Hours*. He was very interested in finding out about *Meisterin* Meyer.'

Reimer was talking to Pappenheim on his mobile. 'The journalist did not come back.'

'I heard most of what Klemp just said,' Pappenheim said. 'Not difficult to fill in the rest. All right, Johann. I'll see to it.'

'Yes, Chief,' Reimer acknowledged, ending the call.

'Now what?' Klemp asked.

'We wait.'

Having taken a deliberately roundabout route, Sharon Wilson drove the BMW along Unter den Linden, in the direction of the Brandenburg Gate; but she was not going there.

As she approached the junction with Friedrichstrasse, the lights turned red. There were several cars ahead of her. Staying in the right-hand lane, she calmly pulled up behind a white van. She did not seem bothered by the fact that she was barely a block or two away from where Pappenheim was in his office, making plans on how to stop her.

There was a turning to the right just before the lights, which led to a small parking area. She glanced at the hotel from the DDR era, to which the car park belonged. Two cream taxis were parked at the hotel entrance.

A police car pulled up, seemingly behind her, lights flashing. She did not panic. She glanced into her mirrors, swiftly located its position, and did nothing.

The patrol car gave a slow duo tone on its siren. Cars to her left moved further left. The police car swung out and raced past, crossing the red lights at speed, heading for whatever incident demanded its immediate attention.

Sharon Wilson smiled to herself as the lights turned green. The traffic ahead of her moved on, allowing her to turn into the car park. She put the BMW into a slot, then left it to go to a taxi.

She told the driver to take her to the Kurfürstendamm.

The driver, clearly assuming she was a hotel guest, asked, 'Where on the Ku'damm?'

'I'll tell you when we get there.' Her tone suggested the conversation was over until she chose to speak again.

The driver got the message, and set off without further comment.

Some time later, as they entered Tauentzienstrasse, the driver began to look questioningly at her in his rear-view mirror.

She said nothing to him until they were approaching the junction with Fasanenstrasse.

'Here!' she said. 'Right here will do.'

The taxi came to a halt in a manner that made the person in the car behind sound his horn furiously.

'Ah, go stuff yourself,' the cab driver muttered, glaring at the other car as it drove past.

A man in his late forties, he was once a minor Stasi operative in the DDR. Driving a taxi had been the only option open to him after the Wall had come down. Years later, it still grated upon him.

Sharon Wilson's predatory instincts were finely honed. She stared at the back of the driver's head.

'You sound like a man who does not like his job,' she said as she took out some money to pay the fare.

Glad she had at last deigned to have a conversation with him, the taxi driver was suddenly loquacious.

'Before this,' he grumbled, 'I was someone in the DDR.'

'And now you sound as if you regret its passing.' She handed over the money, with a generous tip.

'I'm not the only one,' he remarked sourly, then brightened at the size of the tip. 'Thank you!'

'Anything to help a former comrade.'

He twisted round. '*You?*'

'Me,' she lied.

'But you don't look old enough. You must have been what . . . six?'

'I was a little older, but I was already looking forward to serving like my father, in State Security.'

The driver was almost ecstatic. 'A Young Pioneer! Who would have thought it? In my taxi!'

'There must have been a few who have taken your taxi . . .'

'Perhaps. But they wouldn't talk about it these days.'

'All nice democrats now.'

The taxi driver's mouth turned down. 'Exactly. What was your father's department . . .' His voice faded as Sharon Wilson's green eyes seemed to pierce him.

'You would not expect this of me, would you?'

Years of conditioning made him say, 'No! Of course not, Comrade!'

She nodded, then left the taxi without another word.

Sharon Wilson was wearing a lightweight, white business suit whose skirt was deliberately shorter than it needed to be. It hovered high above the knee. On her feet were classic, flat-soled shoes that would not hinder rapid movement. She was again blonde.

The taxi driver watched the movement of her leg muscles as she walked.

He licked his lips unconsciously. 'That,' he said to himself, 'is a comrade I would have liked to have worked with.'

He did not move off until she had turned the corner.

Sharon Wilson knew exactly what was going on in the driver's mind. In fact, she was banking on it.

A tiny smile crossed her lips as she turned the corner.

After an unhurried stroll, she entered a large department store on Tauentzienstrasse, and made her way up to the restaurant floor where many bars and bistros served different types of fare. She went to one that served seafood which was cooked as you watched. The cooking was done within the crescent of the bar at which diners could sit.

Sharon Wilson chose a high stool at the far end. There were three other customers, all at the opposite end.

Five minutes later, a man in his forties took the seat next to her. They greeted each other like old friends. They had never met before. He called her Ellen, which told her he was the person she was supposed to meet. They ordered, and while they ate, they continued to chat like old friends. Never once was the true nature of her business mentioned.

The man glanced at his watch after they had finished. 'I think we should be getting back.'

It was a cue. She nodded, understanding.

'Excellent,' the man said to the chef, who beamed at him with undisguised pleasure.

They left the store and went to where he had parked his car, a high-performance black Mercedes coupé, in the underground garage. There was an identical Mercedes next to it. But there were differences. The second Mercedes was more powerful. It had big fat wheels, quad exhausts, and the brake calipers were red.

'Yours,' he said to her, handing her the keys.

She looked at it with undisguised pleasure. 'You are so good to me. Leather. I love leather.'

'*I'm* not the one who's good. I'm just the messenger.'

Something in his voice made her say, 'And what's the message?'

He pointed to the car she had just been given. 'Get in. Leave the windows closed.'

She did not move for a few stubborn seconds, then squeezed the remote. She got in behind the wheel.

He took the passenger seat. 'The message is short. You call off the hunt.'

She whirled on him. '*What the fuck!*'

'Those are the instructions.'

'Whose *fucking* instructions?'

'Those who pay you . . . and very handsomely.'

'Look. I'm a *fucking* contractor. I'm not one of you. I do my *fucking* job, and you *fucking* pay me for it. I *always fucking* succeed.'

The man remained calm. 'You do your job very well. That is appreciated. As a result, you have a certain degree of autonomy. Facilities are put your way. But do not imagine you are indispensable . . .'

Her eyes bored into him. 'Are you *fucking* threatening *me*?'

'No. I am but the messenger. I am passing on the message. Something has occurred, which brings an unexpected change. The situation is to be studied . . .'

'What has changed? Is Müller *fucking* dead?' She spoke rapidly, as if afraid of having been cheated.

'Müller is not dead.'

'Good. I want that *fucking* bastard myself. And his American bitch?'

'To the best of my knowledge, Colonel Bloomfield is also in good health.'

'*Fucking* bitch! I want both of them!'

'If you do as advised, you will get your chance. In the meantime, enjoy the break. A villa has been . . . acquired for you in the south of France. Go there. Take the time to recharge. When the time is right for further action, you will be advised. You might even find being down there helpful. If you need to, you will not find it difficult to find some . . . amusement. Just don't kill them afterwards. You do not need the attention. *We* do not need the attention.'

The man stopped. Her eyes were still boring into him.

'Is *that* fucking all?' she demanded.

'No. It is not all. Your attack on Müller's colleague was good strategy. It had the element of surprise. She is not expected to survive . . .'

'So I did not *fucking* miss, after all.'

'You did not. But given the . . . ah . . . interest you have aroused, it is suggested you leave today. In fact, the moment I leave this car, you must be on your way.'

'And the apartment?'

'Has already been cleared. All you need is in the boot of the car. Weapons that you may need are already at the villa.'

'I keep my *fucking* guns!'

'No one is going to take them from you. Keeping them

secure till you get to your destination is your responsibility. You will find all information you need in the glove compartment. Details of your next target are in there. Do *not* take action until contacted.'

'So what happened to cause the change?'

'Müller has suffered a major setback . . .'

'*Fucking* good!'

'We do not have all the details as yet. But people we believe he was after – who possibly had information detrimental to us – are dead. He did not get a chance to question them.'

'So he's still in Australia . . .'

'He returned to Berlin, then went back for a second try, we believe. The object of the second trip is not certain. Our contact could not say.'

'Were these people in the general area I was?'

'We're talking of Australia. As a "general area" can cover hundreds of square kilometres, you can say that. Mainauer was originally sent to eliminate Müller, Colonel Bloomfield, and the people they hoped to see. Mainauer has not been seen, nor been heard from, since. He is clearly dead. Take that as a warning when going up against those two. Mainauer was very good. He had never failed before. And remember, they got Dahlberg – a professional of great experience and one of *the* best we ever had – long before they even knew of Mainauer. Dahlberg lost control, and paid the price. Just some advice.'

The man got out before she could respond. He went to his car, got in, and drove away without a glance in her direction.

'*Fuck* you!' she snarled in a low voice at the departing car.

She started the engine of her own car. It growled powerfully into life.

'Oooh,' she said. 'Mmmm!'

Four

At Woonnalla, it was 18.30 local.

Müller and Carey Bloomfield were on the balcony, semi-reclining on the loungers. They still wore their shoulder harnesses, guns holstered. The binoculars were on the small table.

Müller had cooked a meal of baked barramundi down in the Box, as they now called the hidden apartment. An excellent wine from the hundreds of bottles had accompanied it. The plentiful supply of barramundi steaks they had found in the freezer had been a welcome surprise. Both liked fish.

Replete, they had decided to eschew starting on the stored files until later, and had returned to the balcony to watch a glorious sunset. Though the sun had gone down at roughly seven minutes to six p.m., there were still vestiges of its passing, high up in the dark of the sky.

'Müller,' Carey Bloomfield began in a voice made lazy by the meal she had greatly enjoyed.

'Yes?'

'You'll make someone a good wife one day. I hate men who can cook like that.'

'Blame my . . . mother . . . and . . . and Aunt Isolde. One started, the other finished. My . . . father was not a bad cook either.'

'Runs in the family.'

'Looks like it.'

A brief silence fell, then was broken by Müller.

'As for the Lavalieres of Grenoble . . .'

'You've been thinking about that for all this time?'

'Not all the time. Theirs was only a precaution, in case anything happened to them. They've still got the original black boxes from the first crash all those years ago, hidden there. Their intention was to ensure no one gets access to the house. With what we've found in the Hargreaves' Pandora's Box, our chances of seeing no harm comes to them are much greater. Hopefully, circumstances won't force me to inherit.'

'I think they want you to have it, anyway. People keep giving you things, Müller.'

A further silence – this time of several minutes – passed as the night grew darker. The backglow from the lights that had automatically come on outside the main house, and in front of the outhouses, could be seen as a smear on the dark, allowing them to see each other reasonably clearly, even though they had deliberately chosen not to turn on the lights in their part of the outhouse.

The night was itself strangely quiet.

'Shouldn't there be night thingies making all sorts of noises out there?' she said. 'It's so quiet, you'd think they're waiting for something.'

'Perhaps they'll start up later,' Müller suggested.

Carey Bloomfield made herself more comfortable on the lounger. 'Just sitting up here is great,' she said. 'The Hargreaves must have sat here often, just watching the world go by. They really did find their slice of Eden.'

Müller said nothing.

'You OK, Müller?'

'I'm fine.'

'I know I keep asking . . .'

'Not a problem.'

She seemed to accept that. 'I wonder if Graeme Wishart and the Lyserts have gone on to Broome to see if we're there,' she said after a while.

The Lysert brothers had not yet returned to Woonnalla.

'Perhaps. Or they're all still up at Cape Leveque, continuing with the search.'

'In the dark? If they haven't found anything yet . . .' She paused. 'We could go down to the car and try the radio . . . or down into the Box, or the house . . .'

'No.'

'OK,' she said quickly.

'Wishart may have tried to contact us. So he'll probably

76

turn up in the morning . . . or even tonight. If it's tonight, we should go back down before that happens. I don't feel like talking to either the Lyserts or to him. Not just yet.'

'Sure.'

They sat there, enjoying the growing dark as it deepened, and each other's company. Then in a strange metamorphosis, the night seemed to get lighter, as it deepened. Some time later, the stars had become so bright, it was virtually a twilight.

'I could almost read by this light,' Carey Bloomfield exclaimed in soft wonder.

Müller picked up the binoculars and brought them to his eyes. In night mode, they augmented the available light to give a view that was sharp and bright. He could see very clearly.

'Amazing,' he remarked. 'Far in advance of anything we've got. I wonder if they had these on the other side when the Wall was still up.'

'Maybe these are the only ones like it. A prototype.'

'Perhaps.' He did not sound particularly confident about that. 'Perhaps not.' He passed the binoculars over. 'Here. Have a look.'

'Tell you what,' she said as she took them. 'I'll go check the front.'

'Don't switch on any lights,' he reminded her as she stood up.

'I won't.'

She left the balcony, and went through to the room with the fake cupboard. She went up to one of the windows, and put the binoculars between two slats of the lowered venetian blind.

She began looking, then gasped. 'Oh my God!' she said in a rapid whisper. She hurried back to the balcony. 'Müller, the airstrip lights are on!'

'*What?*'

He got to his feet rapidly, and followed her out. She handed the binoculars back to him as they re-entered the room. He went to the window and had a look through the binoculars.

He gave a sharp intake of breath as his gaze settled on the airstrip.

'Someone coming in?' she said from behind him.

'If so, who?'

'Perhaps the Hargreaves . . .'

'Don't even think it. I don't believe in ghosts.'

'Why not? But I wasn't thinking of ghosts. I was thinking what if . . .'

'Don't even think it,' he repeated, remaining zeroed-in on the airstrip. 'Let's see who has decided to pay a visit, despite the police restrictions.'

'So who turned on the lights?'

'Timer. Perhaps this happens each night.'

'At exactly this time? Come on, Müller. You'd flame me for suggesting that.'

'You're right,' he agreed, still looking at the airstrip.

'Perhaps the Lyserts are here, after all.'

'On a night like this, we would have heard engines long before they got here. No voices, and no lights in the second outhouse.'

'Then something's weird.'

'Something is strange, I will admit. Just don't say it has anything to do with ghosts.'

'Stranger things have happened.'

'Let's give this some time. This place is rigged with all kinds of technological toys. A passing animal could have triggered a sensor.'

He lowered the binoculars.

Half an hour passed. The airstrip lights were still on, but no aircraft appeared. Half an hour after that, when Müller was again checking through the binoculars, the lights suddenly went out. There had been no aircraft.

'Timer,' Müller said again, lowering the binoculars a second time and moving away from the window.

'Spooky,' Carey Bloomfield said, giving an involuntary shiver.

'This would be a good time to get back to the Box.'

'I agree.'

Back down in the study with all the files, Müller had again taken out all the papers from the envelope that had been addressed to him. He had spread them out on the desk, as he would a deck of cards. Some were clipped together, in varying numbers of sheets. One of these had previously been folded in three. The indentations of the folds were still strong enough to make the ends rise upwards.

'Looks like a legal document,' Carey Bloomfield said.

He picked it up. 'It is.'

'The deeds to this place?'

Müller nodded slowly, face expressionless.

'For a man who's just inherited a huge piece of valuable real estate, you don't look happy.'

'The circumstances of the inheritance do not make me happy. But even without that, as I said earlier, I am not certain I want it. This document has closed all my avenues.'

'He did say you could do what you want with it.'

'Yes. He did. But as he also knew what was down here, he also effectively tied my hands.'

'Then do what you suggested. Offer the Lyserts the place, except this house.'

Müller put the document back down on the desk, and looked at her. 'I thought you said they would refuse.'

'You never know. You could get lucky. Most people would jump at the chance. Perhaps I'm wrong, and the Lyserts will.'

Suddenly, a noise came out of Müller that sounded like a bitter chuckle.

'What?' she asked.

'All these years, I've laboured under the impression that I was the Graf von Röhnen. I only truly became that last night.'

'It's important?'

'In the grand scheme of things . . . not really.' Müller had been searching through the papers as he spoke. 'Ah!' he said, picking up a clipped, thick sheaf from the pile. 'That's more like it. Instructions for the entire place – meaning Woonnalla as a whole.' He thumbed through. 'Diagrams of the buildings, electrical circuits, itemizing of various switches, what does what, equipment for running the station, the trucks – both coolers rather than refrigerated – notes about road trains that call to pick up produce, delivery schedules, and more and more. Now I do know I don't want this. I can't work this place and be a Berlin policeman at the same time.'

'You can always say goodbye to the badge . . . if you get my meaning.'

'Out of the question.' Müller waved a hand to indicate the room. 'And what about all this? His work of many years. Do I just let it go while I remain here, running Woonnalla in comfort?'

'Running a place like this is not a "comfort", Müller.'

'It is all relative. Do I allow the Semper to do their worst and I turn my back on Pappi, Berger, Greville, Aunt Isolde . . . ?'

'Just checking, Müller. Not everyone wants to be a rich landowner, after all. You're already rich, of course . . . but you know what I mean.'

'I know what you mean. Ah!' he went on, as he came upon a new page. 'Instructions for use of the computer in surveillance. There are micro cameras – just like the ones in the tunnel – all round the house, and three in the wine cellar. And all controlled from here. Woonnalla was also their fortress . . .'

'As you've said, they had to cover all bases.'

He nodded but said nothing, face still.

She grinned at him, trying to cheer him up. 'Come on, Berlin cop. We're in Pandora's Box. Let's see if we can keep whatever furies there are at bay.'

In Germany, one of the furies was speeding southwards, heading for the French border.

Sharon Wilson had long left Berlin and was approaching the Bavarian state boundary. Despite not needing to replenish the tank, she decided to pull off the autobahn and into a service station.

Curiosity had got the better of her.

She pulled into one of the parking areas, choosing one that was practically empty. The nearest car was ten bays away. She stopped, then opened the glove compartment to take out a plain brown envelope. She opened it, and pulled out the photograph of her next target.

'My,' she said. 'Aren't you a pretty little thing. I'm going to enjoy this.'

She was looking at Solange du Bois, Kaltendorf's daughter.

*   *   *

80

Berlin, 15.00 local.

Pappenheim was frowning at one of his phones, trying to decide whether to carry out a particular course of action he had been considering. He felt it might apply some pressure in the right direction. The information on Heinrich Höhntaler, the supposedly innocent banker with possible Semper ties, had not yet arrived. But Pappenheim was twitchy. He felt certain that a visit to Höhntaler sooner, rather than later, was important.

'The longer I wait,' he murmured to himself, 'the less the chances of total surprise. His pals might consider the possibility, and coach him before I get there.' He glanced at his watch. 'Let's try the early bird routine, even if it is afternoon.'

Having convinced himself, he picked up the phone and punched in an extension number.

'Ah, Lene,' he began when Berger had answered. 'Fancy a drive?'

'Where are we going?'

'Banking.'

'You're rich?'

'No. But I know a man who could be.'

'Do you mean we go now?'

'Are those your footsteps I hear heading for the garage?'

'That soon.'

'Sooner.'

They hung up together.

'How are we going to do this?' Berger asked.

She was driving the big, virtually new BMW 645 coupé that Pappenheim had appropriated from the Semper. They had never attempted to reclaim it, as that would have incriminated them. The then falsely registered car had been the transport of a deceased Semper hitman sent to kill Müller, and who had instead been shot by his contractors for failing to do so.

'By ear,' Pappenheim replied. 'Even a banker of his stature should have finished lunch by now. Catch him while he's still feeling good about himself, after lunch with his secretary.'

81

'You don't know that. He could be a happily married man who would never take his secretary out . . . except for perfectly harmless reasons.'

'Or he could be single, and still take her to lunch . . .'

'There's the bank,' Berger said with what sounded suspiciously like relief.

'I was just beginning to enjoy the game,' Pappenheim complained as they pulled into a reserved parking area. 'Take his slot. His name's on it. He doesn't need it today.'

The slot was directly overlooked by Höhntaler's window.

'I don't believe it,' Berger said as she stopped the car, neatly in position. 'Look up, Chief. The window.'

Someone was looking down at them.

'Doesn't look very pleased, does he?' Pappenheim observed, peering upwards. 'Must be our banker friend.'

This was conclusively proved as they climbed out.

'*You!*' the man at the window shouted. '*Can't you read? You have just parked in my slot! Move your car!* If you do not, I'll call security to move you. If you still remain, I shall call the police!'

'Ah . . .' Pappenheim called up. 'Then we can be of service. We *are* the police.'

'Oh!' Höhntaler said, nonplussed. 'Oh.'

'What manners,' he muttered to Berger. 'For all he knew I could have been an eccentric billionaire . . . come to bring him business beyond his wildest dreams . . .'

'Someone's dreaming, but he's not it . . . sir.'

'Hmmm,' Pappenheim said, then called up to Höhntaler, 'It's about your car.'

'Oh,' the banker repeated. 'Then . . . then you'd better come up. A security man will come to take you straight to my office.'

'Thank you.'

'Ah . . . yes. Yes.'

Watching with interest as Höhntaler ducked back rather urgently inside, Pappenheim said, 'Is he suddenly nervous? Or is that me . . .'

'He's suddenly nervous,' Berger said.

'Then we'd better get up there quickly before he starts making phone calls.'

'He can stall us. Make us wait . . .'

'That's where you're wrong. Ah. Here's the stalwart security . . .'

A hard-looking man in a tight but well-cut suit, with a face that was as full of expression as a slab of granite, came up to them. 'You are the police?'

'We are,' Pappenheim replied with a straight face.

The man seemed to spin on his heels. 'Follow me.'

'I like the strong, silent type,' Pappenheim said to Berger.

'Not me. They talk too much.'

The man led them to a door at the side of the bank foyer, and up a carpeted flight of stairs. They arrived at a small but plush reception area. A young woman sat behind a curving desk that practically encircled her. A mahogany-coloured door was directly at her back, about three metres away.

'The secretary,' Pappenheim whispered to Berger, who pasted a fixed smile upon her face.

The young woman beamed at them. 'Thanks, Olli,' she said to the security man.

The security man grunted, then stood to one side.

'Hello,' she went on to Pappenheim and Berger. 'I'm Angie Massen. Will you please take a seat? Herr Höhntaler will be with you in a moment.'

'Hello,' Pappenheim responded blithely. 'I'm *Oberkommissar* Pappenheim, and this is *Kommissarin* Berger and no, we can't take a seat, thank you. Show ourselves in, shall we?'

He began walking towards the door behind her. Berger followed.

'*Hey!*' the security man called Olli began in a loud voice, moving towards them. 'She said you take a seat!'

Berger whirled, gun out. 'Are you interfering with the police?'

The man stopped in his tracks. The secretary, eyes wide, opened her mouth; but no sound came out.

'Thought not,' Berger said to Olli, eyes cold. 'OK, Chief?' she added to Pappenheim.

'I could not have done it better myself. Thank you,' he added to Angie Massen, as he grabbed the door handle, turned it, and pushed the door open.

He entered, closely followed by Berger, who was putting her gun away.

Höhntaler's office was huge, and furnished in a manner befitting a man at the top of the food chain, in a bank that was outrageously successful. A door led off to the right.

Slim, neatly and expensively dressed, he had a tiny goatee, his partial baldness graced by a perfectly retreating hairline. He looked about forty, but his face was remarkably unlined. Dark, piercing eyes stared out at the world.

He was on the phone as they entered and stared at them, momentarily at a loss for words.

Angie Massen rushed in. 'Herr Höhntaler! I'm sorry! I told them . . .'

'It's all right, Angie,' he said to her. 'I'll call you back,' he said into the phone, then put it down. 'All right, Angie,' he said again to the secretary.

'Ye-es, Herr Höhntaler.' She retreated quickly, closing the door behind her.

'Well!' Höhntaler began with a brightness that was at odds with someone who had just been interrupted making an obviously important phone call.

'Aah!' Pappenheim said, inhaling deeply. 'Is that *the* aroma I smell?'

The banker stared at Pappenheim, as if wondering whether the policeman had suddenly lost it.

'Coffee?' Höhntaler asked with some uncertainty.

'No thanks,' Pappenheim said. 'That's not what I smell.' His baby-blue eyes were at their most guileless.

Berger, reading the signs correctly, waited for Pappenheim's performance to get into full swing.

'I'll have the coffee, thanks,' she said to Höhntaler.

The banker stared at each in turn, not certain what was going on.

'I smell Gauloise,' Pappenheim said beatifically.

Dawn broke. Höhntaler suddenly, and unexpectedly, smiled. 'A fellow addict!'

'Ooh yes,' Pappenheim said without shame. 'May I? I really do need one.'

'Please do! You have no idea how difficult it is. Few of my colleagues smoke. In fact, you can't even count them on one hand. And I've never had a client in here in the last twelve months who smoked. Frau Massen doesn't. My wife doesn't. I'm almost afraid to smoke in my own office, in case it annoys an important client. I try to keep it down when I am alone for a while. One feels hounded.'

'I know exactly what you mean. I work in a rigorously policed – no pun intended – smokeless zone. Please indulge yourself.'

'Thank you! I will!' Höhntaler reacted as if the office belonged to Pappenheim, and not to him.

Höhntaler pulled out a drawer, and took out a packet of *Blondes* like a drowning man suddenly given a lifebelt. He and Pappenheim lit up together. They drew on their cigarettes, inhaled deeply, then exhaled with loud sighs of satisfaction.

Berger watched it all with a steadfastly neutral expression.

'We haven't been properly introduced,' Höhntaler said after a second drag. 'I am, of course, Höhntaler . . .' He came round his desk to offer a hand.

'Pappenheim,' the *Oberkommissar* said, shaking it briefly. 'And my colleague, *Kommissarin* Berger.' He dropped ash into a cupped hand.

Höhntaler went over to Berger to shake her hand. 'Frau *Kommissarin*. Please,' he went on to them, 'take a seat. And I'll see to that coffee, Frau Berger. How would you like it?'

'With milk and sugar, thank you.'

'My pleasure.'

Berger sat down in an opulent leather armchair, while Pappenheim remained standing.

Höhntaler went back to his desk and pressed an intercom button. 'Angie . . . could we have a coffee for *Kommissarin* Berger, please? With milk and sugar.'

'Immediately, Herr Höhntaler,' came the response.

'Thank you, Angie.'

He ended the transmission and remained standing. 'So, Herr *Oberkommissar*, who would have thought we both smoked these?' He imitated Pappenheim. and dropped ash into his own cupped hand.

'Who indeed. Wonders, Herr Höhntaler. Wonders. Kindred souls.'

Höhntaler nodded sagely, and drew on his cigarette with undisguised pleasure. Pappenheim and the banker, like schoolboys behind the gym, seemed deeply immersed in cigarette heaven.

Watching them, Berger found it difficult to decide which of the two was putting on the show. She surprised herself by thinking that perhaps Höhntaler was also feeding the pantomime.

Angie Massen entered with the coffee on a silver tray, looked startled to see Pappenheim and her boss smiling through their respective veils of smoke, gave a disapproving frown that belonged more to a censorious wife than a secretary, then switched a smile back on as she approached Berger.

'Your coffee, Frau *Kommissarin*,' she said, placing the tray down on the small table like an offering. A small plate with biscuits was next to the coffee in its exquisite china cup.

'Thank you,' Berger said.

'My pleasure.'

Angie Massen went back out, giving Höhntaler a parting shot with her disapproving frown.

As he had with the first, the banker ignored her.

Berger sipped at her coffee which was unexpectedly good, and continued to watch the performance.

In reception, Angie Massen was frowning.

'Something wrong?' Olli the security man asked.

'He's smoking!'

'So? Everyone knows he's a secret smoker.'

'He's smoking with that policeman!' She made it sound as if a heinous crime had been committed. 'They're like two boys, just standing there . . . smoking! And dropping ash into their hands!' She looked disgusted.

'Are you annoyed that he's smoking?' Olli knew all about her lunches with her boss. 'Or because he's smoking with that fat policeman who looks as if he sleeps in his clothes?' A fitness freak, he added with contempt, 'Addicts.'

'He's big,' Angie Massen said, 'but he's not fat . . . not in the way you mean it. And don't underestimate him, Olli, because he likes to pretend he's a rumpled fool,' she went on with surprising perception. 'And did you see his tie?'

'Why should I look at his tie? It's summer, what does he

want with a tie, anyway? Not as if he's a banker.' Olli smirked as he said that.

She ignored the dig. 'His tie looks better than Herr Höhntaler's. A woman notices these things. A rumpled fool who knows how to choose ties,' she went on, expression thoughtful now. 'I remember a teacher just like that at school. He looked like a tramp, but he was very, very smart. None of us could pull a fast one on him. I think it's the same with this policeman. He's after something.'

Despite himself, Olli looked at the door to Höhntaler's office with renewed interest, but remained silent.

Inside, several minutes had passed. Berger had watched, fascinated, as Pappenheim and the banker had smoked their cigarettes to the very end, in complete silence. Their attention appeared to have been entirely focussed upon the serious business of enjoying the weed, as if mere conversation would have been a sacrilegious interruption.

She waited in anticipation, to see how the subtle sparring would develop.

At last, the ritual was over.

'Aah,' Höhntaler sighed. 'All good things . . .'

'Do pass,' Pappenheim finished. He held the dying butt expectantly.

'Ah yes,' Höhntaler said. 'Ashtray.' He pulled out the same drawer as before, and brought out a pristine ashtray.

'First of the day was it?' Pappenheim commented as he emptied the cupped hand.

Höhntaler looked sheepish. 'Well . . . no, but I always wash it . . . in there.' He too – with seeming reverence – emptied his hand into the ashtray; then he pointed to the side door. 'My . . . er . . .'

'Executive bathroom.'

'Er . . . yes.'

Pappenheim stubbed out his cigarette. 'Seems a shame to send you off to the bathroom again.' He brushed the ashed palm clean against his clothes.

Berger listened to all this with mounting anticipation. She knew that this was the time when Pappenheim's baby blues would be at their most innocent, effectively hiding the unsheathed knife that was ready to strike.

In the event, it was the banker who switched the game.

Carefully covering the ashtray with a hand as if to kill the lingering smell of their smoking, he said, 'Now that the pleasantries are over, I know that two senior police officers are not paying me a visit just to talk about a stolen car. I'll . . . just wash this, then be right back.'

Pappenheim said nothing as he watched Höhntaler go through the door.

Berger began to say something, but Pappenheim held up a quick silencing finger. He did not seem worried that the banker might have another door through which to escape.

They said nothing to each other as they waited for Höhntaler's return.

The banker was soon back, with an again pristine ashtray. He put it away in the drawer and remaining standing, turned to Pappenheim expectantly.

'I am very sorry to have to tell you,' Pappenheim – the epitome of the reluctant bearer of bad news – began, 'but your car was involved in a serious crime.'

Höhntaler's expression gave nothing away, but his eyes did. They were watchful, and uncertain, at the same time.

'What kind of crime?'

'The worst, I'm afraid, Herr Höhntaler. Murder.'

'*What?*' For the briefest of moments, the watchful uncertainty vanished to be replaced by something else: fear. Then it was gone, and the dark eyes hid everything.

'The murder of one of our colleagues,' Pappenheim's voice was suddenly harsh. But the delivery was so unexpectedly low, it made Höhntaler straighten unwittingly, as if an electric shock had been administered to him.

'That's . . . that's impossible!'

'I wish it were. Unfortunately, our young colleague will not have the luxury of enjoying her twenties.'

'A *police officer*? But . . . but . . .'

'If you know something about this, Herr Höhntaler, it would help you to tell us.'

The banker was shocked. '*Me?* Why would I know anything about what happened to your colleague? My car was stolen! Cars are stolen every day. How can their owners know what is subsequently done with them?'

'I'll grant you the point. However, it would seem that the theft of your car was for a specific purpose.'

'Which was?'

'When we find out, we'll be back to you. Thank you for seeing us, Herr Höhntaler. And thank you for the smokers' solidarity. Good to meet a fellow addict. We'll see ourselves out. I know you're a very busy man. Coming, Berger?'

'Right with you, Chief,' Berger said, putting her cup down and getting to her feet. Her own expression studiously neutral.

'That's *it*?' Höhntaler said to their backs.

'That is it,' Pappenheim replied without looking round.

They left Höhntaler staring after them, trying to understand what had just happened.

'Smokers' solidarity!' Berger said, scoffing palpably. 'Even for you, Chief, that was pushing it.' She got in behind the wheel of the BMW. 'I loved the ash-in-the-hand trick.'

'Not really,' Pappenheim said, unrepentant as he climbed in beside her. He shut the door. 'He was watching me as much as I was watching him. He knows a lot more than he's telling. As for that bit with the ash . . .' Pappenheim smiled to himself.

She started the engine. 'He was shocked when you lied to him about the goth.'

'That was real shock,' Pappenheim agreed. 'But only because he was kept out of the loop when it came to that part.'

'So he *knew* his car would be stolen?' She began to reverse out of the parking bay, and glanced up. 'He's looking.'

'Let him,' Pappenheim said without shifting his attention upwards. 'I'm not sure whether he knew what was to be done with it. I got what I needed from him, for now. I think he knew it would be . . . "borrowed", let's say; but I believe his real shock was at the prospect of being thrown to the wolves.'

Berger reversed cleanly out, and drove out of the car park. 'But why would they do that?'

'To deflect our attention from Sharon Wilson . . .'

Pappenheim was interrupted by his mobile.

He got it out. 'Pappenheim.' He listened as someone spoke

urgently. 'All right,' he said. 'Thanks. Tell them not to touch anything until we get there. And warn the bomb disposal boys. OK. Well, well,' he said to Berger as he ended the call. 'Speaking of the devil. We're making a detour.'

'*Bomb* disposal? And where to?'

'Unter den Linden.'

'But that's nearly back to our . . .'

'Exactly. A lot of balls, that woman.'

'Sharon Wilson?'

'Our hitwoman herself. Two colleagues in a patrol car remembered seeing Höhntaler's BMW on Unter den Linden. They were on a call, lights flashing, siren going. They stopped right behind it. Did she panic? Not in a million years. She remained calmly where she was, making no suspicious move. Lucky for them. She would have shot them both. They took off on their call, ignoring her completely. It wasn't until after they had arrived at their callout – a small traffic accident – that they got the news about the BMW. Then they remembered.'

'So we've found it?'

'In a manner of speaking . . . yes. The patrol colleagues remembered where they had spotted it and as no calls had come in about its being seen anywhere else, they backtracked.'

'To where?'

Pappenheim told her.

'You're joking. Right under our noses?'

'She has a sense of humour too . . . if not necessarily quite to my taste. Hence the bomb squad. Perhaps she will try another visit to the hospital,' Pappenheim went on. 'Just to make certain of her kill. People like that hate to fail. She will want to make certain, to her satisfaction, that the goth really is dead. We move the goth today.'

But Pappenheim was very wrong about Sharon Wilson's next move.

They arrived at the car park where Sharon Wilson had deliberately abandoned Höhntaler's BMW, to find the patrol car waiting. Berger pulled up next to it.

Pappenheim climbed out and went up to the two policemen who were standing by their vehicle.

'Pappenheim,' he began, '*Oberkommissar* . . . and just getting out of the car is *Kommissarin* Berger.'

'Yes, sir,' one of the men said. 'We were told to expect you. I'm Norste, *Hauptmeister*, and my colleague is Heinberg, *Meister.*'

Pappenheim nodded at them. 'Good work remembering.'

Norste looked pleased. 'Thank you, sir.'

'Did she give any indication that she saw you?' Pappenheim asked as Berger joined them.

Norste shook his head. 'None that we could spot.'

Pappenheim nodded. 'She's a cool one.' He extended a hand. 'Thank you both.' He shook hands with them. 'We'll take it from here. I'll have a word with your boss.'

'Thank you, sir,' they both said.

Berger waited until they had got into their car and driven away, before saying to Pappenheim, 'Do you really think she wired it?' She stared at the supposedly stolen BMW with some apprehension.

'It might tickle her sense of humour. If it's clean, we'll move it to the garage. Our banker friend will have to wait for his car. Better make sure no one comes close. See if we can find the people who own these cars to move them, just in case. But don't panic them.'

'I'll just rush around screaming *bomb*, shall I?'

'Very droll, Lene.'

By the time the bomb disposal people arrived, Berger had cleared the car park of all other vehicles including a waiting taxi. The two members of the bomb squad quickly discovered there were no explosives in or on the car.

'Someone's having a joke on you, Pappi,' the *kommissar* in charge said, removing his protective gear.

'Hmm,' Pappenheim said. He took out a cigarette, and lit up. 'Hmm,' he said again after a long drag.

Smiling, the *kommissar* and his colleague got back into their vehicle and drove away.

Berger looked at the furiously puffing Pappenheim. She knew the signs, and waited for him to speak.

'She's up to something,' he said at last. Long drag. 'Better tell those people they can bring their cars back.'

'Already done.'

'Hmm.'

'You'll tell me, won't you, when whatever you're thinking about pops out?'

'Mm? Oh. Yes.'

The taxi that had previously been moved was coming back. It pulled to a stop next to them. The driver got out.

'I saw her, you know.'

Both Pappenheim and Berger looked at him. Pappenheim removed his cigarette, and waited.

'I saw her,' the driver repeated. 'The woman who owns that car. I took her to the Ku'damm.'

Pappenheim looked at him with interest. 'Did you now. When?'

'When she parked here. She parked the car, then came to my taxi. She was a Young Pioneer, you know,' the driver added with some pride. 'She was in the Ministry. She told me.'

'Did she now,' Pappenheim said in a soft voice.

'Yes. Imagine. A comrade from the Ministry in my taxi.'

'Must have been quite a thing for you,' Pappenheim said with a straight face. He glanced at Berger whose own face was so neutral it looked frozen.

'Oh yes!'

'You miss the old days, don't you?' Pappenheim suggested, putting believable sympathy into his voice.

'Ah . . . you understand,' the driver said, warming to the theme.

'Oh I do,' Pappenheim said. 'And you are?'

'Ivan Nippe. I was also in the Ministry.'

'Were you now . . .'

'But not as high as *she* was. Her father was in the Ministry too.'

'Imagine. Perhaps, Herr Nippe, you could tell us exactly what happened?'

'Of course. One must always help the police.'

'Of course one must.'

'Oh,' the driver said. He told them what had taken place, then paused.

'Yes?'

'She was wearing gloves. I thought she must be going to a function.'

'Of course she was wearing gloves,' Pappenheim said in a voice that betrayed just how much this news displeased him. 'Well thank you, Herr Nippe. You have been very helpful.'

'One must always help the police,' Nippe repeated.

'"One must always help the police",' Berger mimicked as they drove away. 'Even as he snitches on someone he believes is a "comrade". Old habits die hard.'

'Now now, Lene,' Pappenheim said. 'Sometimes, we need every help we can get . . . even from the likes of Ivan Nippe. We now know what Sharon Wilson was up to . . . to a point. She set the whole charade up. She knew we would find the car, with the taxi driver conveniently waiting to tell all. She set him up, and set us up . . .'

'She made him drop her off where she knew he would not see where she was really going . . .'

'Picking up another car . . .'

'Meeting someone . . .'

'Which means she's not going to be near anywhere we expect her to be . . .'

'Not even after the goth?'

'That's where I part company with that train of thought. It could be exactly what she wants us to think. We still move the goth. I'd rather be overcautious about that, and be proved wrong.'

'No argument . . .'

'And she wore bloody gloves . . .'

'Not stupid. And now? Where to?'

'Another visit to my friend in smokers' solidarity.'

'Back to the banker? *Now?*'

'There's a joke in there somewhere. Let me think about it.' Pappenheim began to hum to himself; out of tune.

When they arrived Höhntaler was again looking out of the window, and down at them.

'Is he stuck there?' Berger wondered, peering up.

'Too low for him to jump to make it effective.'

'Is this where *I* say there's a joke in there somewhere?'

'I'm still your superior. Don't pay back.'

Berger allowed herself a tiny smile as they climbed out.

'No need to send Olli,' Pappenheim called up to Höhntaler. 'We'll find our way.'

'Bet he'll be pleased to see us again,' Berger said as they walked towards the bank entrance. 'Wonder if he'll offer me another coffee? It was quite good. I like those dinky china cups . . .'

'Are you enjoying yourself?'

'*He's* not,' Berger countered.

The unsmiling Olli was already waiting.

'That was fast,' Pappenheim said to him.

'I'm always fast.'

'I'll remember that, Olli,' Pappenheim said.

'Is that supposed to be a joke?'

'A tip, Olli. When I make bad jokes, I'm at my worst.'

Pappenheim moved past the security man, followed by Berger.

Olli had no choice but to trail behind.

At the reception, Angie Massen jumped off her seat as if she had just sat on a pin. Her eyes followed Pappenheim and Berger.

'*Herr Oberkommissar!* You can't . . .'

Pappenheim gave her one of his best smiles, baby blues drowning her. 'Of course I can. We're old smoking buddies.'

'There goes my coffee,' Berger complained in a hiss.

'We'll see.'

Pappenheim opened the door and went in, closely followed by Berger.

Höhntaler greeted them with a tired, resigned smile.

'So good to see you again, Herr Höhntaler,' Pappenheim announced breezily as if he owned the office, and before the banker could utter a word. He fished out his packet of Gauloises and offered it. 'Here. Have one of mine.'

Höhntaler, taken completely off guard, had already stretched out a hand before stopping himself.

'Too soon after the last.'

'Nonsense! It's not often you get to smoke with a brand companion. And anyway, who's in charge here? You? Or those two outside?'

'Of course not!'

'Then?' The pack was still being offered.

'Oh. All right.' Höhntaler took one.

Pappenheim lit them both. 'Do you think Frau Berger could have another coffee. She considers Frau Massen makes fantastic coffee.'

'Of course. I'll see to it. Glad you like it, Frau Berger,' the banker added as Berger took the seat she had previously. 'It's from Guatemala. Some . . . professional colleagues have their own plantation.'

'Very convenient for you.'

'Yes. It is fortunate. I'll just tell Angie.'

Höhntaler ordered the coffee, then said to Pappenheim, 'Twice in one day, Herr Pappenheim.' This time, he brought out the ashtray immediately.

'We found your car.'

'Ah! That's very good. Excellent. Where is it?'

'We had to check it for explosives . . .'

Höhntaler nearly spat out his cigarette. '*Explosives!*'

'Can't be too careful these days. Luckily, your car was clean. So no controlled explosion. Your car is safe.'

Höhntaler visibly relaxed. 'Thank God! When can I have it picked up?'

'Not yet, I'm afraid . . .'

'But you just said . . .'

'I said it was clear of explosives. But there are other tests to be done, to see whether something might lead us to the thief. As soon as they are complete the car will be returned to you, intact. You have my word.'

Höhntaler digested this news. There was not a lot he could do about it.

He nodded, seemingly thoughtful. He drew on the cigarette. 'Very well. Let me know when it can be picked up.'

'I shall personally inform you.'

'Thank you . . . ah . . .' Höhntaler looked in the direction of the door as Angie Massen entered with Berger's coffee. 'Your coffee, Frau Berger.'

Berger gave the secretary a quick smile, and was rewarded with one that was definitely strained. 'Thank you,' she said. 'Very good coffee.'

Berger got another strained smile and Angie Massen hurried out as if she could not leave quickly enough. Berger glanced at Pappenheim, but he seemed preoccupied with enjoying his cigarette.

With a sense of déjà vu, she turned to her coffee.

As before, the two men smoked in silence. She was again reminded of an undeclared psychological war being fought, with both sides pretending it was not.

She finished her coffee before either of them was on the last drag.

The ritual with the ashtray was again re-enacted.

At the end of it, Pappenheim said, 'Thank you again for your time, Herr Höhntaler. We must be leaving.'

The banker stared at him. 'There's nothing more?'

No less surprised, Berger got to her feet.

'Nothing more for the moment,' Pappenheim said with a disarming expression. 'I enjoyed our second smoke, and I'm certain my colleague enjoyed her Guatemalan coffee. Thank you again. We'll see ourselves out.'

Leaving an astonished and puzzled Höhntaler staring, wondering what he had missed, they made an unhurried exit.

Pappenheim beamed at the uncertain Angie Massen and the stoney faced Olli. 'See you two again sometime.'

'All right, Chief,' Berger began as they got into the car. 'What was that all about?'

'Is he at the window?'

She looked. 'No.'

'Now he'll be making another phone call. I hope you were keeping a close eye on him when we were up there.'

She started the BMW. 'I was.'

'And?'

'He's definitely twitchy. It's not the car that's worrying him.'

'Hmm.' Pappenheim's smile was beatific.

'When are you going to tell the boss about all this, and the goth? Have you heard from him?'

'Which question first?'

'Both.'

Pappenheim gave her an odd look. '*Both?*'

'You know what I mean.' She began to reverse.

'He hasn't been in touch. Not surprising. Without the goth

96

to give us a secure channel, we're not going to risk an eavesdrop. That answers both?'

'Yes. Where to now?'

'Back. I need a smoke.'

Höhntaler was on the phone. 'They were here again! They've only just left!'

He paused, listening.

'I am *not* panicking. I'm not that kind of banker. I don't panic.'

'We are well aware of that,' the voice said in his ear. 'Or you would not be where you are.'

'Are you threatening me?'

'No one is threatening you. You are an important member of our organization. You do valuable service. We appreciate it.'

Höhntaler was only a little mollified. 'My car was used by someone who killed a police officer! Have you any idea how serious this is?'

'We are well aware. You have no cause for worry.'

'Perhaps you should speak to Pappenheim. I don't think he would agree with you.'

'Ah yes. Pappenheim.' The voice was filled with a cold rage as the name was spoken. 'We know all about Pappenheim. In due course, he will be taken care of . . .'

'You're going to kill *him*?'

'You look after the bank. That's your job.'

The conversation was ended.

Höhntaler replaced the phone, then looked down at the drawer containing his cigarettes.

'I need a smoke,' he said.

He opened the drawer.

Sharon Wilson was charging across Bavaria in the hot-tuned Mercedes coupé, on her way south. In her mind's eye was Solange du Bois, Kaltendorf's daughter.

Five

In the Box at Woonnalla, Müller and Carey Bloomfield were each scanning through separate files, taken at random. She was in the high-backed chair.

'Jesus!' she suddenly exclaimed. 'Müller! *Müller!*'

Sitting on the edge of the desk, he looked up from his file and turned to face her, waiting, noting the excitement in her face.

'Let me read this to you. It's part of a report. Bear with my German. OK?'

'Your German is excellent.'

'Nice things are always nice to hear.' She began to read:

'. . . there have been rumours that a British agent may have been contaminated just before the lab explosion. Comrade Pyotr, a GRU operative in the area, believes he may know the identity of this agent. If this proves to be correct, it is recommended that the British agent be seized immediately, and tests carried out. If these prove negative, he is to be subsequently eliminated. If the tests are positive, he is to be kept until all testing is exhausted, and then eliminated.'

She paused, then continued, 'There's a gap, then this:

'. . . Comrade Pyotr appears to have been himself eliminated. This could mean that he was correct in his suspicions, and the British agent has taken action to silence him. I request permission to pick up where Comrade Pyotr has left off. It is vital that we find this British agent, whose identity is as yet unknown.

'Whoever it was signed this *Rotbarsch*. There's a written note next to the name.'

98

'Which is?'

'Just the one word. *"Terminated"*. Whoever terminated *Rotbarsch*, saved Greville. It *is* Greville, isn't it? And this report is about the DNA weapon.'

'Given all that we now know, it would seem he does mean Greville.'

'So whoever closed down *Rotbarsch* for good, already knew what was in that lab and, like Greville, didn't want it turned loose. Any ideas?' Her eyes held Müller's.

'You're thinking,' Müller began, 'that *Rotbarsch* – possibly a code name – submitted the report to Jack Hargreaves, who was his superior officer in the DDR. Hargreaves knew what it would mean if the report went beyond him. So he stopped *Rotbarsch*, permanently; then he made certain the report never went beyond him, and eventually brought it here.'

'We think alike,' she said. 'Müller, this means your fa . . . Hargreaves knew all about Greville! Perhaps they even met!'

'Greville would have said. We spent that time in the Eifel looking through some of the papers in the briefcase Aunt Isolde had been given years before I was even a policeman, to hand over to me when the time was appropriate.'

'Why would he? Greville is one of those rare birds, Müller . . . a spy on the front line who has lived to a ripe old age – for them, that's anything over thirty. People like that never trust anyone completely . . . even people they like. It's called insurance. You're good at that yourself, Müller.'

'Can I see that?'

'Sure.' She passed him the file.

He studied the name of the agent who had submitted the report. '*Rotbarsch*.'

'You're looking thoughtful,' she said. 'You've heard that name before? Apart from seeing it on a menu, that is.'

'So you know what *rotbarsch* means?'

'Sure. It's an ocean perch.'

'Not many people who understand both English and German know what it means in English. I'm impressed.'

'I'm glad you're impressed. What's going on in that mind of yours, Müller?'

He passed the file back. 'Put this to one side for us to

look at in greater detail. There might be more about the DNA weapon.'

'You did not answer my question.'

'No. I did not. Grab another. See what turns up.'

'Sir, yessir.'

But Müller did not respond, and went back to the file he had been reading. After about five minutes, he decided to put it back for later and eased himself off the desk to get another. He chose a box file. And returned to the edge of the desk.

Carey Bloomfield had also chosen a box file. She was leafing through the top papers, when she came to a familiar envelope underneath. It was similar to the one that had been left for Müller. Curiosity aroused, she took it out of the box.

'Photographs,' she said, almost to herself, touching it with exploring fingers.

Müller paused to look at her. 'Did you say something?'

'Photographs,' she repeated. 'There are photos in here, I think.'

'Then let's have a look.'

She tipped the envelope over. Several photographs slid out. Most were colour prints, the rest black and white. There were slides as well.

She stared at them. 'Oh boy,' she said.

Müller had stopped reading and was also staring at them, in astonishment. All the photographs were of him: from childhood, right up to a recent one of him getting into his car.

'Jesus, Müller,' Carey Bloomfield said. 'What the . . .' She stopped and looked at him, eyes wide.

It took him a while to bring himself to say, 'They certainly kept their tabs on me.'

'But as they were hiding out here, they must have had someone . . .' She paused. 'But who would that be? The "one other"?'

'Perhaps. Perhaps not.'

'They could have destroyed this,' she said. 'They wanted you to know.' She began to rummage. 'There's a note here . . .'

'Read it out.'

She did so.

'This was easy to do. Be more careful. At the last count, there were forty snipers . . . (Forty! My God!) . . . operating globally. This means forty SVDs out there. I have the forty-first. It once belonged to another sniper. He has no further use for it. (Guess that means one dead sniper.) He had many kills over the years. The kills are set down in a dedicated file. There were more snipers, but their numbers have been decreased . . . (No prizes for guessing who may have "decreased" some of them.) . . . although new ones may have been added since I "retired". There is an exceptional one who has a modified scope which takes photographs of the kill. It is his/her way of providing evidence that the job has been done. He/she is extremely successful. You may one day come up against this person . . . if he or she is still alive. All that I know of this individual will be in the dedicated file. This is the SVD file.'

Carey Bloomfield stopped reading, took a deep breath, and again turned her eyes on Müller. 'If that's not a warning, I don't know what is.'

Müller appeared to be staring into space.

'Müller,' she began, a tentative edge to her voice, 'could it be that he didn't "retire" . . . fully?'

'Are you suggesting that he may have continued, while they were down here?' He did not look at her.

'Could be. They had that plane. They could have gone anywhere, met with anyone. No need to go all the way back to Europe . . .'

'All things are possible.' He tried to cut the bitterness in his own voice, and failed. 'Any more in that note?'

She shook her head slowly.

'Put the photographs back into the envelope, with the note, then put it to one side with the other. That's another we'll look at in more detail later.' He eased himself off the desk to replace the file he had been studying. 'Let's find that SVD file.'

It did not take long, and turned out to be another box file. He took it to the desk, and opened it. It was full almost to the point where it would have been difficult to shut properly. He raised the retaining lever, and removed the first four sheets.

They were full of listed names, with dates next to them, some of which even had timings. Next to each date was a small, black cross. Next to that was the nationality of the victim, with a single word describing what he or she had been. The list had a two-word heading: *Semper Kills*.

'The kills,' Müller remarked. He gave the list a quick scan, expression grim. Then he handed the four sheets of paper over to her. 'You may recognize some of these names.'

With a curious glance at him, she took the sheets of paper, and began to read the list in silent horror. She said nothing at all, until she reached the last name.

'Oh dear God,' she said in hushed tones. 'I do recognize some names on here. These were people from all over the world. American, Brit, Chinese, Japanese, Australian, people from the Middle East, South America . . . even kids . . .'

'Pressurizing those with children who would not play, into realizing they meant business.'

'I'm glad you're not going to let up on these bastards, Müller.'

'That was never in question.'

She searched out a few names. 'Even those sniped Romeos are listed here. How did your . . . er . . . Hargreaves get to know of this? Those Romeos are recent . . .'

'Remember that communications array outside, and his sometimes house guest. And as you've suggested, perhaps he was only in semi-retirement.'

She studied the list again. 'All walks of life – politicians, bankers, military, scientists, doctors, cops . . .' She glanced at him. '. . . priests, journalists, spies . . . There are even criminals listed . . . people who fouled up on contracted jobs? And look at this . . . even some poor waiter in Brazil, and a plantation worker in Guatemala . . .'

'They must have been witnesses to something they should not have seen. Or overheard conversations they should not have. Wrong places, wrong times. The Semper are not squeamish when it comes to elimination . . . even their own, as we do know.'

She handed the list back to him. 'I recognize some of the

American names as people whose disappearance, or killings, got the police and FBI scratching their heads at the time.'

'More unsolved cases,' Müller said as he took the list.

'There must be two hundred on there,' she said.

'At least.' Müller idly turned the four sheets over as one. 'Well, there's more.'

'*More?*'

'A scribbled note says this is a small sample.'

'Jesus . . . So has he been able to list all those as well?'

'We'll have to see. But the names he set down on here are people he knew would cause a reaction when put into the public domain, or at least when they became known to . . .'

'Guys like you.'

'And guys like you.' Müller put the sheets to one side, and took out two more from the box file. 'Here's another list, but not what we expect.'

This one was headed *My Kills*. It was itemized in the same way, except for an important difference. The victims were all labelled Semper.

'You will be surprised,' he said, handing the new list to her. He did not elaborate.

She gave him another curious glance as she took it.

Then a soft gasp came from her. 'Colonel Lysker was Semper?' The exclamation mark after the question could almost be seen. 'I don't believe it.'

'Did you know him?'

'I knew *of* him. He was my brother's contact man . . .'

'Now you know whose betrayal caused your brother to be captured.'

She digested this, taking long moments as she remembered the state in which she had found her brother.

'That *bastard!*' she raged, as the gruesome sight of her brother's living corpse, the skin having been peeled off in strips under torture, came back into her mind's eye with a vengeance. Unbidden tears popped into her eyes, moistening them. '*Bastard!*' She wiped at the tears angrily. 'If Lysker hadn't been killed, I'd kill him myself and to hell with the consequences! I'd have shot him in the officers' club, the *bastard!*'

She shook her head once, vigorously, as if coming up from under water.

'You know what this means, don't you, Müller?' she went on. 'And don't look at me. My face is smeared.'

'What does it mean?'

'If . . . if Hargreaves did kill the man who betrayed David, then it means he was still hunting out the Semper . . .'

'While they thought he was dead. Yes. Being dead was a good way to hide.'

Carey Bloomfield looked down at the list again. 'Some snipers on here too, with the names of the people *they* had killed. Some of those names go back years . . . when you were still in your teens. No wonder they wanted to get him when they found out . . .'

'Someone betrayed him . . .'

'And no wonder they wanted to get *you*, when you started on them. Like father, like son . . .'

'They dragged me in. I had no idea they existed. Their mistake.' Müller's voice had the familiar chill in it that always gave her the shivers.

Wordlessly, she returned Hargreaves' list of kills.

Müller took another list from the box file. This one was a single sheet. It was headed *Other Kills*.

His eyes widened for a brief moment as he read it.

Carey Bloomfield was looking at him. 'What?'

He passed it to her without saying anything.

Her eyes also widened as she read the first line. 'How did he . . .' She stopped, then began to read in astonishment, '"*Dahlberg – von Röhnen, Bloomfield*". See? *He* considered you were already the *Graf*.' She said this with a mild air of triumph, before continuing, '"*Heurath – von Röhnen. Von Mappus – von Röhnen, Bloomfield*" . . .'

'That one is rightfully yours. You shot him with that Dragunov . . .'

'You tracked him down. I was just the back up. So yours too.' She continued down the list, murmuring the names. Then almost at the end, she said, 'He credits me with Mary-Anne. Remember that scrawny psychopath? Screeching at me like something out of a horror movie as she came at me.'

'How can I forget.'

'How the hell did he get that information, Müller?' she said as she returned the list of their kills. 'Dahlberg, Mary-Anne, von Mappus . . . even Mainauer, and those guys we got on the Great Northern. He's right up to date. Do you think it's Grogan?'

'Until we know more, Grogan seems the most likely. He too has infiltrated the Semper. At least, I hope it *is* an infiltration. But it could also be someone we know nothing about.'

'Any more in there?'

Müller had no need to look. 'A lot more.' He picked up two clipped sheets. 'For example, this. He's called it "*Some Semper Members*". . .'

'*That* should be dynamite.'

'There's a short preface:

'The core of what would become the global organization known as the Semper began with diehards like von Mappus, after the war. They arose out of the ashes of our ravaged country, like something malignant that refused to die. They believed they had been cheated of victory and sought to rectify that by planning a long-term infiltration of Germany, at all levels. Time, they felt, was on their side. Many of these people had remained in the East, working for the Soviets, as well as the DDR. There were also those of like minds in the then West Germany and, even during the Cold War, began to forge their ties. As the organization grew, new members were added, including internationals.

'Why Germany? Given its then recent history, Germany was the perfect breeding ground. It became even more ideal as it grew into Europe's strongest economy. It became the prize worth picking. The plan was, and still is, to secure control of Germany by stealth, reaching into every corner of the nation so that no one is aware it is actually happening. Overt action is a choice of last resort; but they do not hesitate to take it, if the occasion demands. Their plans are far reaching, to the eventual detriment of both the nation and the international community. Their people are everywhere: the person on the train next to you; the bus, tram, plane, café, or cinema. The person who drives a taxi you have taken . . .

'There were others who, having learned the bitter lessons

of the war, were alert to this danger, even at the early stages, and who were determined to counter the Semper. Also German, and international, this extremely small group of individuals, unable to trust many outside their own tiny circle, then approached me . . .'

'He stops there,' Müller said. 'Beneath that is the list of known members of the Semper.' He did a quick scan of the two pages. 'As you said . . . dynamite. The Semper would certainly kill if they had the slightest suspicion that what is in this room existed. Calling this place Pandora's Box was an understatement. Names from your side of the pond as well. But it does not stop there. Other nationalities are represented. People in seats of power in many professions and callings. Another nightmare coming up . . .'

He handed them to her.

She read it through in total silence, now and then pursed her lips in disgust. When she had finished, she put them down in a manner that gave the impression she felt contaminated.

'Follow the money,' she said, 'and the power. At least one name on here is Pentagon. And I'm not forgetting Toby Adams, my own instructor, who had been like an uncle to me. I trusted that man with my life. I see he's not on this list. Must be on the "deceased" list,' she said with bitter irony, 'although it was Semper who killed him; one of their own, and one of Mary-Anne's kills. The bastards tried to pin that on me.'

'I well remember.'

She rubbed at her eyes. 'Hell. I'm beat and I don't even know it. Been a long day, Müller. It feels like I've been up for more than twenty-four hours.'

'In a way, you have. You go off. I'll hang on here for a while, then I'll get some sleep.'

'You look as tired as I feel,' she said, peering at him. 'Call it a day. It's way, way past midnight. The morning could bring more surprises.'

'I'll be fine.'

'OK.' She looked uncertain. 'OK,' she repeated.

She was standing close to him. She leaned forward

suddenly, to kiss him lightly near the corner of his mouth; then left without saying anything further.

Müller remained where he was, unmoving, for a good two minutes after she had gone. Then returning all the papers to the box file, he left it on the desk and sat down on the chair.

He again picked up the envelope with the photographs of himself, and tipped them out. Searching through them, one made him stop. He drew it closer. It was a picture of a family group of three: his mother, father, and himself at the age of twelve; the age still fixed in his mind that he had last seen them alive. All were grinning at the camera.

Müller felt a sudden moisture in his eyes. Something *pocked* as it hit the photograph. He realized a droplet had fallen, making a splash on the print. He wiped at it with a slow, careful thumb.

He did not see Carey Bloomfield ease her head round the door to look at him, nor the look of helpless pain in her eyes. He did not hear as she withdrew and moved quietly away.

Some time later, the sound of a shuddering intake of breath came out of him. He at last got to his feet, returned all the photographs to the envelope, and left the room to go into the main bedroom. He looked about him, seeing all the framed photographs of himself and his parents when he was a boy. He stared at the carefully made bed.

'I can't sleep in here,' he said to himself.

He went to the room-wide built-in wardrobe, looked for and discovered a section full of spare bed linen. He had a quick shower, then grabbed two pillows and a summer-weight duvet out of the wardrobe. Naked, he carried the pillows, duvet, and his clothes, back to the file room. He dropped his clothes on the chair, then laid duvet and pillows on the floor. He found a reading lamp which he plugged into the socket near where he had put the bedclothes, and switched it on.

He turned off the main lights and taking the box file with him, lay down on the duvet, which he then wrapped about himself. He opened the box file, and began to search through the papers in there. An ordinary white envelope with nothing written upon it caught his attention. Frowning slightly, he took it out. It was not sealed. He opened it and took out the single handwritten sheet it held. The note was surprising.

107

Carey Bloomfield is a lovely young woman. What a remarkable resemblance to Mina! If anything we say still matters,
we could not have chosen a better person for you. Treat her
well.

There was no signature; but there was no need for one.

Müller folded the note slowly, put it back into the envelope, then buried it beneath the entire contents of the box
file, which he then closed.

He switched off the light, and was sound asleep within
less than a minute.

In Berlin, it was 18.45 local.

The wide armoured door rolled itself upwards. The blue
Ready Group van with the grille-protected darkened windows
drove beneath it and down the ramp, into the underground
police garage. The door immediately rolled itself back down
as the lights automatically came on, and was shut and secure
before the van had stopped.

Two officers in full gear stepped out of the front. The back
door opened, and Berger and Reimer climbed out. The two
Ready Group men came round the back to help them unload
a wheelchair, in which the goth was sitting.

'I'm not an invalid,' she protested.

'Be quiet, Hedi,' Berger commanded. 'You're staying in
there until we get you upstairs.'

'I *can* walk, you know.'

'We know you can walk. You're getting what you wanted
. . . being back here . . .'

'This *is* the safest place while I'm like this.'

'There's another one, but never mind.'

'And I can work . . .'

'You won, Hedi. Enjoy it. Now are you going to be quiet?'
Hedi Meyer smiled. 'For now.'

'Let's take her up before she changes her mind,' Berger
said to her colleagues.

'So she's OK?' Pappenheim asked.

They were in Pappenheim's office.

'Strong as an ox,' Berger said. 'The doctor who attended to her said she'll be fine as long as she doesn't do any heavy physical stuff. He's dressed the wound again and is amazed how well she's doing. So much for the "frail" goth.'

'It hides the real steel. Good camouflage. Her Beetle's safe in the garage downstairs,' Pappenheim went on, 'out of reach of those who might be interested in prying. She's got some clothes?'

Berger nodded. 'I picked some up at her place. I used my own car.'

'Good idea. A police vehicle pulling up might have excited anyone watching out for that.'

'Her place is . . .' Berger paused.

'Her place is what?'

'Interesting.'

'Meaning?'

'Not what I expected. Oh it's goth . . . ish, with bright and dark colours . . . but it's very nicely done, and well furnished. I didn't expect that. She's got taste.'

'I don't find that surprising . . . but I think you're leading up to something.' Pappenheim's eyes fastened upon her.

'She's . . . got a picture.'

'Of?' Pappenheim waited.

'The . . . er . . . boss.'

'Ah. You've been *prying*?'

'Not prying, Chief. Honest. I was just hauling out some clothes quickly, when it fell out . . .'

'Fell out.'

'Yes! It really did. It was in a drawer. I pulled out some clothes . . . and . . . it fell out. I put it back exactly as I found it.'

'She's a police officer, Lene. She'll check.'

'I was really good. She'll never know.'

'It's your neck. So how did she come by it?'

'Now who's prying?'

'Rank first. You answer my questions, I don't have to answer yours. So?'

'It looks like something she took with a handy.'

'Those things with cameras.'

Berger nodded. 'I'm certain he doesn't even know.'

Pappenheim sighed. 'Well, she's a grown woman.'

'That's right,' Berger said with meaning.

'Don't start that again, Lene. Did the doctor say anything about checking on her?' Pappenheim went on quickly, stalling any comeback.

'Nice footwork . . . sir.'

'Big people are supposed to be light on their feet,' Pappenheim, at his most shameless, said.

'The doctor said he would be on call any time we needed him.'

'That's good to know, even though we have our own medical team. And no one at the hospital suspects?'

'Only the doctor knows. He helped us. And he's not going to tell anyone.'

'Good,' Pappenheim said.

'So she got her way in the end.'

Pappenheim squinted at her through wreaths of smoke. 'You don't approve? The other absolutely safe option in a situation like this would have been Jens' apartment. It's like a fortress to get into; but Jens has always given me the entry code. She would have been perfectly safe in there, and with no need to have people hovering around as bodyguards, as would have been necessary at a safe house. That would have alerted Sharon Wilson's paymasters that the goth was still alive. So that put other safe houses out as choices. But do you think it would have been a good idea to leave her at Jens' place?'

'Knowing how she feels about him . . . no.'

'So we had no choice. Besides, she wanted to come here. In the end, it turned out to be the best option. We have the two holding apartments for protected witnesses. They are comfortable, and private. She has the best one. She can recuperate in peace until we get Sharon Wilson.'

'You know she'll want to work, don't you?'

Pappenheim gave another sigh. 'I know.'

'She'll keep pestering you.'

'I know that too.'

As if on cue, Pappenheim's phone rang. He picked it up. 'Pappenheim.'

'Sir? When can I start?'

Pappenheim shut his eyes briefly. 'Tomorrow will be soon enough, Hedi. You have yourself a good rest.'

'You won't forget?'

'I won't forget.'

'I'll hold you to that.'

'I know you will.' Pappenheim looked at Berger as he hung up. 'And don't you start.'

Berger made a zipping motion across her lips.

'So you should,' he said, taking one of his longer drags. The phone rang again. Pappenheim picked it up with a sigh. 'Hedi, I said—'

'Who're you calling Hedi?' the sergeant at the front desk said.

'Ah! Margo. You're on duty . . .'

'Believe it or not,' a dry female voice retorted.

'Everybody's rude to their superiors these days.'

'You haven't seen me rude. This is nothing. Anyway, do you want your package, or not?'

'I have a package?'

'What did I just say?'

'I have a package. Who brought it?'

'Some strange, shadowy man. "For Pappenheim" he said. Just that. Nothing more. So? Shall I have it sent up?'

'No. I'll come down.'

'Must be important.'

'Don't get nosy, *Obermeisterin.*'

She laughed.

Pappenheim hung up with a sigh. 'They're not frightened of me any more.'

'It's because they know your bark's worse than your bite.'

'It's the other way round,' Pappenheim insisted. 'And don't you forget it.'

She ignored that. 'I'll get the package,' she offered.

'Now who's being nosy?'

'Of course.'

She was out of the door before he could respond.

'Where's the respect?' he called to the closed door.

He thought he heard a faint laugh.

'Might as well smoke,' he said to himself. He lit up afresh, and blew several smoke rings at the smoke-stained ceiling. 'The question is . . . what is Sharon Wilson up to, and where is she?'

Sharon Wilson had made very good time in the souped-up Mercedes coupé and was approaching the Europort junction, prior to crossing the border into France.

At the hospital where the goth had been, a man walked through the main entrance to go up to the reception desk. He had checked out the person at the desk, and the nearby security guard, before venturing in.

'Hi,' he greeted. 'I'm Jörg Kirschberg.' He held out an ID. 'Journalist . . .'

The woman at the desk, older than the previous incumbent, made a wry face. 'Another one.'

'What do you mean?'

'Journalist. That's what I mean. You want to know about that policewoman as well, don't you?'

'Well . . .' Kirschberg said, looking confused, 'er . . . yes.'

'You're too late.'

'What do you mean?'

'What I mean, young man, is that she's gone.'

'*Gone?* Where? I don't understand.'

'To her grave,' the receptionist answered with ghoulish humour. 'Now do you understand?'

'Er . . . er . . . yes. Yes. I see. Well . . . thank you. Thank you.'

Kirschberg hurried out in apparent confusion, while the receptionist shook her head pityingly.

'You sometimes wonder how they get their jobs,' she said to the security man.

'Someone has to do it.' He was also not the same one who had been on duty earlier in the day.

'That's the problem,' she said, and went back to what she had been doing.

Kirschberg was the same person who had called himself Max Erling.

A few minutes later, a tall man walked past the desk from within the building. ''night, Trudi. 'night, Harald.'

'Goodnight, Herr *Doktor*,' Harald replied.

'Goodnight, Doctor Hammerstein. I thought you had long gone home.'

Hammerstein paused, saying lightly, 'When is work ever finished?'

'I know what you mean,' she said in sympathy. 'Oh . . . a man was just in here, asking about that poor girl.'

'Really? Who?'

'Some journalist. Kirschberg, he said his name was. Like vultures, these people. Can't leave her alone.'

Hammerstein seemed to be more sharply alert than would be expected for such a remark. 'What did you tell him?'

'That she was dead, of course . . .' She paused, looking anxious. 'Did I talk out of turn, Doctor Hammerstein?'

He gave her a work-weary smile. 'No. Of course not. Goodnight again, you two.'

'Goodnight, Doctor.'

'Goodnight, Herr *Doktor*.'

Berger entered Pappenheim's office with a thickish, brown A4 envelope.

'Feels heavy,' she said. 'Must be a lot in there.'

'I hope you didn't try to look inside.'

'I've only just made it to *Kommissarin*. I don't want to lose it.'

'Smart,' Pappenheim said, holding out a hand.

She handed him the envelope.

He paused, looking at her.

'Oh come on, Chief. Don't send me out.'

'All right,' he said after another pause. 'But you stay where you are.'

'Deal.'

'*Deal?*'

'Must be Colonel Bloomfield's influence.'

'Ouch,' Pappenheim said, opening the envelope. He pulled out a thick folder with blue borders. 'This looks interesting. Let's see what the Blue Folder Boys have to say about our smoking banker.'

He began to read, and soon became so engrossed, he put out his unfinished cigarette. Minutes went by.

He looked up suddenly, peering at Berger. 'You're fidgeting.'

'Are you going to tell me anything?' she said, looking at the folder with pointed deliberation.

'Ah. Yes. This will interest you. Stay back.'

Berger had begun to move closer. She stopped. 'I'm staying.'

'Hmm. All right. Listen to this.' Pappenheim returned his attention to the folder. 'Your tasty Guatemalan coffee comes from a plantation owned by a company called *Deutsche Kaffeeverein Guatemala*. There are many coffee plantations out there – big, small, subsistence – but none associated with this group. But according to the Blue Folders, the DKvG is something else entirely. It is a genuine plantation . . . but it is a cover, it seems, for another kind of operation.

'The place is surrounded by armed guards. The local workers are stringently searched and checked – going in and going out – every single day. This will interest you – our banker friend is responsible for the DKvG accounts, running into hundreds of millions. The upper hundreds of millions . . . valued in pounds sterling. A billion euros easily.'

'Oh.'

'Thought you might say that. Must be some coffee plantation.'

'Is there more?'

Pappenheim shut the folder, and looked at her.

'I get the message, Chief.'

'Lene . . . this is for your own safety, and your career. The less you know, the less the Great White will be able to use against you . . . if it ever comes to that.'

'If he ever asks me, which I doubt – too low down the pecking order – I don't know anything.'

'Which means . . . the less you know, the more believable your denial will be.'

'If you say so.'

'I do say so.'

Berger knew when she was beaten. 'OK, Chief. What's next?'

'What's next is that you go home and relax. I'm going to have another smoke, and continue reading this little gem. See you in the morning. And watch out for a crazy hitwoman. You're on her list.'

'She's on *my* bloody list,' Berger said with some viciousness.

'Hmm,' Pappenheim said, lighting up before she was out the door.

Half an hour into his study of the folder, his phone rang. It was again the sergeant at the front desk.

'There's a Doctor Hammerstein here. He wants to speak to you.'

'I'll be down . . .'

'He says there's no need. He can speak from here.'

'All right. Put him on.'

'Herr Pappenheim?'

'Doctor Hammerstein . . . everything all right?'

'I thought I'd drop by to let you know of something that happened at the hospital.'

Pappenheim straightened in his chair. 'What happened?'

'A man calling himself Kirschberg, journalist, was asking about her. The receptionist informed me as I was leaving. She gave Kirschberg the correct answer.'

'Understood. Thank you, Doctor. I appreciate your coming.'

'Is . . . she all right?'

'Given your ministrations, she is doing excellently.'

'Very good to hear.' Hammerstein sounded relieved. 'Strong constitution. Impressive.'

'It's her good living. She does not smoke for a start.'

'Wise. I won't give you advice you already know.'

'Thank you, Doctor,' Pappenheim said with more than a hint of dryness.

'Goodnight, Herr Pappenheim,' Hammerstein said, sounding as if he too were being dry.

''night, Doctor. And thank you for coming. Take care as you go.'

'I will,' Hammerstein said, understanding.

Carey Bloomfield awoke to the smell of fresh coffee.

She took her time before opening her eyes. She was lying in a loose foetal position, the lightweight sheet that covered her delineating her body, almost as if painted over it.

The smell of coffee was coming from behind. She opened her eyes at last, turned her head, and saw the cup on the bedside table, a wisp rising from it. There was no one in the room with her.

She gave a gentle smile. 'Ah, Müller,' she said. 'You really will make someone a good wife.'

Keeping the sheet about her, she rose to a sitting position, picked up the cup, and had a sip. She savoured it.

'Mmm! Now that is coffee.' She had another sip, swallowed that, then called, 'Müller!'

He was there within seconds. 'You rang?'

She stared at him. 'You're dressed!'

'Showered, dressed, and that aroma you smell apart from the coffee, is breakfast being prepared. You've got ten minutes. We have a long, interesting day ahead of us.'

'*Ten* minutes? Müller . . . !'

'Ten.' He turned to go.

'What time is it? And where's my watch?'

'Probably under your pile of clothes.'

'Ah shaddup . . .'

'And it is now nine o'clock precisely,' he said, mimicking the speaking clock.

'Oh very Pom. *Nine!* Müller! Why did you let me sleep so long?'

'You needed it . . . and besides, do you have a rush hour to beat?'

'Ah shad . . .'

'You've already said that.'

'Müller . . . how was I when you came in . . .'

'The door was open.'

'There's no door to close.'

'Oh yes. So there isn't. How were you? Curled up.'

'And the sheet?'

'Covering you. Fully. Why?'

'I'm in the buff, Müller.'

'I could see that . . .'

'Müller!'

But he was already in the hall, on his way back to the kitchen.

'Nine minutes,' she heard.

'Well . . . at least he's getting back to normal,' she muttered as she got out of bed. 'Or what passes for normal.'

'My God!' Carey Bloomfield, empty cup in hand, exclaimed when she saw the breakfast spread on the central table in the vast kitchen. 'What is this?'

'Breakfast?' Müller suggested.

'Yes. Well. I can see that. But it's food for ten!'

'Exaggeration. What you're looking at is part Aussie, part Aussie bushman's, part English, and part bio. A healthy, well-rounded breakfast. Make the most of it. We've got a long day.'

'So you said.' Carey Bloomfield stared at the table in some wonder, as she sat down. 'You made all this? Smells great.'

'Everything was nicely stored. It was just a matter of preparing. That did not take long. Much as I like a cup of tea in the morning—'

'Old Oxford habit?'

'Old Müller habit. However, I felt this deserved coffee. Aussie breakfast blend. You've already had some.'

'And that *was* good.' Her eyes roved about the table. 'Sliced melon, sliced apples, sliced orange, grapes, orange juice, bacon and eggs, sausages, mushrooms . . . and what's that?' She pointed.

'Grapefruit marmalade. Hot toast when you're ready. And that bread you're looking at is coconut bread. I didn't do that. It was already baked.'

'This, Müller, is disgustingly sybaritic . . . and I'm going to eat my fill. Just like last night. I've warned you before, I'm not one of those women who pecks at her food like a bird.'

'For which, I am truly grateful. Now dig in.'

'I'm spoiled for choice,' she protested as she tried to decide which took her fancy most. 'The fruit before, or after?'

'Any order that suits you. We're not standing on ceremony.'

'Ceremony? What's that?' She made her choices. 'So when did you get up?'

'At six . . .'

'*Six?* Müller, you spent *three* hours doing this?'

'Do you think I'm mad? I spent most of the three hours discovering new and interesting things about the files, working the surveillance system, and discovering some hot items on the computer.'

'You have been busy.'

'When we're finished here, I'll show you.'

'What did you discover about the files? And where did you sleep, by the way? The main bedroom?'

Müller shook his head. 'I went in, looked around, and decided I was not ready to sleep there. So I found some bedclothes and slept in the study.'

'On the *floor?*'

'There isn't a bed in there.'

'You know what I mean.'

'I was quite comfortable.'

The unspoken words were almost palpable between them. Both chose to make no mention of what was on their minds.

'After I had showered and dressed,' Müller continued, 'I decided to check out some more files. I felt certain Hargreaves might have set down a more comprehensive list of Semper members? and kills. It seemed logical. But file after file showed nothing like that; and as you've seen, there are just too many to look through for now. So I stopped and decided to try the computer. Nothing on there. Then I opened a drawer in the desk and found several CDs in storage cases. They had no markings, except for numerals. No titles of any kind. At first, I thought they were empty. I put number one in, just to see . . .'

'Paydirt?'

'Paydirt. All those CDs contain the full Semper directory, and a lot more . . . including kills.'

Carey Bloomfield stopped eating. 'Holy . . . *wow!* You're kidding.'

Müller was smiling. 'Not kidding. It's all there – from the top of the tree all the way to the bottom. Ten CDs of 700 megabytes of storage each, all full. We have the lot.' He grinned suddenly. 'From now on, it will be a matter of finding ways to reel them in, in a manner that allows no escape, no matter how many high-powered lawyers, or friends, they can call on. The entire Semper organization – including its cover companies and organizations – is on those discs.'

'Müller, all the information you've now got back there . . . the files, the pictures, the discs, the notes . . . they'd really kill for this, and not pause for breath. If they ever suspected . . .'

'If they ever got to know, what we have already seen from them would be kindergarten games by comparison. Because if we add all that is in the study – including those discs – to what we already have in the rogues' gallery in Berlin, then we are looking at the eventual downfall of the Semper. Jack and Maggie constructed a very big timebomb . . . for the Semper.'

'Any recognizable names pop up during your quick scan?'

'Oh yes,' Müller replied. 'Which brings me to betrayal.' The levity was now gone as if it had never been. 'Ever since the plane went down, I've been wondering who could have been responsible, and now, I've got the confirmation. The person who zeroed Mainauer on to us, who got Jamie Mackay killed, who made it possible for Sharon Wilson to find us in all of Australia – a country that covers Europe from Norway to Greece – so quickly, who made it possible for those people on the Great Northern Highway to be waiting for us and who, I am now certain, directed whoever planted that bomb on the Hargreaves' plane . . . is Waldron.'

Her eyes widened at him. 'Are you *kidding* me? That's Pappi's old friend who helped us out the first time we got here . . .' She stopped. 'Jesus, Müller. Pappi saved his life all those years ago. Why would he do a thing like that?'

'Tell me why he's on the list, then I might try to find a way of explaining it. Hargreaves would not have made such a mistake. But given what has happened, it explains a lot. Yes . . . Waldron did smooth our way here. He was so helpful with everything: arranging the Explorer, our flights from Perth to Broome, our introduction to Graeme Wishart . . . even making certain we were not bothered by officialdom. He was indeed very good; for a very good reason. He knew enough to guess where we were eventually headed. It was just a matter of setting the hounds loose after that.'

119

She still refused to accept it. '*Waldron?* Come on, Müller. That's reaching.'

'He's on the list of Semper members. His *father* is on that list. That is not "reaching". Do not forget your own experience with Toby Adams. Would you ever have suspected him?'

This made her pause for thought. 'God,' she said after a while. 'Who the hell can you trust these days?'

'Not many people . . . especially when you see some of the names on that list.'

'Grogan there?'

'Yes. But we know – I hope – that he's an infiltrator. It was smart to leave his name. If for any reason – however remote as far as the Hargreaves were concerned – the discs did fall into Semper hands, Grogan would be protected. Leaving his name off would have been like a beacon.'

Müller buttered a slice of toast as he continued, 'Coffee . . .'

'Not quite done . . .'

'I did not mean do you want a refill. Coffee features on the list. It caught my interest for two reasons: one of the victims on the first kill list we saw, was a Guatemalan coffee plantation worker. That same plantation also happens to have connections to a bank in Berlin, not far from our own offices. The *Deutsche Kaffeeverein Guatemala* is a plantation with an account that seems incredibly large, even for a successful coffee company.'

'How successful is "successful"?'

'How about an account worth a billion euros?'

'*What?*'

'That's what is on there; and this is only *one* company owned by the Semper. I would think Hargreaves knew what he was talking about. And the man in Berlin with responsibility for that little treasure is someone called Heinrich Höhntaler, banker.'

'Nice work, if you can get it.'

'Höhntaler is not an innocent banker administering funds for clients whose *bona fides* he has taken at face value. Höhntaler is Semper. We've got it all, Carey. We've got it!'

'Müller?' she said after a long pause. 'You've called me Carey . . . without my having to beg.'

He stared at her. 'Didn't you hear what I just said?'

'I did. I just thought this was worth mentioning.'

He gave her a wary glance. 'You're dangerous.'

'Of course. I'm a woman.'

'Pappi will try to contact me today,' he hurried on. 'I'll ask him to find out about Höhntaler. There must also be a secure way to transfer the information on the CDs to the rogues' gallery computer . . . and perhaps a few bits of the other information as well. The goth should be able to work a little of her magic. That way we'll have some vital information to hand, while the originals remain safe and secure down here. We have the big stick.'

The corners of Carey Bloomfield's mouth were tucked back in a tiny smile.

'Care to share the joke?' Müller asked.

'It's nothing.'

'Why do women always do that?'

'Do what?'

'And that too. The "innocent" question that is anything but.'

'You guys have a long way to go . . . but don't let that worry you.' She gave his hand a quick pat. 'Ease up, Müller. I'm teasing.'

'Is that good? Or bad?'

'Depends.' Her smile widened.

'I give up.'

'I should, if I were you. You'll lose.' He gave her another wary glance as she continued, 'If you can find a way to freeze their assets, you've got a hell of a lot more than a lever. You've got yourself a very big gun.'

'But only one target, so far. The CDs should give us plenty more. But the very first one we attack will set off alarms right through the entire organization. They won't take it lying down. We'll have to maintain surprise. That means hitting them in several places at once.'

'How do you arrange that without alerting them? They have people in all sorts of places of influence.'

'And *we* know who they are . . . thanks to the CDs.'

Six

France, Hautes Alpes. Route Napoleon 202, 03.12 local.
Sharon Wilson smiled as the little car behind her struggled to keep up. It had latched on to her tail just after passing Digne-les-Bains, and had been trying to pass her ever since. Enjoying the contest, she had speeded up and slowed down at intervals, speeding up again every time it had made it close enough.

Since leaving Berlin, she had stopped only for petrol and quick snacks. During one of those stops she had dozed briefly to recharge. She never used hotels on the road. Hotels meant leaving a trail to be followed. With her destination now less than two hours away, she felt alive, pushing the big coupé to its limit in the darkness, its bright lights spearing the night. She enjoyed the growling roar of the engine against the unseen mountains beyond the glow of the lights.

Then just ahead, on the right side of the road, she saw a large patch of gravelled, open ground. A lay-by like a huge car park, in the middle of nowhere. The place was quite empty. Beyond it, were the dark waters of a vast lake. Here, at its northern end, it was narrower, spreading southwards into the gloomy distance.

She glanced in her mirror. She had left the little pursuer far behind in her recent burst of speed. Its lights were not even visible. She decided to pull into the parking area, to see what would happen when the car caught up again.

She smiled to herself, parking the Mercedes nose-on to the water, and turned off the lights. She switched off the engine and climbed out. Barefoot, and in minimal shorts and a transparent sleeveless blouse of white linen, she stretched luxuriously. It was a clear night and as her eyes grew accustomed, she began to make out the shapes of the surrounding mountains and the high ground about her.

She walked to the edge of the parking area to look at the water. The ground sloped steeply away for about five metres, to the lake. As her eyes grew even more accustomed, she could see the amorphous shape of a track that went precipitously downwards. It looked safe enough to try only in daylight.

She smiled again when she began to hear the screaming engine of the little car, its driver racing to catch up. No other vehicle was on the road.

She remained where she was, facing the lake. She made a decision, depending on what the little car did, and who was inside. With calculated deliberation, she opened the blouse fully.

Soon the screaming engine, echoing in the night, grew louder. A blaze of lights, and the car shot past.

Sharon Wilson waited, still smiling.

Then came the screech of brakes.

'Mm-hmm,' she said. 'Fun.' She continued to remain where she was.

Before long, she could hear the car turning; then it slowly began to return. It turned into the car park. It came close, like an animal uncertain of what was ahead, but still curious enough to check it out.

The little car pulled up almost parallel to the Mercedes coupé, a few metres away, its engine idling.

Sharon Wilson still did not move.

Then a youngish male voice called in English. 'German?'

'It's a German car,' she replied, not turning round.

'I never thought a woman could drive like that. You are very good.'

'I am very good at many things.' She could sense he was looking at her legs.

The lights on the little car went out, and the engine died.

'Mm-hmm,' she said under her breath. 'Fun.'

She heard the door of the car open.

'You should be careful,' he said. 'A woman like you, alone, on this road at night and standing out here . . . anything can happen.'

She turned, slowly, knowing that with his own eyes

growing accustomed to the gloom, he would see the opened blouse.

'What can happen? Are you going to attack me?'

'No!' He sounded astonished that she would suggest it. He had been approaching. Now, he stopped, and swallowed. It was a faint sound. 'I . . . I think you . . . should not be out here like . . . this . . . dressed like . . . this. I would not like my girlfriend . . .'

'So you have a girlfriend.'

'Yes. I am going to meet her in Castellane. We are going to the coast in the morning.'

'Then you should hurry to get there.'

'Castellane is not too far from here.'

'I see. What's your name?'

'Maurice Baudouin.'

'Your English is very good, Maurice.'

'Thank you. I learned it for my job.'

'Which is?'

'I am a guide. You know, for people who come for their holidays.'

'I see,' Sharon Wilson repeated. 'Do you meet a lot of women in your job?'

'Of course. Many.'

She could almost hear what he was thinking. Rich, bored woman, husband not giving her enough attention, looking for crazy sexual adventures. Everyone knew how some women behaved on holiday. And when he was finished, he would brag about it to his male friends.

'Of course,' Sharon Wilson said. 'Do you really have a girlfriend, Maurice?'

'Of course!'

'But you want to *fuck* me. Is that it?'

Surprised by the directness of it, Baudouin could only say, 'I . . . I . . .'

'Fine. I'm leaving.'

He hurried closer. 'No! Wait! I mean . . .'

She let him get close enough for her proximity to completely unnerve him. 'You mean . . . what?'

This time, he swallowed loudly enough for it to be easily heard.

'Goodbye, Maurice. I only like men who know what they want.' She began to move back to her car.

'No . . . wait . . .' Instinctively, he reached out to put a hand on her arm.

She stopped. 'If you touch me, this has to mean something. If not . . .'

Baudouin was not a male spider and so foolishly, threw caution to the winds. Ruled by something much stronger than his head, he allowed himself to be seduced by Sharon Wilson.

She reclined the passenger seat of the coupé and, scarcely believing his luck, Maurice Baudouin almost scrambled on top of her in his eagerness to get what was being offered, and what he certainly wanted.

No vehicle passed while Baudouin had his wildest fantasies fulfilled. He could not believe how this sexually hungry, unknown woman whom he had met in the night could contort herself with such inventiveness. Temporarily putting the girlfriend in Castellane out of his mind, he abandoned himself to the wildness of it and let the fiercely energetic woman consume him.

'Mmmm,' Sharon Wilson said. 'You *are* so . . . *strong.*' The last word was a drawn-out wail.

When it was over, Baudouin hurried out of the car, doing up his trousers. Shorts on the floor of the car, she followed.

'Maurice,' she called softly. 'I'm very warm inside. Do you want more?'

He paused, hands at his still-open zip, and peered dreamily at her half-naked body. He looked as if he would be happy for a repeat performance.

She went up to him, and cupped his face in her hands.

'Do you want more?' she said again, her voice seductive and soft. 'You'll never forget this. Your girlfriend in Castellane will be a piece of cardboard by comparison.'

He thought she was about to kiss him. It is doubtful he knew what was happening as she snapped his neck.

She took her hands away as he fell. Quickly, so as not to leave any drag marks on the gravel, she rolled the body over the edge of the lay-by. She was already moving back to the car as Baudouin's body tumbled down the rough slope to the water's edge.

She put her shorts back on, got in behind the wheel, pressed the switch to bring the passenger seat back to its normal position, then started the engine. She spun the car to disturb the gravel and obliterate the indentations of the wheels where the Mercedes had been standing.

'It *fucking* stinks in here,' she said. 'And I need a *fucking* bath.'

She drove away from the lake, Elgar's *Nimrod* swelling powerfully and loudly out of the car's twelve speakers.

There was still no other traffic. With just under 110 kilometres of her journey left to go, she would have had her bath and be soundly asleep between soft sheets, before Baudouin's body was discovered.

Woonnalla, Western Australia.
When Müller and Carey Bloomfield had finished breakfast and had loaded the dishwasher, they made their way back to the study. Most of the food had gone.

'Wooo!' she said. 'I feel like I've eaten ten horses. One would have been enough. You cook too damned good, Müller. Not fair. You must let me boil you an egg some time.'

'I await that with anticipation.'

'He thinks I'm kidding. And here we are in the study,' she went on quickly before he could say anything. 'Time to show me what you found.'

'All right,' Müller said with his own tiny smile.

He sat down at the computer. It was already on, but had gone into energy saving mode. Movement of the mouse brought the huge plasma screen monitor back to life. Next to the mouse was a small, joystick-like lever in red, with a black button on top. Its small base was fixed to the desk.

'Before breakfast, I did a routine check of the entire environs. We have no visitors . . . so far.'

He hit a key. The monitor divided itself into nine windows – each equivalent to a nineteen-inch screen – in rows of three.

'This is the basic mode,' he went on. 'The middle screen of the bottom row is the working screen for the computer. As you can see, the other screens monitor different camera locations.'

'Work while you survey.'

'Nice line . . . but essentially, yes. You can't be surprised, even while doing something else . . . if you've got surveillance mode on. Each screen can also subdivide itself into as many windows as is visually practical. I'll show you.'

Moving a hand to the joystick, Müller pressed the button once. Instantly, a pulsing red border framed one of the screens. He pressed the button again, and it subdivided.

'In this mode, I can click the button as many times as is practicable until the screens become too small to be of any visual use. However, if I do this—'

He hit another key, and a small white cross appeared in the centre of the screen. He clicked the button once, and kept it pressed. The screen zoomed in until the spot marked by the cross filled the entire screen, with razor-sharp definition.

'I can do this with any screen . . .' He moved the joystick. '. . . or pan in any direction. I can select any camera . . .'

He hit a third key, and a window scrolled down showing a series of small bars, indicating the location of each camera. He clicked on a bar. Instantly, the particular location came onscreen.

'The system can also do this automatically if I press this key to activate auto mode.'

He did so, and let go of the joystick. The system began to loop through all the camera locations.

'If something interests me, a click on the joystick stops the auto function at the screen, and again I can zoom in, out, or pan. If I leave the stick for thirty seconds, auto mode returns. There is also a record mode, and everything can be saved on either the main or the external hard drive. The external is in one of the drawers. There's some material on it. I'll check it later. You never know. We might see who their visitors were.'

'Neat system,' Carey Bloomfield said. 'I could use that where I live. And I'm not joking.'

'I thought you lived in a good area.'

'I do . . . but you can never be too careful. I didn't know you were good with computers, Müller.'

'I'm not. The goth would sneer at my efforts; and besides, I had a little help. The dots were joined for me.' He reached

127

into a drawer, and pulled out a ring-bound file. 'Fifty pages of detailed instructions. As you've said, they were prepared for my eventual arrival.' Müller's voice went very quiet as he continued, 'Even though they suggested they might not be here, I think they hoped they would be.'

Instinctively, she placed a gentle hand upon his shoulder for a few moments. 'You OK, Müller?'

'I'm fine.'

'OK. Show me some of what's on those CDs.'

'Coming up. The CD I was talking about is already in.'

Müller switched back to standard computer working mode. The lower middle screen now became the computer monitor. The other screens showed real time surveillance of different parts of the property, in auto mode.

He clicked on the CD icon, and opened it; then opened one of the folders displayed. This was captioned *DKvG Dokumente*. He opened that, and several other folders were displayed. He opened one. Several photographs of the plantation came onscreen. At first glance, it seemed like any other coffee plantation. Then the photographs began to show other aspects – satellite shots, close-ups from various angles, armed gate and perimeter guards, armed men on horseback, armed men training, various buildings with armed men about them, large sections of genuine coffee growing areas.

'*Armed* men?' Carey Bloomfield said in astonishment. 'And I'm not talking about the gate guards.'

'Interesting, wouldn't you say? Whoever took those photographs is – or was – someone who could either move around in there freely, or had some very powerful equipment. Either way, it must have been dangerous. The satellite shots could only have come from people who knew the Hargreaves well enough to pass them on . . .'

'Or was one of the updaters.'

'That too.' Müller selected a group shot in front of a building, and expanded it on the image of a woman in combat fatigues, long blonde hair gleaming. 'Recognize her?'

'My God! The late, unlamented Mary-Anne!'

'Seems as if this is where the Semper killers do their refresher training. Not all are, of course. Some of those

128

armed men on horseback may be perimeter guards. The entire plantation is fenced off . . .'

'Must have cost plenty to fence off that piece of real estate.'

'A fortune. But they can certainly afford it. While all of the armed people may not be the Semper's killer elite, some definitely are. They have also got contracted people. Those who are not strictly Semper, but who do it just for the money. You'll see a couple of other old friends: one Semper, one mercenary. I'll be back to Mary-Anne. First, this one.'

Müller switched to a photograph of another woman, this time on horseback. She was in shorts, and was barefoot. She rode the horse without a saddle. Just a blanket was between her and the back of the animal.

Carey Bloomfield stared at the image. '*Sharon Wilson,*' she said in a tight whisper. 'I'll be damned.'

'One of the contracted assassins. The Semper sometimes pair them with one of their own . . . as they did with her . . .'

'The guy who was with her when she pulled that motorbike stunt at Gantheaume Point . . .'

'And whom she was not too bothered about abandoning when it suited her.'

'I hope I meet up with her again soon,' Carey Bloomfield said. It was a prayer.

'I do not think you'll need to worry about that. I am quite certain she wants a return match. A word of warning . . . she has a great number of kills.'

'So have I.'

Müller looked at her.

'I'm not a shrinking violet, Müller.'

'Never said you were. Now here's another friend.'

The new photograph was of a man in full sniper gear. He had removed his camouflaged headgear, and was grinning into camera.

'*Mainauer!*' she exclaimed. 'Another late, and unlamented.'

'Some more photographs of him were sent to us in Berlin.'

'From unnameable sources?'

'That kind. Yes. This photograph looks remarkably as if it belongs to the same batch.'

'More infiltrators?'

'Possibly. Remember what my . . . Hargreaves wrote. There is a small group dedicated to destroying the Semper. *He* was, after all, an infiltrator working for them. There are bound to be others. Perhaps one of those took the photographs.'

'And Hargreaves arranged to have a few sent to you.'

'Perhaps.'

'Back to Mary-Anne. Take a look at that building. What would you say it is?'

'Do *you* know?'

'Yes.'

'It's fenced off . . . a compound within a compound. A specialist indoor firing range?'

'Try again,' Müller suggested.

She studied the building. 'Could be any number of things – from a storage area of some kind, to living quarters . . . but I don't think it's living quarters. Looks too heavily protected.'

'Your instincts are telling you something, but I'll put you out of your misery. It's a laboratory.'

'A lab? For . . . what . . . ? Oh no.'

'Oh yes.'

Müller closed the photo folder, and opened another. This contained a series of diagrams, all fully labelled, of every building on the plantation. He highlighted and expanded the diagram of the building in front of which Mary-Anne's group had been standing. Above it was the caption: *PS0*.

She stared at it. 'This is where they cultivated that DNA nightmare? This is where they hid their damned lab?'

'This is one of the places,' he corrected, 'where they tried . . . and failed. The picture you just saw is old. Mary-Anne was still alive and kicking. The data with which they were trying to recreate PS0 was still in existence . . . until the goth got into their systems and killed it. Now they have nothing . . .'

'Which is why they will renew their search for whoever is carrying the original in his own DNA.'

'Greville. Unfortunately for them – and fortunately for Greville – they still have no idea of his identity, any more than *Rotbarsch* did.'

'And if they ever found out . . .'

'They'll never take Greville alive, nor get his body to run tests upon.'

'I'm almost afraid to ask this, Müller. If it came to it . . . would you kill Greville to prevent them from getting hold of him?'

'Greville would kill himself first, and I would dispose of his body as he has already asked me to.'

'But if for any reason he was unable to . . .'

'I don't think I want to answer that,' Müller said.

She looked at him for long moments. 'If that time ever came . . .' She paused. 'I'd . . . I'd help.'

He turned to look sharply at her. 'Do you know what you're saying?'

'I know exactly what I'm saying. And I know that Greville is absolutely right when he says this DNA weapon should never be let loose on the world. He's been carrying it for all those years, and has kept it even from the people who sent him out to that original lab, to get hold of it in the first place.'

'Let us hope we will never *ever* arrive at the point where we must make that decision.'

'Amen to that,' she said. Then movement made her glance at one of the monitor screens. 'Company,' she said urgently.

Müller selected the screen, and zoomed in. The Lyserts' pick-up truck, followed by Wishart's police vehicle, were on the approach road.

'They'll be here soon,' he said, moving rapidly. 'I'll leave it on record mode, then shut down everything else. They'll see the Explorer when they get here. We ought to be upstairs before they arrive.'

They made it in plenty of time, and were already waiting at the front of the house when the two vehicles came to a slow halt, a short distance from where they were standing.

'You'd think they were scared to come any closer,' Carey Bloomfield said in a low voice.

Müller said nothing, watching as the three men seemed to take longer than was necessary to get out of their vehicles. They came forward with a strange diffidence.

Wishart stopped closer than the Lyserts who stood to one side, watching Müller with some apprehension.

It was Wishart who spoke first. He addressed Carey Bloomfield, but he looked at Müller. 'So you persuaded him.'

'I'm not sure I had much to do with it,' she said.

Wishart finally addressed Müller. 'You OK, mate?'

Müller nodded. 'I'm fine. How did the search go?'

Wishart looked embarrassed and grim at the same time; the Lyserts as if their world had come to an end. All three looked tired.

'Nothing,' Wishart said. 'We found no sign of bodies. Bits of plane were found close to shore, but it looks as if the explosion took place further out than we thought. Deep water, currents . . . Whatever. The divers were down all day yesterday. More sections of the plane have been brought up . . . but there's a lot still missing.'

'Black boxes?'

Wishart shook his head. 'Nothing.'

'I see.'

'Sorry, mate.'

'Not your fault, Graeme. Not your fault. I brought this to you. Excuse me for a few moments, I . . . want a few words with Paul, and with Pete.'

Müller left a puzzled Wishart to stare after him as he went over to the Lysert brothers.

They observed his approach warily.

'Can we have a little walk?' he said to them. 'Something I need to discuss with you.'

They exchanged glances, before Paul said, 'Sure, mate.'

Watching them move away, Wishart said to Carey Bloomfield, 'What was that all about?'

'Woonnalla.'

'I reckon it belongs to him now, him being Jack and Maggie's son.'

'He wants to give it all to the Lyserts.'

Wishart stared at her. 'He *does*?'

She nodded. 'Yep.'

'They won't accept.'

'I told him.'

'He must understand. Their respect for Jack and Maggie would never allow them to take this from their real son.'

'I told him that too. He said they worked the place since they were teenagers. It rightfully belongs to them.'

'He'll never get them to agree. Look at them.'

She turned to look. The Lyserts were shaking their heads vehemently, while Müller was trying to convince them; and failing.

'He won't move them from that position,' Wishart insisted. 'It's a matter of pride, and respect. He'll have to think of something else.'

'He has a Plan B.'

'He'll need it.'

'This looks like it's going to be a long session,' Carey Bloomfield said. 'Why don't we go on to the terrace? I'll burn some coffee.'

Wishart gave a slow smile. 'I like burned coffee.'

'He thinks I'm joking.'

Later as they sat down to coffee on the terrace, Wishart tasted his. 'This is good brew.'

'Don't tell Müller. He cooks so damned good, I could strangle him.'

Wishart grinned. 'I never interfere in a domestic quarrel, if I can help it. Old police motto.'

'The world over . . . with good reason.'

'So how's he taking it?' Wishart asked.

Both knew what he meant.

'He keeps calling them the Hargreaves,' Carey Bloomfield answered. 'It's his way of handling this whole thing. I sometimes get the feeling if he allowed himself to call them mom and dad, it would finish him. I don't know that. I'm just guessing.'

Wishart sighed. 'Yeah. I can't even begin to understand what he's feeling right now.'

'No sign of the bodies at all, Graeme?'

He shook his head slowly. 'Not a thing. I thought we might see some shreds of clothing. Oh I'm sure some of that will wash up, somewhere. But the only thing I can guess happened to the bodies is that out there in deep water, in the dark, sharks – perhaps great whites – got them. Or even salties. We can only wait. All round these coasts, people can disappear out there without trace –

currents, sharks, crocs, incapacitation by sea-snake bites, or stingers – anything could have happened to Jack and Maggie. They wouldn't have hit the water still alive, or even in one piece. Any sharks around would have a feed . . .'

'Ugh!'

'Sounds horrible, but we have to consider that.'

'I know. But the picture is still grim.'

'Yeah.'

Outside, Müller was still trying to persuade the Lysert brothers, and was meeting with stiff resistance.

'Pete . . . Paul . . . I'm a Berlin policeman. What do I know about running a place like this?'

'You could learn,' Pete suggested.

'Yeah,' Paul said. 'We could teach you.'

'I appreciate the offer, but you know I can't. I have a job to do that will take me some time . . .'

'You mean dealing with the people who sent that fella after Jack and Maggie?' Paul Lysert asked.

'Yes.'

'We can look after the place, just like always,' Pete said, 'just like when Jack and Maggie had to go away.'

Müller looked at each in turn. 'Go away? What do you mean?'

'Sometimes,' Pete began, 'they'd take off for weeks. We always ran things then. They trusted us.'

'Looking at this place,' Müller said, giving no indication of the questions their comments had raised in his mind, 'I can see the trust was justified.'

'We can just carry on,' Paul said, 'as before. You do your coppering in Berlin, we look after Woonnalla.'

'You're really not going to take the place, are you?'

'Nope,' they said together.

'We saw the look on Maggie's face when she saw you,' Pete said. 'We saw the way she cried. You cannot ask us to take Woonnalla from you. Anyway, do you know how much this place is worth?'

'I have a fair idea.' Müller's sigh was one of resignation. 'All right. How about this? Let us say the house, its garden, and the nearest outhouse now belongs to me. Everything else, we share. Equal partners.'

Paul gave him a sideways look. 'What does that mean exactly?'

'Exactly what it says. The three of us are now the new Woonnalla management, and owners.'

'Do you have a lawyer, back there in Berlin?' Paul asked.

'Yes. Old family firm who have always represented my family.'

'Would they let you do this?'

'No one "lets" me. I will inform them of my decision. They will take it from there. You deserve it, for what you have done here.'

'You're not going to back down?'

'As much as you backed down on my original offer.'

Suddenly, the brothers grinned at him.

'You're Jack and Maggie's son all right,' Paul said. 'Just as hard-headed when the mood takes. OK. We will do it like that. We'll run things as before. But there's one thing.'

'Which is?'

'We need a new plane . . . a 337,' Pete said, 'just like the old one. I've been flying it for years, so I'd like the same. Great plane to fly.'

'Can we afford it?'

The brothers laughed.

'I think you'll find you can,' Pete said.

'Do you know where to get one?'

'Sure. And I can get everything done – registration, certification, insurance . . . anything that needs doing.'

'So we're agreed?'

'We are,' the brothers said together.

All three shook hands on the deal.

'Let's talk some more,' Paul added.

Carey Bloomfield and Wishart were starting their second cups of coffee when Müller joined them on the terrace.

'Freshly burned coffee?' she offered.

Müller glanced at Wishart.

'I'm staying out of it,' Wishart said, straight-faced.

'I'll risk it.'

Carey Bloomfield glanced at Wishart. 'See what I mean?'

'I'm staying out of it,' Wishart repeated. 'How did it go?' he went on to Müller.

'Those brothers drive a hard bargain,' Müller said as he sat down.

'Did you get them to agree to something?'

Müller nodded. 'Finally. We shook on what I thought was a deal, then Paul said we should talk a little more. You're looking at one of the new partners in the management and ownership of Woonnalla.'

'Which is?' Carey Bloomfield said as she handed Müller his coffee.

'Thanks,' he said to her, then continued, 'First, I offered the entire place, except this house and the first outhouse. They refused outright, and would not budge. I then suggested a three-way partnership. Again, except for the house and the area around it.'

'Plan B,' Carey Bloomfield said to Wishart.

'To which they agreed,' Müller said. 'Or at least, I *thought* they agreed, having shaken hands on it.'

'So what have you ended with?' Wishart asked.

'They took less than I offered. Amazing people. The fixed deal is now twenty-five per cent each . . .'

'But there's just the three of you,' Carey Bloomfield said.

'In physical presence, yes. In spirit, no. They decided I am the embodiment of Jack and Maggie Hargreaves. I am the representative of their twenty-five per cent each. I therefore control fifty per cent and the brothers fifty per cent. That way, no one has a controlling vote. In their books, fair equity.'

Wishart was smiling. 'The People's way of doing things. The brothers are showing that to them Jack and Maggie will always be here. They have honoured you. Take it seriously.'

'I do. After all, Jack and Maggie were my . . .' Müller paused, then went on, 'I have made them promise that they should *never* make any reference to the fact that I have any connections here . . . either past or present. It's for their own safety. My lawyers will use another firm as executors of the Hargreaves' estate. Everything will be done correctly, but I will not be identified. As I've said, it is for their own safety.'

'So apart from that,' Wishart said, 'it will be business as usual?'

Müller nodded. 'Everything carries on as before. They have it all under control. They've told me about the seasonal harvesters who regularly come to help with getting the produce out. I've left it to them to carry on as before. No point disrupting anything. I've got the house in perpetuity, with a hundred-metre zone beyond the garden. And . . . we've made our first executive decision. We're getting another aircraft, a 337, fitted out similarly. Pete seems to know where to get one.'

'He should,' Wishart said. 'If anyone does. So we'll be seeing you in Oz more often now.'

'For a while . . . not as often, unless the situation demands it. There is still plenty to do.'

'Not leaving the force then.'

'Not yet. No.'

'Well, you know where I am . . . if you need anything.'

Müller caught the extra meaning in Wishart's words. 'Yes. Thank you. And you know how to reach me in Berlin.'

Wishart nodded. 'I do. Anything I have that might interest you, I'll get in touch. When are you thinking of heading back?'

'Within the next forty-eight hours . . . probably sooner. It all depends.'

Wishart rose to his feet. The others followed suit.

'I'd better be heading back myself,' he said. 'Miles to go. Carey, thanks for the coffee.'

'You're welcome.' She gave him a quick embrace. 'Look after yourself, Graeme.'

'See that *you* do,' he said. 'And this fella here,' he added, glancing at Müller.

'Count on it. Twice.'

Wishart held out a hand to Müller. 'Nothing I can say can make it better, so just watch your step as you take on these people.' He gave Müller a brief grip on the shoulder as they shook hands. 'Anything you need. OK?'

Müller nodded. 'I'll remember. Thanks, Graeme.'

'I'll go see Pete and Paul before I leave. I'll make my way out. Have a good flight back, you two.'

137

'We will. Good man,' Müller continued after Wishart had gone.

'Yes. He is. Hope the Semper never get him in their sights.'

'Let us not even think it. Here. I'll help you take these things inside.'

After they had put everything away, they went back down into the Box.

'Müller,' she said as they entered the study, 'are you really going to kit out the new plane exactly like the old one?'

'Not exactly, as I'm certain the Hargreaves had equipment on there that the Lyserts will not have known about. There should be some documentation down here about precisely what was added. In fact, given a piece of news from the Lyserts, there's bound to be.'

'You've got my radar excited,' Carey Bloomfield said. 'What piece of news?'

'When I said to them I'd be spending nearly all of my time on the other side of the world, they more or less said no worries. They can handle things just as they did when Jack and Maggie were away. It seems the Hargreaves went away quite often . . . sometimes for weeks.'

There was a short pause as Carey Bloomfield took this in.

'Are you telling me . . .' she began, choosing her words as if feeding them through a minefield, '. . . they were still hunting out the Semper?'

'It would explain some of the up-to-date information. They could have easily disguised themselves. The best wigs are indistinguishable from the real thing these days.'

'We haven't seen any wigs here.'

'We haven't looked.'

'They were playing a dangerous game,' she said.

'They certainly were . . . but remember, they were supposed to be dead. Anyone likely to recognize them would probably have walked right past without a second look.'

He sat down at the computer and glanced at the surveillance screens.

'Müller . . .'

'I know what you're going to say. As soon as I realized the connotations of what the Lyserts had said, I have considered that sometime during the past twenty or more years,

138

the Hargreaves might well have been on the same street, or even in the same building as I was, at any given time. And no, I don't feel particularly good about it.'

'Look,' she said, trying to do some quick repair work, 'we don't know any of this for certain. They're just wild guesses, based upon what the Lyserts said. The Hargreaves may have taken a few long holidays . . .'

He shot a glance at her. 'What do your instincts tell you?'

'That what we just said is possible,' she admitted with some reluctance. Trying to change the subject, she went on, 'Do you remember that politician who tried to bribe you and Pappi with accelerated promotion?'

'Because he wanted us to stop probing the Semper. We won't forget him in a hurry. He has a few sordid secrets he would not like to see the light of day. Pappi found them.'

'Is he on the Semper list of members?'

'He is. I made a point of looking. And thanks for the diversion.'

'I just thought . . .'

'It's all right. I'm fine.' Müller, sitting, gave a short laugh that contained no real humour. 'I seem to be saying that to you quite often. Look,' he went on. 'Graeme's leaving.'

On one of the screens, the police vehicle could be seen trailing dust as it left the sealed section of the approach road.

'I wonder what his reaction would be,' Carey Bloomfield said, 'if he ever found out this was down here. Or the Lyserts.'

'Their reactions would certainly be interesting . . . but as they never found out in all those years . . .'

'And as they're not likely to . . .'

'Precisely.' He glanced at his watch. 'It's one thirty p.m.; Berlin time is seven thirty in the morning. Pappi will be trying to reach me soon, if he's going to do so at all. I'll put in a new password – all courtesy of the join-the-dots manual . . .' He patted the ring-bound file. '. . . to give the goth access. Then we should go up to the room near the balcony to wait for Pappi's call, in case he can't reach my mobile down here.'

'How long do we wait up there?'

'Not very long, if I know Pappi.'

* * *

'This is madness, *Meisterin* Meyer,' Pappenheim said. 'You're not fit enough.'

Pappenheim was pushing the goth's wheelchair along the corridor that led to the rogues' gallery.

'You let me be the judge of that,' she retorted. 'Now stop making a fuss . . . sir. We've been through all this already.'

Pappenheim had received a call in his office, promptly at 06.00.

'You're still here, sir?' he'd heard the familiar voice say.

'Why are you awake, Miss Meyer? You should be asleep. Getting some rest.'

'I've had enough rest since that cow put that hole in me. I've been awake since five.'

Pappenheim had become anxious. 'Are you all right? Shall I call one of the medical—'

'Don't panic! I'm OK. We've got work to do . . .'

'"*We*"?'

'We. How are you going to manage a secure connection to the boss, without me?'

Pappenheim had thought about that, then had said, 'Go back to sleep. Let me think about it.'

'It's long been daylight over there. I'll call back in an hour.'

'I'm sure you will.' Pappenheim had hung up with a sigh. 'She won't give up.'

He had then lit his second cigarette of the day; but as his night had been broken by just two hours' worth of dozing, it could also have been seen as a continuation of the previous day's smoking.

Exactly one hour later, the goth had called and Pappenheim had given in. He knew she was right.

'You will tell me if things get uncomfortable for you?' he now said to her.

'Yes,' she said in a voice that might have been reserved for a tiresome child. 'I'll tell you if that happens. Now, sir. *Please.* I . . . am . . . O . . . K.'

'And how were you able to dress yourself, anyway? You could have called one of the female colleagues to . . .'

'Female ingenuity. I'm not an invalid.'

'And can you type with one hand . . . ?'

'*Sir!*'

'Oh all right.'

He stopped outside the armoured door, and punched in the entry code. The door sprang slightly open, and lights came on inside a large atmosphere-controlled room where all the sensitive documents and other items of information were kept.

Pappenheim pushed the wheelchair through and entered. The door shut behind them with a soft hiss that was not unlike that of the Pandora's Box on the other side of the globe.

He pushed the chair to the computer console. The goth tended to spend as much time as she could upgrading it with programs she had developed herself, and by tweaking its hardware. It was by far the most powerful and advanced computer in the entire building.

'Do you need the standard chair?' Pappenheim asked, solicitude itself.

'I'm OK like this. Just give me a few minutes to power up, and establish a secure path for the call.'

'All right,' Pappenheim said again, feeling out of his depth as usual.

He marvelled as she appeared able to hit the keys with one hand, almost as fast as with two.

'How can you do that?'

'Do what?' she asked without turning round.

'Use the keyboard so quickly with one hand.'

'Practice makes perfect.'

'I knew that.'

'Your channel is open,' the goth said, temporarily taking her hand off the keyboard to point at the phone next to the computer. Each fingernail was painted a different colour. Her eye-shadow was blue. 'Time to call the boss.'

At Woonnalla, Müller and Carey Bloomfield were waiting in the room next to the balcony. He had not opened the French doors, to lower the risk of being overheard from outside.

His mobile rang.

'So you know Pappi,' Carey Bloomfield said.

He favoured her with a tiny, fleeting smile as he accepted the call. 'Yes, Pappi.'

'There you are,' came Pappenheim's voice, full of relief.

'I'm here. As you're calling, I take it the goth has got us a secure transmission.'

'Very secure. According to her, she has some nasty surprises in store for any ambitious eavesdroppers.'

'I'm sure she has. Good thing she's there. I have some very good news to transfer.'

'Good news is always good to have. Any bad news?'

'Very.' Müller did not expand.

'I . . . see. I take it this will be for later.'

'Correct.'

'Understood. And the good news is?'

'The best you could wish for . . . and more.'

'I like the sound of that,' Pappenheim said.

'Ask the goth, if I give her a password, whether she can take control. I have access. She'll know what I mean.'

'Let me ask . . .' Pappenheim came back almost immediately. 'I quote "can a baby suck sweets". Don't ask.'

'I won't, I'll take that as a yes. Password coming up. Then give me half an hour.'

'Done.'

In Berlin, the goth said, 'He has access to a computer out there, that he can turn over to me? Where is this thing?'

'He didn't say. But he must have some very special information to send. He would not even tell me on the phone. Can you do this . . . "takeover" securely?'

'I won't even bother to answer that.'

Pappenheim cleared his throat. 'Sorry.'

'Not your fault you don't understand computers . . . sir.'

'That's right, *Meisterin* Meyer. Rub my face in it.'

'Well,' she said, which could have meant anything. 'Password in . . .' she went on, '. . . and accepted. We're in.' The single hand seemed to skim across the keyboard. 'Now if he will just . . . point me . . . to the drive . . . ah! Got it. Downloading. This won't take long.'

It did not.

'Saved to the server,' she said. 'Do you want to see?'

'Of course. Call it up.'

She opened one of the multitude of folders.

Pappenheim gaped. 'My God! Where did he get all *this*?'

The goth was herself dumbstruck.

'Try another folder,' Pappenheim urged.

The new one continued the effect of the first. After four more folders, Pappenheim called a halt.

'My God,' he repeated in a gleeful whisper. '*He's got it all!* We have them now! But how did he manage . . . ?' Pappenheim paused. 'Can you set up a chat with him?'

'Can a baby suck sweets?'

'Thank you, Hedi. A yes would work just as well.'

'Yes.' She was setting up the connection even as she spoke.

Woonnalla, Pandora's Box.

'Hey,' Carey Bloomfield said. 'Someone wants to talk.'

SO HOW IS IT OUT THERE IN AUSSIE LAND?

HOT, Müller typed.

HOT IS RIGHT! THE CHIEF WANTS TO KNOW WHERE YOU GOT THIS HOT STUFF FROM.

LATER.

UNDERSTOOD.

WHEN BACK?

SOON.

GOOD. MISSING YOU.

'That,' Carey Bloomfield remarked, 'was not Pappi.'

'He's missing me.'

'I'm sure he is.'

'Stop fighting,' Müller said. 'She's over there . . .'

'And I'm way over here with you, and she hates it.'

'You're imagining things.'

'I'm a woman. I know my fellow woman. Trust me.'

Shaking his head slowly, Müller typed, WHAT NEWS YOUR END?

I'VE BEEN SHOT.

WHAT!!!

Müller was shocked.

Carey Bloomfield stared at the screen. 'What the . . .'

HOW? Müller typed. WHERE? BY WHOM?

143

OUTSIDE OUR BUILDING. SHARON WILSON. AMBUSH.

'*Jesus!*' Carey Bloomfield exclaimed.

Grim-faced, Müller typed. PHONE. 15 MINUTES. GOING OFF.

OK.

They hurried back to the balcony room, via the tunnel. Pappenheim rang exactly fifteen minutes after Müller had shut down.

'What happened, Pappi?' Müller asked immediately. 'And how is she?'

Müller listened without interrupting and with a still expression, as Pappenheim gave him the grim details of the attack, the second try at the hospital, the apparent involvement of Höhntaler in the charade with the 'stolen' BMW, and of the goth's being moved to one of the witness apartments.

'This was Sharon Wilson's message to you,' Pappenheim went on, 'personally delivered. Oh . . . and the rest of us are on her list too – you, me, colonel Bloomfield . . .'

'I'm flattered,' Müller said in his coldest voice. 'And so, I am certain, is the colonel. We can barely wait.'

'There's a queue. Berger wants her strike too, then me, then the goth, then . . .'

'She's making plenty of friends, our Miss Wilson.'

'So she is. With friends like us, she'll go a long way. Permanently.'

'You'll find her listed, along with the other luminaries.'

'I look forward to that.'

'All right, Pappi. Tell the goth from me that she is to return to bed as soon as you're finished. It's an order.'

'I'll tell her, but she's being stubborn. As long as we need communication . . .'

'No more communication till I'm back. That should stop her.'

'I'll pass it on. To digress – why do I have the feeling there's something else, very important, that you're not telling me?'

'Later,' Müller said. He was thinking both about Waldron and the Hargreaves.

'Like that, is it?'

'Necessity.'

'Understood.'

'You'll also see some interesting details about the banker.'

'He's *on* there?'

'He's there.'

'This gets better.'

'Or worse, depending on your point of view.'

'As I said. Can't wait. Watch yourselves out there, Jens.'

'We will. And you do the same. All of you.'

'Doing that.'

'What was all that about "the Colonel"?' Carey Bloomfield asked when Müller had ended his conversation with Pappenheim.

Müller gave her the full breakdown of what Pappenheim had reported. She was silent for some time after he had finished.

'Poor kid,' she said. 'She was lucky.'

'Very.'

'And she's got guts.'

'We know that. Remember how she disarmed that electronic belt Heurath had put around Kaltendorf's daughter.'

'Ah yes, the winsome Solange du Bois.'

'Is that the unsheathing of claws I hear? She's a child.'

'She was a seventeen-year-old woman,' Carey Bloomfield corrected. 'Now she's an eighteen-year-old woman . . . and counting.'

'Sympathy for the goth, and not Miss du Bois?'

'Don't misunderstand me, Müller,' Carey Bloomfield said. 'If I have Sharon Wilson in my sights and she's about to shoot the goth, Sharon Wilson would be dead meat. I'm certain the goth would do the same for me. In the other combat zone, all bets are off. Understand the nature of the beast, Müller. Which reminds me,' she went on, 'why would the Semper feed us one of their bankers so deliberately? To divert attention from Sharon Wilson? If so . . . why?'

'Pappi suggested he was having an affair with his secretary. Perhaps they frown on that. Bad for security.'

'They could just shoot him. He would disappear one day, and that would be that. Not as if it hasn't happened to others. Bankers can become expendable.'

145

'I think they're playing a more devious game,' Müller said. 'First, they would not imagine in their wildest nightmares that we would have information about their Guatemalan activities. Secondly, if we moved against Höhntaler, they would have a regiment of lawyers ready to tie us up in knots. This would fit with a diversion, in order to let Sharon Wilson run free to hunt. She has not been spotted again since that taxi driver last saw her. She could still be in Berlin . . . or . . .'

'Long gone from there . . .'

'Change of tactic,' Müller suggested. 'Perhaps the attack on the goth was considered enough for now. The shock effect worked . . . but we're now alerted. What would you do next if you wanted to keep up the pressure, but also wanted to strike without warning to have the same effect?'

'Find a weak spot.'

Müller nodded. 'Exactly. An unprotected flank. All of us can shoot back. Who can't?'

She stared at him. 'Aunt Isolde?'

'I've thought about that. But she's got two colleagues from the Ready Group on a kind of working holiday, staying down there. They can certainly shoot back, and Greville is very deadly with a weapon. I've seen him at work. Impressive, despite his age. He's quick.'

'No,' she said after a while. 'You got to be kidding me.'

'I think,' Müller said, 'we've arrived at the same destination. Back down we go. For once, I'm hoping the goth is as stubborn as I know her to be when it comes to that computer, and she's still there.'

Seven

The goth was arguing the matter with Pappenheim.

'Look, sir,' she was saying with heavy patience. 'You know it makes sense for me to copy all that information to CD, for security. We cannot afford to lose any of this because of any possible accident. Dealing with electronics is my field. I believe the old rule that if anything can go wrong, it will. With computers, it's not just a rule . . . it's a way of life. It's crazy not to back this up now. Whoever set up this info base, did it well. It is neatly segmented for burning to CD in numbered batches. I've already created a program, which has been installed on here for some time now, that will do this safely, and *fast*. It won't take very long to do all the stuff that I downloaded from the computer the *Hauptkommissar* was using.'

Her changeling eyes were pitted against his baby blues.

'You're not going to give in, are you?'

'I'm staying here till I faint. Then where would you be?'

Pappenheim looked at her, aghast. 'You'd really *do* that?'

'Try me and find out.'

'You're disobeying . . .'

'Sorry to interrupt, *sir*. But I'm not. I am suggesting . . . *recommending* . . . saving this very sensitive information that the *Hauptkommissar* got hold of under God knows what circumstances. We can't risk losing it. You can put the CDs in there with the other stuff.' Her eyes did not waver.

'In there' was one of the floor-to-ceiling banks of solid steel cabinets that lined most of the room, each cabinet having its own keypad.

'Whatever gave me the impression you were frail?' Pappenheim at last said in wonder.

'Not me.'

He sighed, knowing what she said made sense. 'If you fainted, he'd probably take away my cigarettes. All right. Burn away. I'll put the copies in the cabinet.'

It was while she was burning the information that something blinked onscreen.

'Sir!' she called. 'The boss is back on! I left a warner that would pick up the signature of the computer he's using.'

'See what he wants . . . if it's us he wants to talk to.'

She typed, LOOKING FOR US?

YES. PAPPI . . . SHARON WILSON MAY BE FLANKING. CHECK ON DU BOIS.

'Sir?' the goth said. 'What does he mean?'

'Something I should have considered. Answer "will do immediately".'

She did so.

GOOD. GLAD YOU WERE STILL THERE, came the response. OUT.

The goth turned to face Pappenheim. 'Sometimes, it's worth being stubborn.'

'All right, Miss Meyer. Point taken. Don't rub it in. I have a call to make. I'll do that in my office. But first, pause in your burning. I need an email address. Alphonse La Croix, retired high-ranking *gendarme* . . .'

'As in France?'

'As in France. Can you find it?'

'I'll have to hack. But I have a program that should make things easier.'

'Imagine.'

The goth turned her program loose. Soon, what appeared to be hundreds of people with the name La Croix began to scroll at high speed. Then the scrolling stopped. Five names were highlighted. One email address used LaCG@ . . .

'This is the one,' the goth said.

'Are you sure?'

She shot Pappenheim a glance that was full of pity. 'What do you think? "LaC" must stand for La Croix. The "G" for *Gendarmerie*. Easy. Even though he's retired, he can't let go.' She shot him another glance. 'Someone I know will be just like that when it's time to retire.'

'Look who's talking. So you got into his email *account*, to find his profile?'

'Do I have to answer that?'

'No,' Pappenheim said. 'You can cage your program again. Keep burning those CDs. Will you be all right for a short while? I'll be back with a message to send.'

'I'll be fine while you have your cigarette.'

'And my phone call. Don't forget that. I won't be long.'

'Those things will kill you . . . sir.'

'So *everybody* keeps telling me. What can I say?'

Pappenheim made good his escape.

Once in his office, he lit up, picked up one of his phones, and dialled a Grenoble number. La Croix was there.

'Alphonse! *Bonjour, mon vieux . . .*'

'*Qui est . . .*' La Croix began, then switched to English. '*Pappi!* Nice to hear, you old chimney! Still smoking?'

'Says the man who makes me look like a novice. What about you?'

'Ah. My doctor, a young man – a child by comparison – tells me my lungs look like chimneys with no sweeper to clean them out. But if I stop now, the process of reversal will begin. Of course, he also says I need twice as many years as I have smoked . . .'

'And have you stopped?'

'As I do not expect to live for another hundred years, I decided his advice was useless.'

They both laughed at this.

'So, Pappi,' La Croix said when their laughter had subsided, 'how can I help?'

'I have a message for you.'

Pappenheim imagined La Croix's ears priming themselves. 'Business for a reluctantly retired person?'

'Something to break the boredom of days.'

'Like the last time?'

'Similar. If I say LaCG, would that be correct?'

'It is very correct,' La Croix replied in astonishment. 'How did you . . .'

'Do you really want to know?'

'On second thoughts . . . perhaps not.'

'The message will be on its way in a few minutes.'

149

'I will wait for it.'

'Thank you, Alphonse.'

'Thank *you*, Pappi. I always like something to break the days.'

Pappenheim hung up with a thoughtful frown. 'Retirement can be difficult,' he said to the phone quietly.

By the time he returned, the goth had copied all the information to a stack of CDs – each neatly numbered like the originals at Woonnalla – which she had then put into storage boxes.

'All done?' he asked.

'Naturally. I am fast. Is there anything you'd like to see before we shut down? I can do that from the server. No need to use the CDs. When you want to get at any part of this information, you'll need the password. Please *don't* forget it, sir. And you shouldn't write it down anywhere. It can't be broken, because there is only one chance allowed. I wrote it like that deliberately, just in case someone we don't want to manages to get in here for a try at it. If I'm not here and you make a mistake, it will be locked down. I have a key, but it's very complicated. If I give it to you, you might do some damage.'

'Thank *you*, *Meisterin* Meyer.'

'Just don't forget the password, and you'll be fine,' she responded without a shred of sympathy.

'Thank you for putting me in my place.'

'Just guiding you through, sir,' she said with a sweet little smile.

'I don't know which should worry me most – your smile, or when you're trying to nail me to a wall with that stare of yours.'

'A smile can be the sweetest honey, or the worst of poisons.'

'Where does that little quote come from?'

'A boyfriend said that to me when I dumped him.'

'Why did you dump him?'

'He was seeing another woman when he was with me. He regretted it.'

'Serve him right. Obviously suicidal. No mercy, eh?'

'Not for that. No. What would you like to see?'

'First, the message.'

Her hand flew across the keyboard. 'Ready.'

'"Dear Chimney" . . .' Pappenheim began.

'*Chimney?*'

'Are you going to interrupt me at each word?'

'A person can wonder . . .'

'A person should take the message.'

'Carry on . . . sir.'

'"To break the days. Find a secure way to reach another retired colleague, du Bois, in Cap Ferrat. His granddaughter, Solange, is at risk from a professional assassin, female. For security reasons and your own safety, I'll not give you the name we know her by . . ." Don't want him to go asking anyone about Sharon Wilson and maybe warning the wrong people . . . ". . . but she has many aliases, and is extremely dangerous. She is very good at changes to her appearance, but here is a general description".' Pappenheim gave it. When the goth had finished setting that down, he continued, '"This may not be of much help, but should at least give du Bois some advance warning. Perhaps serving colleagues can help him. The important thing is for Solange du Bois to be extremely wary of being approached by any woman she does not know . . . even someone who appears to be a tourist seeking help.

'"What does a young doctor know? Pappi."

'All right, Hedi,' Pappenheim said. 'Send that. As secure as you can.'

She hit the enter key. 'Sent. No one will have time to get at it.'

'Good,' Pappenheim said. 'And thank you. Now if you wouldn't mind, call up Höhntaler, Sharon Wilson, and the *DKvG.* Let's see how they fit together.'

When the information that Müller and Carey Bloomfield had already seen at Woonnalla came up, Pappenheim uttered softly, 'My God in Heaven. Look at her kills! Look at those notes: one shot, one shot, one shot . . . You were *very* lucky, Hedi.'

She swallowed. 'So I see.'

'All right,' he said some minutes later. 'Close everything down. If I need to see this again, I promise not to forget the password. Now to get you back. I don't want to lose my cigarettes.'

She smiled again as she shut down. 'He wouldn't do that.'

'If I let you faint in here? Who knows?'

In Grenoble, Alphonse La Croix read his mail from Pappenheim twice. Then he did so a third time.

'A secure way,' he murmured. 'What is the most secure way? Take it myself,' he said in answer to his own question. 'And what better way to break the boredom of days?'

La Croix was a widower with a married daughter, and lived alone in a big, comfortable house on the outskirts of Grenoble. His daughter lived within the city itself. He thought of telling her where he planned to go, then remembered the need for security.

'I spent most of my professional life avoiding prying journalists,' he muttered to himself, 'and what do I get? A daughter who becomes a journalist!'

Telling her would only excite her innate curiosity.

'Worse,' he continued, 'she marries a boy doctor who presumes to lecture me on my smoking!'

Going south for a few days was definitely the best option, he decided. She always checked up on him. He'd leave her a note, but would not say where he had gone.

'She treats me like a fragile child,' he grumbled as he began to get ready for the journey. '*Me! A gendarme!* I've been in places that would make her hair stand on end in fright. Now where are my car keys? Ah. There.'

He picked up the keys, then went to the computer and deleted the mail from Pappenheim.

'Never know with her. She wouldn't think twice about trying to break my password to read my mails.'

Despite his grumbles, father and daughter had a warm relationship. Each worried about the other more than was necessary. She about his solitude in retirement; he about the kind of people she might have to meet while doing her job.

Having made himself ready, he wrote her a hasty note, then went into the garage.

He wanted to leave quickly, in case she decided to pay him one of her surprise visits.

'She should have a baby,' he said. 'That would keep her occupied.'

In the Pandora's Box at Woonnalla, Carey Bloomfield was idly looking through a far corner of the study. In a slot about a foot wide between the shelves, she saw six large, flat shapes in plain brown wrapping. They appeared to be larger than the slot should allow. She peered closer, and realized that there was an extra deepness to the slot at that point.

'Hey, Müller!' she called. 'Have you been down this end?'

'Not yet. Why?'

'You should see this.'

When he arrived he reached for one for the packages, and moved it slightly away from the others.

'They look like paintings,' he remarked with some uncertainty.

'Whatever they are, they're yours now.'

'You want me to unwrap it.'

'Of course I want you to unwrap it. What do you think?'

Müller pulled it out and after feeling for the back, lay it flat on the floor. 'Definitely a painting,' he said. Very carefully, he began to remove the wrapper. 'If it is, I want to be able to wrap it up again,' he explained.

The wrapping came open like a flower. It was a painting, but what a painting.

'Ooh wow!' Carey Bloomfield said.

Müller stared at it, his astonishment undisguised. 'The Monet!'

'*The* Monet? You *know* this painting?'

'Yes. It was one of their favourites. For years, I thought Aunt Isolde had it safely in a bank somewhere. I just never asked.'

'Come on, Müller. You're not suggesting she knew?'

He kept staring at the painting. 'What? No. I think they just took it with them when they planned to . . .' He paused. 'It was their favourite.'

'I know. You just said. Do you want to check the other five?'

'Might as well,' he said, after some hesitation.

Four of the five paintings were a second Monet, a Matisse, a Mondrian, and a Pissarro.

'I can see what influenced your taste in paintings,' Carey Bloomfield observed. 'What's hanging in your office right now?'

'The Mondrian.'

'That figures.'

The fifth painting was signed by a Norwegian artist Müller had never heard of. It was an unusual painting: a vast snowscape with a single, darkly gleaming rock, upon which was a solitary, huge snow eagle. Its head was cocked to one side, its proffered right eye a startling, golden orb. Its fierce-looking beak was slightly open. It was the epitome of the merciless predator. A small caption at the bottom left-hand corner, in script, defined it as *Snow Eagle on Rock*.

'Jeez,' Carey Bloomfield said. 'That's a mean-looking bird. It looks like a bald eagle . . .'

'Your country's emblem . . .'

'But there's something different. Same dark body, with white head and tail . . . but still different.'

'It is bigger than your eagle . . .' Müller said, '. . . which may be a deliberate choice. And look at this – the nictitating membrane is closed, giving the impression of a golden eye; but in real life, an eagle can still see through that. So this effect is also deliberate in the picture, as in the meaning. The bird is imposing . . . and menacing.'

'It sees all.'

'Exactly.'

'Strange thing to have with this set of paintings,' she said. 'Do you know these others?'

'Not in the family. No. They must have bought them later.'

'Investments?'

'Possibly.' Müller was studying the eagle closely.

'How much do you think they're worth?'

'Together . . . perhaps millions.'

'Money goes to money,' she remarked.

Müller said nothing, continuing to stare at the eagle.

She lowered herself next to him. 'What are you doing with that bird, Müller?'

'The eye.'

'What?'

'Take a look at the eye. Tell me what you see. Look closely. It has been very subtly done. Easy to miss.'

She peered at the painting. 'I see an eye. That's it. Wait a minute. Wait . . . a . . . minute. I see a design of some kind, *in* the eye. What is it? Do you know?'

'The Semper seal.'

She pointed at the eagle. '*The* Semper seal?'

'The Semper seal,' he repeated. 'You've seen it before. Grogan put it on an envelope sealed with wax. In it was a note he gave you to pass on to me.'

She sat back on her heels. 'I remember. When those Romeos were being killed by snipers.'

He nodded.

'So what is the significance of this painting?' she asked.

'Hargreaves rose very high in the Semper, as you know. He became one of the elite. I'm guessing . . . but I believe high-ranking members probably have one of these. Unless you know what you're looking for, it's just an ordinary painting . . . not to everyone's taste but to a Semper member, a recognizable sign of extremely high rank . . .'

'Looking at it gives me the shivers. It really is a mean-looking sonofabitch. It looks like it's the master of all it surveys.'

'I would say this describes the Semper intent precisely.'

'They left it here so you would know . . .'

'So that I would spot the people at the top, if I saw one of these anywhere. They could be in offices, homes . . . anywhere. Semper rankings are not given in the lists on the CDs, or the XD. Perhaps there's something in the files we have not yet seen.'

'Have you ever seen a painting like this since you started chasing these guys?'

'Never. This is the first . . .'

'What if it's the only one?'

'Then someone, somewhere, is missing it.'

'Unless it belonged to your . . . to Jack Hargreaves himself.'

'That would have made him *the* top man. Makes no sense, given what has just happened. Either there are a few of these around, identifying the people at the very top of the tree . . . or this is the only one, and it was somehow "acquired" from the rightful owner. It is a potent symbol of the Semper. Whoever this really belongs to – assuming it *is* the only one in existence – will be less than pleased.'

'"Less than pleased". Nice line in Brit understatement, Müller. I'd think such an owner would be spitting blood with rage, and just about everything else.'

'That's what I said . . . more or less.' Müller began to carefully rewrap each painting. 'Might as well leave them here. Safest place for now.'

The N202, France.

Like most locals, La Croix used the back roads instead of the toll-plagued autoroutes; which was the reason he was on the N202 heading for Nice on his way to Cap Ferrat, just ten kilometres further along the coast.

Which was also why he came upon the two motorcycle policemen who were off their bikes and waving traffic on, in both directions.

La Croix stopped just at the edge of the big lay-by. A huge lorry was parked in exactly the same spot where, unknown to La Croix, the Mercedes had stopped. Its large wheels had effectively obliterated any trace of imprints that might have been left, even after Sharon Wilson's thorough efforts.

La Croix also saw the police car parked a short distance from the truck, and next to that, an ambulance.

Then one of the motorcycle policemen was approaching with the kind of stride that said he was not in a patient mood.

He motioned for La Croix to lower his window.

La Croix did, and Earl Bostic's blasting sax in *Flamingo* slammed out. The biker cop reeled back. Even the non-uniformed police by their car paused to look.

'Earl Bostic!' the motorcycle policeman said in astonishment. Then he recovered himself. 'Turn it down, sir.'

'Certainly. You know your jazz, eh? You're a bit young to know Earl Bostic.'

'My father is a fan. I picked it up from him . . .' Again, the policeman checked himself. 'You can't stop here. You must move on!'

'Let me introduce myself. I am La Croix, *Gendarmerie.*'

The policeman's eyes widened. 'Er . . . yes, sir. One moment.'

He glanced at the Peugeot's licence plate with its suffix number of thirty-eight, and to the curious gaze of his colleagues, hurried over to the police car where a man, obviously in charge, was looking at him with sharp interest.

'What the hell was that?' his superior asked.

'Earl Bostic, sir.'

'The jazz saxman?'

'Yes, sir.'

'And who's the old fool with the taste for old jazz?'

'He says his name's La Croix, sir . . . *Gendarmerie . . .*'

Now it was the superior's turn to widen his eyes. '*The* La Croix from Grenoble?'

'He has a Grenoble licence plate.'

'I thought he was retired. Or dead. How did he get here so fast? We've only just arrived ourselves. And why would the *Gendarmerie* be interested in an accident to a drunk stupid enough to take a pee at the edge of this place, in the dark?'

The policeman shrugged.

'I suppose I'd better see what he wants,' his superior remarked, none too pleased. 'Just what I need . . . bloody interfering *gendarmes*. All right, Marais, go back to getting those gawpers moving.' He began walking towards the Peugeot.

'Sir.'

La Croix watched him approach. 'I'll bet he thinks I've come to meddle.' He got out of the car and lit up a Gauloise. He never smoked in his car, whose leather seats were pristine.

La Croix was not a big man; but despite his age, he looked tough, and battle-hardened. He still had a full head of longish, dark hair, with more of the grey than the dark. He also sported a luxurious moustache. It gave him an almost comical look; until one saw the milky grey eyes. They were very good at making anyone who thought of making fun of his moustache think twice.

'La Croix,' he said, introducing himself as the other drew up. He extended a hand.

'Vieuxjean,' the policeman said. 'I thought you were retired,' he added, as they shook hands. Vieuxjean did not smoke.

'Or dead,' La Croix added. 'I can see it in your eyes. I am surprised you have heard of me. And don't worry, I am not here to interfere.'

'Many have heard of you in our circles. So what interests the *Gendarmerie* about this? And are you really retired? Or have they called you back?'

'I'll answer all three questions. The *Gendarmerie* are not interested. I am retired, and I have not been called back.'

Vieuxjean looked puzzled, and seemed as if he did not quite believe La Croix. 'I don't understand. We only just got the call. And here you are . . .'

'Coincidence. I'm on my way to the coast on another matter entirely.' La Croix took out his ID. 'See? I am really retired. I'm a pensioner.'

Vieuxjean still did not look as if he believed that completely.

'So what happened here?' La Croix asked.

'Why don't you walk with me? I'll give you the details.'

'Thank you.'

'A call came in this morning,' Vieuxjean began. 'Castellane. Seems a young woman's boyfriend had gone missing. He was due to meet her. They, like you, were going to the coast. She checked that he had actually left, before reporting it. He had. Then the driver of that truck . . .' Vieuxjean jerked a thumb, '. . . stopped to have a pee. He looked down, and saw the body, and reported it. Marais and his colleague over there were first on the scene. They were on patrol and were diverted. It looks like the boyfriend, one Maurice Baudouin, stopped for a pee, and tumbled off. His . . . er . . . zip is still open. Neck broken by the fall. We've only just arrived ourselves . . . which is why I'm surprised to see you here so soon. Coincidence?'

'Believe it or not . . . yes.'

'Vieuxjean!' a female voice called up from beyond the edge.

'That's the doctor,' he told La Croix. 'Yes?' he replied to the doctor.

'I think we have something else here,' she said loudly. 'Not a pee. He *was* relieving himself, but in a different way, if you understand me.'

There were suppressed titters from the policemen.

'Perhaps he was thinking of his girlfriend,' someone else said, equally loudly, 'and couldn't wait. Nice way to go.'

The titters were louder.

'Enough!' Vieuxjean ordered, glancing at La Croix, who wore a steadfastly neutral expression.

'I won't know more until a proper examination,' the doctor called.

'That should give her some fun,' someone whispered. One of the motorcycle policemen.

Vieuxjean glared at the culprit.

'I heard that!' bawled the doctor. She sounded as if she were on her way up. Presently, she came into view. She stared at La Croix. 'My God! *La Croix!* I thought you were dead! So the smoking didn't get you, either.'

Vieuxjean gaped from one to the other. 'You *know* each other?'

'About twenty-five years ago,' La Croix said.

'More like thirty,' the doctor corrected.

'Hello, Josephine.'

'Good thing your name's not Napoleon.'

Vieuxjean was looking confused. 'Is this an old war?'

'War was never declared,' she said, staring at La Croix. 'Why are you here, La Croix?'

'Just passing through . . .'

'Like old times.'

'Josephine . . .'

'Why are the *Gendarmerie* interested in this poor boy?'

'They are *not* interested. I really am passing through. Going somewhere else . . .'

'Like old times.'

La Croix took a deep breath. 'All right. Just to prove it. I'll leave. Thank you,' he said to Vieuxjean. He nodded at the doctor. 'Josephine.'

He killed the cigarette by grinding it underfoot. He picked up the dead stub, and turned away from them to walk to one of the rubbish bins that was near where the truck was parked.

He dropped the stub into it, then without looking back, returned to his car.

'Just like old times,' the doctor said for a third time, watching as he got in behind the wheel.

Vieuxjean looked at her. 'What's going on between you two?'

'None of your damned business,' she snapped. 'Now let's get that boy up here.' She turned away from him and went to the ambulance.

Vieuxjean watched as with a slight wave, La Croix drove away, not seeing Baudoin's car, which was hidden by the big lorry.

'I don't believe he's retired at all,' Vieuxjean said to himself.

As he headed towards Nice along the N202, La Croix reflected upon the vagaries of life. If he had not heard from Pappenheim, he would not now be motoring along this route; and he would not have seen the woman with whom he had fallen in love, thirty years ago.

And he would not now be taking a message to a colleague he had not seen since their twenties, when they had served together in the Overseas Department.

The boredom of days had been effectively broken.

The Box, Woonnalla, Western Australia.

Müller and Carey Bloomfield had been continuing their work with the files. They swapped tasks from time to time, each taking turns at the computer, while the other checked the files. They were looking for information that was both within the files and on the computer so that Müller could have those which were urgently relevant, picked up by the goth in Berlin.

It was again Carey Bloomfield's turn at the computer. She had been doing a search, when she discovered an oddly named file: 'Follow the body trail'.

Curious, she opened it.

'Sharon Wilson's weakness,' she began to read. 'Follow the trail of male bodies.'

She read on a little further, before yelling, '*Müller!* You've got to see this!'

Müller stopped reading the file that had been engrossing him, and went over to her.

160

'Read this,' she said.

He read the introduction through in silence, then began to read the first of the itemizations. He stopped, staring at the screen.

'She leaves a trail,' he remarked softly. 'And she does not even know she's doing it . . .'

'Or doesn't care, since no one – she *believes* – knows about it.'

'Except Hargreaves knew, and he set it all down . . . and in detail. All those she killed for private reasons, not necessarily contractual . . . although it seems some *were* part of the job. She was more careful about those.'

'People who would make waves if they were killed off carelessly.'

Müller nodded. 'The ones the Semper needed out of the way. She would make certain those contracts were professionally carried out. Her playthings, on the other hand, are a different matter altogether. How many men, I wonder, thinking they were on to a good thing, never lived to regret it?'

'If this file is anything to go by . . . looks like she's going for some kind of record.'

'Killings? Or the other?'

'Both. But it's probably not the sex that's the real turn on. It's the power trip.'

'Woman's intuition?'

'Think about it, Müller. There are a lot of women who would like to snap a man's neck when they're done with him.'

Müller suppressed a smile. 'As Hargreaves himself says on here, the list is not complete. He began to set it down, but wasn't sure at first . . .'

'Until a pattern began to emerge.'

Müller, still looking at the screen, nodded once more. 'This will lead us straight to her, if she indulges herself this time. Pappi should have this as soon as possible.'

'She must have some spider genes . . . with an appetite to go with them.'

'Males are certainly not safe around her,' Müller said with a straight face.

161

'If they can't control themselves, that's their funeral.' She bared her teeth without looking at him.

'I can see those claws.'

'See what you want, Müller. But those guys were after a fast lay. They got it, and paid in a way they never imagined. They walked into it. They get no sympathy from me.' She paused. 'Sure it's gruesome. Many got their necks broken. No frail angel, she. But no one forced them.'

'There's force, and then there's force. But I get the point.'

'The goth would agree with me.'

'That is a low blow.'

'Sure.' Carey Bloomfield was unapologetic. 'I'm a woman. See? I'm smiling as I say it,' she said through her teeth and a stretched grin.

But Müller was thumbing through the instruction file.

'What are you doing?' she asked.

'Looking through the join-the-dots instructions for the computer. There must be something . . . in here . . . about . . . ah! Found it. This machine,' he continued, 'can be configured, and timed, to switch itself on and off, automatically. Perfect.'

'Meaning?'

'Meaning it can be made to switch itself on and even go online, within any specified set of timings. You can even do this remotely, once you're in. Meaning, it can be accessed from Berlin, by the goth, at those specified times, whether we're at Woonnalla or not . . .'

' "We"?'

Müller looked up from the file. 'One would expect you to be here from time to time.'

'Would one?'

'You know what I mean.'

'Do I? Tell me.'

'Behave,' he said.

'Coward,' she said.

He ignored that, continuing to study the instruction file.

'Something else here,' she said, 'on Sharon Wilson.'

'What is it?'

'A sort of addendum on the weakness. I'll read it out: "A secondary weakness is her aversion to water travel. She is

162

prone to violent bouts of seasickness, irrespective of the size of vessel". Guess if we can't get her the normal way, we can always put her in a life preserver and rock her to death.'

'Well, at least we know she won't plan to attack on the water.'

'Are you smiling as you say that, Müller?'

'No,' he replied, and keeping the relevant section of the file open, went on, 'Let me see if I can make this work.'

'Yes, sir,' she said, leaving the chair so he could sit down at the computer.

'Would you like some coffee?' he asked.

'You'd like me to burn some? Sure you can take it?'

'I'll survive,' he replied, eyes studying the instructions as he tentatively began to reconfigure the machine.

'Careful,' she said as she went out. 'It bites.'

'Mmm hmm,' he said, not really listening.

Half an hour later, he thought he had it.

'Here goes . . . whatever,' he said. A half-empty cup of coffee was on a small mat next to the keyboard. He got to his feet, and picked up the cup. 'It should shut down in a minute, then switch itself on again five minutes later. It's just a test run to see if I've done it properly. Coffee's good, by the way. Not burned at all.'

'I wasn't really trying.'

'I don't think you burn coffee at all. It's a ploy to avoid making it. When you were a freshly minted officer, all the senior men asked you to make coffee. You made it so badly, they got the message and stopped asking. How am I doing?'

'I hate guys like you.'

Müller grinned.

Then right on cue, the computer shut down.

'Let's hope it comes alive again,' Carey Bloomfield said, looking at it with some uncertainty.

'If it does not, we've got problems. I can't call on the goth to fix it.'

'What's this "we"? *I* . . . was burning coffee at the time, officer. Dunno nuthin'.'

'It will work.'

'Is that hope? Or certainty?'

'Certainty.'

When the five minutes were up, the computer switched itself on.

'Certainty,' Müller repeated.

'Aaargghh shaddup,' she said.

'Settings are saved,' he remarked, smiling with some pride in his work. 'I'll take it off auto mode. All I've got to do before we leave is put in the required timings, put it into auto mode, and everything's set.'

'The goth would be proud of you.'

'That was a needle of some kind.'

'You bet.'

'Now that you've had your fun, let's dig some more into Pandora's Box of horrors, shall we?' Müller looked slowly about him. 'One thing still puzzles. We've dug into these files, both on and off the computer, studied recordings . . . yet there is still no mention – or image – of the person who has visited them over the years.'

'The "one other". The updater.'

'And possibly the person who also worked in the field with Hargreaves, during his absences from Woonnalla.'

'There's a lot of stuff to get through. We've been here for less than two full days. We need months. It could be in there . . . somewhere.'

He nodded, still looking about him, as if hoping to see what he was looking for.

'Müller . . . do you think they were both involved in this? I mean both Jack *and* Maggie.'

He took a long time to respond. 'I can't say anything with much certainty about them any more. My certainties have taken a tumble. Perhaps she was also involved, perhaps not. But she will certainly have known the fine details of what he was engaged upon. It is not unlikely that she was also involved. Perhaps she was the one who physically created this database, and not Hargreaves himself. As far as the Box is concerned, they certainly worked at it together.'

'The other side of their Eden.'

'The dark side. Do you remember,' he went on, 'that contact Pappi had in Grenoble?'

'La Croix, I think his name was. *Gendarmerie*, wasn't he?'

'That's the one. Retired.' Müller was still looking around. 'Do you remember what the Lavalieres said about him?'

'That he was helpful to them . . . which probably cost him his job in the end.'

'That is what I remember too. "Early retirement". This means La Croix must have had his own suspicions; which someone, somewhere did not like . . . and pulled some strings. Exit a too curious policeman. We never got the chance to meet with La Croix. This is something we should do as soon as the circumstances allow.'

'What brought this on, Müller?'

'You mentioned the Lavalieres. It set off a train of thought, starting with the crash when I was twelve, and coming – if not quite full circle – to a point that has led us here to the Hargreaves' Pandora's Box . . . after another plane crash . . .'

'And still tied to you.'

'And still tied to me. Am I the lucky one.'

She heard the bitterness in his voice, despite his attempt to disguise it with some levity, and understood that this conflict within him would go on for some time. The bereavement and sense of deprivation that would have hit him as a child when he had believed his parents dead; the sense of continuing loss, that had now been slammed head on by the discovery that they had really been alive all those past years, would have been replaced by a sense of anger and betrayal.

Then having forced himself to confront them with his anger, they had died again, this time for real, and right before his eyes. He would have been filled with remorse for his anger; then guilt for having brought danger to them; then a further sense of loss before he could have made his peace with them. Then more anger – this time against himself; against them for leaving him as a child, despite his growing realization of what they had sacrificed, in order to combat the malignant growth of the Semper.

The anger of the child was in furious conflict with the rationality of the adult.

'The lucky one,' she heard him repeat.

Having a very real idea of the turmoil within him, she wanted to go up to him and hold him tightly; to give him comfort.

But unsure of how he would react, she held back.

'Hey,' she said brightly. 'Let's see what other pleasant stuff we can find in this box of horrors. And while we're busy doing that, why not let the computer do its on-off thing? You never know, Pappi and the goth might be keeping watch and might spot us online. Then you can pass on what we've just discovered about Sharon Wilson.'

'That,' he said, 'is a very good idea.'

'I'm pretty good at good ideas,' she said.

'Don't get big headed.'

That's my Müller, she thought with relief.

The bitterness in his voice was gone. For now.

Müller glanced at his watch. 'Are you hungry? We haven't had lunch. Perhaps an early dinner?'

'Now that you mention it . . . it's horse-eating time.'

'Then how about this . . . you keep up the hunt and watch out for any signs of Berlin trying to reach us, and I'll bundle something together for dinner. Give me a yell if they come on.'

'Deal,' she said.

In Berlin, the goth called Pappenheim.

'I've had enough rest, sir. Perhaps we should stay online, just in case.'

Pappenheim looked up at the three smoke rings, nicely suspended above his head, and restrained the sigh he felt coming.

'*Meisterin* Meyer . . .'

'I'm *not* an invalid . . . sir. I am OK.'

'So you keep saying. You'll keep ringing, won't you?'

'Yes.'

This time, Pappenheim did give in to the sigh. 'All right. I'll come and get you.'

'No need for you to do that, sir. Just send one of the colleagues . . .'

'I need the walk.'

'I can tell you're being dry, sir. But I'll be ready.'

'So kind of you, *Meisterin* Meyer.'

Half an hour later, at the computer in the rogues' gallery, she exclaimed, 'What did I tell you? He's on!'

Pappenheim peered at the screen. 'Are you sure?'

She favoured him with a derisive snort, and began to type.

In the Box at Woonnalla, Carey Bloomfield yelled, '*Müller!*'

'On my way!'

Seconds later, he hurried into the study, wearing an apron. She looked at it critically. 'Nice, dark suit. Slate grey.'

'It matches the kitchen. What's the excitement?'

She pointed at the screen.

ANYBODY HOME?

'Seems you were right,' she said. 'Again.'

'I just know my colleagues well,' he said, as he began to type.

YES, he wrote.

In Berlin, the goth said in some triumph, 'Hah! What did I tell you?'

'You told me so,' Pappenheim said. He watched, as more letters appeared onscreen.

SOME INFO FOR ACCESS. DRIVE D.

ACCESSING, the goth typed, and proceeded to invade the computer at Woonnalla.

She extracted a highlighted file.

GOT IT, she typed.

GOOD. KEEP A RUNNING WATCH. MORE FILES FOR EXTRACTION WILL BE HIGHLIGHTED ON THIS DRIVE.

OK.

SIGNING OFF.

As Müller signed off, Pappenheim said, 'He's getting good at this.'

'Kindergarten stuff. It's the least he should be able to do on a computer. You too.'

'*Me?*' Pappenheim sounded shocked.

'You.'

'My idea of hell is fiddling with a computer.'

'You won't know till you try.'

But Pappenheim was looking at the title of the file the goth had just picked up. '"Follow the body trail". What kind of a title is that?'

'This kind,' the goth said, opening the file. 'Oh!' she continued as she did a quick scan of its contents. 'Sir . . .'

'Yes,' Pappenheim said in an astonished voice. 'I see it.'

They both read it silently, as the goth scrolled through.

'She *breaks* their necks?' Hedi Meyer said in horror when they had read it all.

'Perhaps that's where the real kick comes from.'

'That's sick!'

'Whatever it is,' Pappenheim remarked, 'this is the kind of person who shot you, with a clear intent to kill.'

For a moment, the goth's changeling eyes looked more dangerous than Pappenheim had ever seen them. It made him pause. He had never imagined that such fury lived within her. Then it was gone.

'One day,' the goth said.

'One day what?'

'I'll get her.'

'Remember, there's a queue.'

'I've not forgotten. Shouldn't you get this piece of news to your friend the *gendarme*?' the goth went on. 'He might need it.'

'I should indeed,' Pappenheim agreed. He looked at the expression on her face. 'Don't say it.'

'I wasn't going to say anything about this giving you a chance to smoke.'

Pappenheim shook his head slowly as he went out. 'No respect for rank.'

Eight

Back in his office, Pappenheim immediately lit up, then called La Croix's number.

There was no reply.

He let it ring for some moments and was just about to hang up, when someone picked up at the other end.

'*Hello*,' a female voice began in French. '*Residence La Croix.*'

Pappenheim decided to hang up without saying anything.

'Whoever that was,' he said as he put down the phone, 'it wasn't his wife . . . unless she's come back from the dead.'

He leaned back in his chair and stared at the ceiling, sending a plume of smoke boiling towards it.

'Where are you, Alphonse?'

Alphonse La Croix was in Cap Ferrat.

He stood on the balcony of his room, in the small hotel which appeared to be the only such establishment with the best view in Cap Ferrat. The hotel was high above the little port, with an almost bird's-eye view of its colourful buildings in pastel and bright shades and terracotta roofs, its marina chock-full of expensive yachts and all manner of other craft, and the expanse of the Mediterranean beyond. All this was spread out before him in unashamedly glorious technicolour.

The ground dropped almost perpendicularly beneath his feet.

Over to his left, the high ramparts of the Alpes Maritimes carried the three corniches towards Monaco and Italy. The bay indented deeply towards Beaulieu-sur-Mer, out of sight beyond the corner of his eye. Straight ahead and just beyond the marina, was another hotel; big, low-lying. A palace of luxury, it boasted a history of decades as a watering-place for the legends of the big screen, and other luminaries. A flotilla of gleaming yachts, some looking like corvettes, rode quietly at anchor on what seemed like a surface of glass.

In the middle distance, a pair of jet skis towed high plumes as they threaded their way between the anchored yachts. Closer inshore, a gaggle of small training skiffs with brightly coloured sails slowly traversed the waters beyond the marina like ducklings in trail formation.

From his position, La Croix looked down upon the tops of tall trees, seemingly close enough to touch. Far below the hotel, the landscaped grounds of a neighbouring villa bordered the road that led down to the port. A very short stretch of the road was visible between the greenery. One of the many ubiquitous mopeds screamed its raucous, two-stroke song along it, on its way down.

'What a magnificent view!' he enthused.

The hotel was perfect for his needs. Clean and neat, it served only breakfast, and beverages as and when required. There was no bar or restaurant. He could not have asked for a better place to stay.

Despite the high position of the hotel, it was only a few minutes' walk, steeply down to the marina, where he would be meeting with du Bois. He had called the completely astonished former policeman from his room, and had arranged the meeting.

La Croix now glanced at his watch. Time to leave. A leisurely stroll would get him there in plenty of time.

He left the hotel, walked past a closed, small chapel at the roadside and down the short, curving stretch of the Avenue Albert 1er. The high green railings of an unseen villa with large grounds to his right were patrolled by a huge Alsatian which raced along below, speeding to reach the high and wide closed gate before he did. When he got there, the dog was waiting. It glared at him, and barked in manic rage.

La Croix paused. '*Shut up!*' he yelled at the dog.

Taken aback by his temerity, instead of becoming even more enraged, the dog gave a tiny whimper, and settled on to its stomach. It looked at him, as if waiting for further orders.

'Good boy,' he said, and walked on. 'Damned dogs.'

Just past the gate, he turned right and down a short flight of steps that led to the Avenue Denis Semaria, the narrow, multi-turn main road that went down into the port itself, and which he had to cross. An open bus-stop was on the other side, next to a narrow alleyway.

A grassy central section divided the road at that point and he stood briefly on that, as a small rush hour of three cars following the one-way system turned a corner to his right, to head up out of the port. They were led by another moped. The rider wore no helmet, neither did his female passenger on the pillion. Indifferent to the cars he was slowing down, the rider had turned his head slightly, to chat with her. Remarkably, there was no irate blowing of horns.

'Patient people,' La Croix observed.

The cars behind the moped were a French-registered BMW SUV, a Jaguar XK with Monaco plates, and a gleaming black Mercedes coupé with German plates.

His mind on the coming meeting with du Bois, La Croix paid them scant attention. Luxury cars were common fare in the area.

When they had all passed he crossed over, and headed down the alleyway which was flanked on one side by the high sides of houses, and on the other by the large, berailed grounds of another of the many secluded villas of Cap Ferrat. The light and shadow of the alleyway gave it the air of a medieval passage.

La Croix went through and came out on the continuation of the Avenue Denis Semaria which would eventually take him all the way down to the port.

The Mercedes coupé had not followed the rest of the traffic. Instead, it had turned sharply left to go up the Avenue Albert 1er that La Croix had just walked down. It kept going as the road changed into the Boulevard du General de Gaulle. It continued past another big luxury hotel until the road made a wide curve to the right. The Mercedes then took a left turn which led towards the Cap Ferrat lighthouse, then turned left again up a steep private road, that led to a villa hidden behind high walls and among tall pines.

The car paused before a solid gate which opened silently.

The gate was shutting again as the car drove through and up a short, winding drive that curved its way through landscaped gardens. The ground levelled out before a colonnaded entrance. The car stopped, and a woman in thick-rimmed glasses climbed out. Her hair was tied in a loose, careless bunch. Her clothes were smart, but spinsterish.

Sharon Wilson removed the fake glasses and smiled to herself as she entered the building. As she went into the atrium-like hall, the smile widened to a grin.

She had seen the man standing on the central divider, waiting for the traffic to pass. He had not excited her interest. To her, he had just been another pedestrian on his way to the port.

What had made her smile was the fact that she had seen Solange du Bois.

She climbed the wide, gently curving staircase to the top floor, and made her way to the master bedroom. She put the keys to the car and the glasses she did not need on a polished bedside cabinet, then went into the ensuite bathroom. There, she began to remove the perfectly fitting wig.

Saint-Jean-Cap-Ferrat is a peninsula with peninsulas, with inlets that had their own inlets. At its neck, were the shoulders of Villefranche-sur-Mer to the west, and Beaulieu to the east. It was an unraucous haven of exclusivity, and it suited Sharon Wilson's requirements to perfection.

The sumptuous villa was high up on the western side of the Cap, with a spectacular view of Villefranche and its deep-water inlet which allowed even cruiseship behemoths to enter. The large bedroom window looked out upon the deep bay, which was currently packed with motor cruisers.

A steeply descending series of steps, hidden by high walls, went down in a zigzag pattern to the water, far below. The steps were themselves accessed via a gated entrance. At the bottom was a boathouse, protected by a breakwater. Within the boathouse was a powerful Sunseeker Superhawk 48 speedboat, there for her use whenever she needed it.

There was a strange thing about Sharon Wilson's aversion to boats – any boat, from the smallest skiff to the biggest liner – that was not in the file. She was never seasick . . . if she were herself in control. She could power a speedboat all day, in the choppiest of seas, never once feeling the slightest bit ill. It was a fatally important omission in the file.

There were no staff at the villa. They had been told that the villa resident, victim of a traumatic divorce, wanted strict solitude. After preparing the villa, they had been given time off for the duration of her stay, and paid handsomely for it. Highly discreet and experienced in looking after the very wealthy, they had not given the requirements a second thought, and were more than happy to have the free time and the generous extra money.

Again, this suited Sharon Wilson perfectly.

When she had first arrived, the staff were already gone; which meant no one around to see her, or remember her time of arrival. The weapons she would need were already there, in a hidden safe to which she had been given the combination in her instructions. She had gone to bed immediately after a long bath, and had slept soundly. She had woken during the late morning, prepared herself for her outing, then driven down to the port. After breakfast at a roadside café, she had gone for a walk around the marina, deciding to amble along the curving mole, where several motor yachts were berthed.

She had gone to the very end of the mole, and had sat down on one of the huge rocks that formed the breakwater.

It had been while she'd been sitting there, that she had unexpectedly seen Solange du Bois. She now knew how she would carry out the contract, when the time came. Until then, she would spend the time unobtrusively studying her target.

In Berlin, Pappenheim tried La Croix's number for the third time.

On that occasion, no one answered, but an answering machine came on. Pappenheim paused, as the prerecorded instructions, in La Croix's voice, suggested he leave a message. A woman's voice had answered before. Now an answering machine?

Despite his wariness, he decided to leave a short message. 'Call Chimney,' he said, and hung up immediately.

*　　*　　*

173

In La Croix's Grenoble home, his daughter frowned at the machine.

'"*Chimney*"? Who is "Chimney"? And why is he so anxious to reach you? What are you up to now, Papa?'

She had seen the vague note La Croix had left, but still decided to call his mobile.

In Cap Ferrat, La Croix followed the road as it curved right towards the centre of the little port. He crossed over, and walked on towards a display of sculptures near the Place Clemenceau where, unknown to him, was the café that Sharon Wilson had earlier had breakfast.

The Place opened out into a multi-level raised promenade that went all the way to the edge of the marina, where it was bordered by a railing. Beneath the promenade deck were the many restaurants which lined that side of the marina. A narrow street with speed reducing bumps bordered the water's edge.

Leaning against the railing, and gazing at the many boats, was a man La Croix recognized.

He made his way down some steps towards a currently silent and brightly coloured children's merry-go-round, went past it, and towards the man he had come to see.

'Marcel,' La Croix greeted in a quiet voice.

Du Bois turned his head slowly, then straightened. He was taller than La Croix, had short silvery hair, and was clean-shaven. Deep, dark eyes, almost eagle-like, peered out on the world beneath white, bushy eyebrows. The eyes, almost like La Croix's, looked as if they had seen more in life than they had wanted to. Years of Côte d'Azur sun had topped up those spent in the overseas territories to give du Bois a polished, tanned look that would never fade.

A wiry man, he wore a white, short-sleeved shirt out of his jeans, and sandals mercifully without socks.

Du Bois gave a slow smile of pleasure, and held out a hand. 'Alphonse!'

They shook hands, then went through the cheek routine.

'So you really are still alive,' du Bois said.

'People keep saying this to me,' La Croix protested. 'I'm younger than you are.'

Du Bois' eyebrows did a brief upwards dance. 'A year

'. . . two years . . .' he shrugged. 'What is that . . .' He grinned.

'And what about you, you old dog . . . how are you keeping?'

'How do I look?' du Bois countered.

'Fit. I must say.'

'And I am fit. My life is stable, and my granddaughter plans to be the curator of the Villa Ephrussi one day. This means she will stay here. For that, I am happy. And you?'

'I lost Eloise, years ago . . .'

'Sorry to hear.'

It was La Croix's turn to shrug. 'Life. I have a married daughter who is a journalist, and more inquisitive than anyone has a right to be.'

'I wonder where she got that from,' du Bois said with a straight face. 'And the husband?'

'A young doctor who keeps trying to get me to stop smoking.'

They both leaned on the railing and looked out upon the boats.

'What does *he* know?' du Bois said.

'My thoughts exactly. Do you still?'

Du Bois shook his head. 'Solange made me stop.'

La Croix stared at him. 'I don't believe it.'

'Believe it. I stopped six years ago. Stubborn when she wants to be. Just like her grandmother was. I lost her too, when our daughter was very young.'

'Sorry, Marcel. Always bad when that happens.'

'Yes. It is.'

Both men retreated into their memories of their respective wives, then La Croix said, 'So? Where is she . . . your paragon of a granddaughter?'

Du Bois moved his head in the direction of the jet-skiers. 'Out there, on one of those things. One of our young colleagues is with her. He's crazy about her; she's not interested, but looks on him as a friend.'

'We both know how that feels,' La Croix commented.

'All men, at some time in their lives know it,' du Bois agreed ruefully. 'She's eighteen . . .'

'Dangerous for young men.'

175

'Oh yes.' Du Bois spoke with fondness, and pride. 'Unfortunately, she has an infatuation for someone older.'

'Oh-oh. But this is also normal for young women that age.'

Du Bois nodded. 'Yes. That is true . . . but in her case, it is a little more complicated than I would like it to be.'

'How?'

Du Bois became abruptly reticent. 'We haven't seen each other for more years than Solange has in her short life. What could be so important that you needed to be here yourself? I'm sure you did not come all the way here, just to listen to stories about my granddaughter.'

'That's just it, old friend. I *am* here about your granddaughter.'

A spark of fear came into du Bois' eyes. He darted a glance out to sea, anxious gaze following the jet skis. 'What do you mean?'

'I bring a message . . .'

'Message? What message? And from whom?'

'Some years ago,' La Croix began by way of explanation, 'I went to an international police conference in Berlin . . .'

'*Berlin?*' Du Bois said the word with a real sense of foreboding.

La Croix stared at him. 'Yes. Why . . .'

'Finish what you have to say. Then I'll know.'

'Well . . . I met a German colleague. We hit it off. We had the same attitude to senior officers who were more politically motivated than was good for them, or for us especially.'

Du Bois nodded in sympathy. 'I've met a few of those in my time.'

'The German colleague and I kept in touch,' La Croix went on, 'but not very often. Earlier this year, he got in touch about a very strange incident that had occurred when we were still young men . . . a plane crash in the mountains near Grenoble. The crazy thing was . . . I was involved in the original investigation. Unfortunately, I asked too many awkward questions at the time. I must have made the wrong impression in some quarters. Long memories in those quarters.' La Croix spoke with bitterness. 'Years after that, I was retired early . . . with no logical explanations given.

'Someone, somewhere, managed to stop my career before I was ready to stop. Then I got that call from the German colleague.' La Croix paused. 'Life has so many surprises. It turns out my colleague's superior is none other than the son of those people who were killed in that crash . . .'

'Name of Müller.'

La Croix again stared at du Bois. 'But how can you know this?'

Du Bois made a rueful sound. 'The man with whom my granddaughter is infatuated is a German policeman, *Hauptkommissar* Müller. I have met him. What was that again about life's surprises?'

'But I don't understand . . .'

'Let me fill in the blanks for *you*, old friend. As you know, when we were serving in the overseas department, I married a girl from the islands. We came back here with our daughter. *She* met a young German who was on holiday. She was the same age as Solange is today . . . and as beautiful.' Du Bois loudly cleared the lump that had suddenly come into his throat. 'They fell in love. Of course they did. She was so . . . beautiful. He wanted to marry her. Well . . . that soon died when he told his family. He did not have the guts to stand up to them.' Du Bois' expression grew hard. 'Unfortunately, my daughter was pregnant. Her shame made her go back to the island to kill herself, after the child was born. She walked into the sea, and never came back. We were left with our little Solange.

'Then one day, this man appears at our home. The same man who had abandoned our daughter. He begged forgiveness. He actually cried. I wanted to kill him, but I was . . .' Du Bois raised his hands in a gesture of helplessness. 'God help me, but I forgave him. I let him see Solange. He looked at her, and began to cry again. It was a strange thing to see, La Croix. The tears just fell. I was looking at a man who hated himself even more than I hated him. So I allowed him to visit Solange. As she grew older, she began to love him. Nothing was too much for him to do for her; no expense too great. He gives more money for her than is necessary. In those early days, she would look up at him with pride, and was always so happy to put her hand in his. She still does, and still is.' Du Bois gave a shrug. 'What can I say? He *is* her father. Then I let him take her to Berlin once or twice. By then, he had risen very high in the police . . . yes, he is a policeman,' Du Bois finished with dry humour.

La Croix was looking at him wide-eyed. 'My God.' He looked out to sea, searching out the cavorting jet skis. 'And this man, this senior policeman . . . he knows Müller?'

'He's his boss. They belong to some kind of special unit.'

'My God!' La Croix said again.

'So what is this news that is so important that you have brought me?'

La Croix told him, stressing the need for absolute security.

Du Bois gave a long sigh. 'I have been afraid of this for a long time, after what happened before . . .'

'*Before?* You mean she has already been in danger . . .'

'She was kidnapped, and nearly killed. Müller saved her, and brought her back here. Which explains the infatuation. He's her knight in shining armour.'

'She'll grow out of it,' La Croix said, almost without thinking.

'Most young women, perhaps. Solange is very strong willed. I hope you are right.' Du Bois was again looking out to sea, anxiety etched upon his face. 'She should come in. She's been out there long enough.'

'You must not let her see you are worried.'

'Of course not! But I can worry while I'm here, and she's out there.'

As du Bois continued to stare out to sea, La Croix diverted himself by looking at a snorting speedboat that was manoeuvring towards its berth, right in front of him.

Then his mobile rang.

He got it out, and looked at the display. 'My daughter,' he said to du Bois. 'I knew she'd do that. Yes, Chantal,' he answered.

'Papa! Where are you? What are you doing? Is that a speedboat I can hear?'

'This is France. There are swarms of speedboats . . .'

'*Papa!* I'm not a fool! *Where* are you?'

'And I am not a senile child! I am retired. I can go where I please. I am fine. Nothing for you to worry about.'

She paused. 'You had a phone call. He was determined. He rang *three* times . . .'

'That must have made you curious . . .'

'*Papa!*' she scolded again.

'As you obviously took the call, what did he have to say?'

'He didn't. He wouldn't talk when he heard me answer.'

'Smart man,' La Croix said under his breath.

'What did you say?'

'I'm just muttering. So? What happened?'

'I put on the answering machine . . .'

'And?'

'He left a message. "Call Chimney". What does that mean? Papa! Are you there?'

'I'm here,' La Croix said after a while.

'What does it mean?'

'It's just a joke,' La Croix said. 'Nothing important.'

'But . . .'

'Goodbye, Chantal. It was really not something you needed to call me about. I am going to hang up now. I am fine.'

He ended the call, and switched off the phone.

Du Bois was looking at him. 'Daughter trouble?'

'Not the kind you mean, alas. She's prying again. But I lied about the message she had. It *is* important. It was from the German colleague. I need to get in touch with him urgently. Do you have a computer?'

'We have minitel . . . but you don't mean that, I can see. Solange, of course, has one. It's a youngsters' world. I leave such things to her. We'll wait till she gets back . . . if you can wait.'

'It concerns her. We'll have to.'

'Not for long,' du Bois said with some relief. 'Look.'

The jet skis were approaching the marina, side by side.

'As you're more relaxed now,' La Croix began, 'I've got another example of how life can hit you in the face when you least expect it. On the N202 on the way here, I saw someone I have not seen for nearly thirty years . . . someone I was in love with . . .'

Du Bois turned searching eyes upon him. 'You mean Josephine Vallennes. But what was she doing on the N202?'

'How do *you* know about her?' La Croix asked, astonished.

'She comes out here sometimes. It's not far.'

'That still does not answer my question.'

Du Bois appeared slightly ill at ease. 'She tracked me down.'

'*Tracked* you down? Why?'

'All those years ago, you talked about me to her, and our time overseas. When you disappeared from her life, she wanted to know why. She decided to try and find me, to ask. I couldn't give her the answers she wanted, but we kept in touch.'

'You *knew*? All these years?'

'What would you have had me do? Call you up wherever you were with your new wife to tell you that your ex was asking about you?'

La Croix fell silent. 'I made a mistake,' he said at last.

'Yes. You did. She never married, you know. Josephine.'

'I . . . didn't know,' La Croix admitted in a slow, regretful voice. 'No wonder she hates me.'

'They say love and hate are very close.'

'I've made some mistakes in my life but this . . . was one of the very worst.'

'It was.'

'You don't have to be so quick to agree,' La Croix said.

Du Bois was unrepentant. 'The truth tends to hurt. Come on. Let's go down to the water to meet them.' As they began walking eastwards along the promenade, he went on, 'What was she doing on the N202, anyway? She's a doctor. Forensics.'

'I know.'

'You actually *talked*?'

La Croix explained the circumstances. 'So if I hadn't got that message for you, I would not have been on the N202, and I would never have seen her . . .'

'For another thirty years.'

'If I lived that long.'

They went down some steps to street level, and began walking towards the slipway.

'Strange way for that boy to die,' du Bois said, 'breaking his neck like that.'

'Something about it does not feel right.'

'Your policeman's nose twitching?'

'He was not drunk,' La Croix said. 'Why would he go for a pee so close to the edge . . . ?'

'He didn't only pee . . . according to what you've just said. He got excited. It was dark. A fall like that all the way to the water – especially in his aroused state – could easily break his neck. Perhaps he should have waited till he got to his girlfriend. And here they are . . .'

Solange du Bois was indeed beautiful. Anyone who knew Kaltendorf would not have believed it possible; but the far greater part of her beauty came from her mother's island genes, and from those of her French grandfather. What there was of Kaltendorf seemed to come from the man he once was, and not the one he had subsequently turned out to be.

Solange's gleaming dark hair could easily be seen as an inheritance from her mother; and her pale grey eyes came from the Kaltendorf side of her ancestry. Hers was an outstanding natural beauty that caused many a second, and third, look. Added to this was an almost unnerving calmness, and an unforced aura of self-confidence that went far beyond her eighteen years. She seemed far wiser than she had a right to be.

Both Solange and her companion were in wetsuits. The blue and black neoprene clung to her as if for dear life.

My God, La Croix thought as he watched the dangerous but natural movements of her approach. *Du Bois has every reason to be worried. If she really is after Müller . . . that poor cop is in trouble.*

'Who's your new friend, Grandpapa?' Solange was saying.

'A very old friend,' du Bois corrected. 'Alphonse, my granddaughter Solange, and her friend Antoine Reze. Solange, Antoine . . . my old colleague from the overseas days, Alphonse La Croix, retired *gendarme*. Careful, Antoine. He was *very* high up.'

Solange gave La Croix a warm, but enquiring smile. 'I've heard of you.' She took his hand, and kissed him on the cheeks.

'All good, I hope,' he said.

'That depends,' she said, eyes giving nothing away.

He realized that as she would have met Josephine Vallennes, she would be aware of what had happened.

'Things are usually more complicated than they at first seem,' he said.

'I know.'

Then Antoine Reze was holding out a hand and saying with great respect, 'Monsieur La Croix.'

'Antoine.'

After they had shaken hands, du Bois said to Reze, 'Antoine . . . a little talk . . .'

'Grandpapa!' Solange began, misunderstanding. 'He hasn't done anything wrong . . .'

'I know he hasn't, or I would not let him see you again. Excuse us for a moment,' he said to Solange and La Croix. 'Come, Antoine.'

Staring as they moved away, she said to La Croix, 'What is that about?'

'A little precaution . . .'

'Precaution? What precaution? Antoine hasn't done anything . . .'

'It's nothing to do with something he has done.'

Solange turned her pale grey eyes upon La Croix. 'Why are you really here? It's not just a visit to an old colleague, is it?'

La Croix gave an awkward laugh. 'You are very direct . . . and perceptive.'

'For one so young?'

'I did not say that.'

'It was in your eyes. I saw it.'

'Then I must learn to hide my thoughts better.'

'That won't help,' she said.

'You are too old for your years, child.'

'And I am not a child, Monsieur.'

'No. You are not. My apologies.'

'Now may I know why you are here?'

After a quick glance at where du Bois and Reze had stopped, he gave Solange the gist of his reasons for being in Cap Ferrat. He told her as calmly as he could.

She said nothing for long moments, then asked, 'This warning comes from Jens Müller?'

'Indirectly. Yes.'

'He saved me, once.'

'I know. Your grandfather told me.'

'Will he be coming here?'

'I don't know. But you must be careful.'

'I'll be careful.'

Astonished by her calmness, La Croix said, 'Are you not afraid?'

'Of course . . . but it would be stupid to allow that to paralyse me.'

'You are a remarkable young woman.'

'I'm just ordinary.'

'I very much doubt that.'

'There is something I want you to do for me, Antoine,' du Bois was saying to the young policeman. 'And for Solange . . .'

'Anything! Just name it.'

'Don't promise the world before you know what's coming,' du Bois admonished. 'You're a policeman. Be more cautious.'

'Yes, sir.'

'And don't "sir" me. I'm not your boss.'

'No, s . . . no, Monsieur du Bois.'

'Now, Antoine . . . I am not one of those grandfathers who decides on a boyfriend for his granddaughter. *She* makes that choice . . . well, unless it is so outrageous, I am forced to intervene. But I am not thinking of you as the outrageous choice. I know how you feel about her, and if left to me, I would not be disturbed if she responded in kind. Your family background is not important to me.'

'Thank you, Monsieur. I appreciate the sentiment. I can wait for her,' Reze, whose mother had part Algerian ancestry, added gallantly.

'Then let us hope you will be fortunate.'

'Yes, Monsieur.'

Du Bois took a deep breath. 'Now Antoine, what I have to ask of you could be dangerous.'

Reze's eyes narrowed briefly. 'How dangerous?'

'To be honest, I don't know. I need you to watch over Solange for me, for a few days, until the danger is past.'

Reze's eyes widened. 'She is in danger?'

'She could be.'

'I'll guard her with my life,' Reze vowed.

'Let us hope that won't be necessary. My colleague and I will be watching too. What I shall tell you cannot be told to anyone else . . . unless it is to someone whom you can trust absolutely, to help you. *No* one else. This is very important. If you cannot promise me this, we will stop right here.'

'You have my word. I have a colleague who is also a close friend . . . Etienne Bertrand. He is very discreet. He will not talk if I warn him not to. And he will help, if I ask him.'

'Very well. The four of us should be enough.'

'If this could be dangerous, will we need weapons?'

'I hope not . . . but perhaps to be safe . . .' Then du Bois told Reze about the chameleon who was Sharon Wilson.

What neither could know, was that Reze's vow would turn out to be prophetic.

The du Bois house was no villa but was a big two-storey building, comfortable, with a small garden of orange trees, on a narrow street of mainly low-lying buildings that ran parallel to the Avenue Denis Semaria, where it went past the Place Clemenceau. Distance from the marina was barely a five-minute walk.

La Croix and du Bois were having a coffee in the living room, its French doors opened wide to the orange garden. The warmth of the day and the brilliant blue of the sky gave the place the air of a haven of tranquillity which, under normal circumstances, it was. Reze had gone off to talk to his friend, and Solange was up in her study, setting up the computer for La Croix to use.

'Of course,' du Bois was saying, 'we don't know that this . . . professional killer *is* down here.'

'True,' La Croix agreed. 'The warning is a precaution. But it would not be wise of us to assume she isn't already here, or on her way.'

Du Bois nodded. 'Better safe than sorry. The important thing is to keep her unaware that we know about her . . . if she is down here. Our presence near Solange must seem natural, so as not to alert her.'

'And once we spot her, we warn my German colleague. He can then make discreet arrangements to have her picked up. If we're lucky, that is all we'll have to do.'

'Then I hope we *are* lucky,' du Bois said with feeling.

'Computer's ready!' Solange called from upstairs.

'We're coming up,' du Bois responded.

They finished their coffee, and went up to where Solange, barefoot in jeans and T-shirt, was waiting.

The study was a large room with prints of famous paintings covering one wall. The second sported a single large window which overlooked the port. This was where she had her desk and the computer. The third wall was entirely taken up by a floor-to-ceiling bookshelf, mainly filled with books on art. The wall with the door was reserved for posters of her favourite bands and singers.

Du Bois pointed to the bookshelf. 'She takes her work very seriously. She was given time from her studies to do what she calls a field study at the Villa Ephrussi . . .'

'Grandpapa, I'm here. No need to talk about me in the third person.'

He smiled at her. 'Allow me to play the proud grandfather once in a while.'

'More like every day,' she said to La Croix.

'But you enjoy it.'

'Of course,' she said, giving du Bois a fond glance. 'The computer is all yours.'

'Thank you . . .'

'If you would prefer, I can leave . . .'

'No need for you to go. After all, this does concern you.'

La Croix sat down at the computer and began to hunt out his mailbox. When he had accessed it, he took out his mobile.

In Berlin, Pappenheim was chafing with impatience and anxiety, and smoking faster than normal; which was something.

He was just about to persuade himself that he should try one of his contacts in the Blue Folder lot, when his phone rang.

He grabbed at it like a drowning man.

Before he could speak, he heard La Croix's voice. 'Ready to receive.'

185

'On its way,' Pappenheim said, and hung up immediately after.

He got to his feet, killed the cigarette after a final puff, and hurried out to the rogues' gallery where the goth was already waiting.

In a room in another part of Berlin, a listener with headphones shook his head.

'Their automatic scrambler broke it up. And the call was so short, it might never have happened. They expect to be eavesdropped.'

His companion swore viciously. 'Not a hint of an idea where that call came from?'

The other shook his head once more.

'Shit, shit, *shit!*' his companion snarled. 'They've been having communication like there's no tomorrow, for the last two days. Something's up, and certain people want to know how this is going to affect us.'

'I can't work miracles.'

'*Then damned well try!*'

In Cap Ferrat, La Croix put away his mobile.

'I should be getting a mail soon. I must do it quickly in case Chantal is still in the house, and tries to find my password.'

Solange was standing a discreet distance way. 'She would do that?' She was genuinely surprised.

'Oh yes. After she has persuaded herself she is doing it because she is worried about me.'

Solange was so shocked by this, she said nothing.

'How's your English?' La Croix asked du Bois. 'The mail will be in English.'

'My English is very fine, thank you,' du Bois replied in the language. 'I sometimes pretend not to understand,' he went on, reverting to French, 'when I don't feel sympathy with the tourist who is asking me, or who talks loudly and slowly, as if that will help.'

They both exploded into fits of laughter.

'You too, eh?' La Croix said as their laughter subsided.

'Me too.'

Solange looked from one to the other. 'I think I'll leave you big boys alone.' She began to make her way out of the room.

Du Bois looked at her. 'Solange . . .'

'It's all right, Grandpapa. I'm not going out. I'll be downstairs.'

La Croix glanced at du Bois.

'It's OK,' du Bois assured him. 'She's just more worried than she's letting us know.'

'The kind of person we're dealing with, it's not surprising. Ah. Here's the mail.'

La Croix opened it, and read it in silence. 'Oh God,' he muttered softly, when he'd finished. He leaned back. 'Have a look,' he added to du Bois.

Du Bois read Pappenheim's mail in stunned silence. When he had finished, La Croix deleted it immediately, and closed the mailbox. Then he went offline.

Face grim, he turned to du Bois, and waited.

'We must not put two and two together, and come up with three,' du Bois cautioned. 'But seeing this,' he continued, 'I have to admit that your feeling about something being wrong about that boy's death is beginning to look . . .' He paused. 'She *breaks* their necks! What kind of a woman is this?'

'One who wants to kill your granddaughter, and do it to contract . . . without emotion. She does not feel, that one.'

'But *why*? And why do they want to hurt Solange again?'

'Her father's unit is obviously upsetting some powerful people. Remember how I was magically given early retirement. This is an international network of criminals, Marcel. Yes, criminals . . . but of a very special kind. These are not the type of people we have dealt with in our careers as policemen. These are people who move in the shadows, and they've been at it for decades. Fighting them is not easy.'

'Which is what Solange's father, and Müller, and your German friend are doing.' Not knowing about Kaltendorf, du Bois lumped him with Müller and Pappenheim.

'I am assuming this, yes. As I am sure you already have.'

'The truth is, I know very little about it. The first time this came home to me was when Solange got kidnapped. I tried to convince myself it was an accident. She was in the

187

wrong place, at the wrong time. An innocent bystander. Well, at least this . . . this . . . woman,' du Bois continued, 'hates going on the water. Solange can still use her jet ski. She'll be safe at sea . . .'

'But not alone. Antoine must still accompany her.'

'That goes without saying.'

'I have an idea how to settle the question of Maurice Baudouin. Do you have Josephine's office number?'

'Are you tired of life? She'll bite your head off.'

'Perhaps. But she will have done more tests by now. She won't have DNA results as yet; but she might have found more than she did at the scene. Her curiosity might make her give me some answers.'

'I'll get her card,' du Bois said. 'It's your neck.'

He was soon back with Josephine Vallennes' business card.

La Croix took it. 'Thanks. May I use this phone?'

'Of course.'

La Croix dialled the number.

'Vallennes,' came the familiar voice immediately.

La Croix hesitated.

'Hello!' The voice became irritated. 'Speak, or hang up!'

'Josephine . . .'

There was a pause. 'So it's you.' Now her voice had grown cold, by several degrees. 'What do you want? Absolution? And how did you get my number, after not bothering all these years?'

'Josephine . . . look . . . can we use the daggers at another time? I'll do nothing while you throw them at me. I deserve it.'

'An *apology*? Surely not . . .'

'Josephine . . . I have some information that might be relevant to the Baudouin incident.'

That brought her up short. Her intake of breath was clearly heard.

'I *knew* it!' she said. 'You're not retired at all!'

'Whether I am retired or not does not matter. What matters is what happened to Maurice Baudouin.'

'What is your interest, La Croix?'

'Let me ask a question of my own, Josephine,' he countered. 'Have you found any evidence that Baudouin was with a woman just before he died?'

This time, she could not hide her gasp of surprise. *'How did you know?* There were dried elements of a fluid on his . . .' She paused. 'Yes. He was with a woman . . . but I don't understand how. There was no second car, and there is no evidence – so far – that she was in his. Perhaps he picked her up, had his fun, then on his way to his girlfriend, stopped for a pee. His bad conscience prevented him from looking where he was going, and . . . you know what happened. He was a tourist guide. Perhaps he found someone looking for some easy sex and he obliged.'

La Croix did not correct her reading of the situation. 'Perhaps.'

Josephine Vallennes seemed to pause for thought. 'La Croix . . . how do you know all this? And where are you?'

'Sorry. I really can't say more . . .'

'Like old times.' She slammed the phone down.

'No absolution for me this century,' La Croix said, putting the phone down. He turned to du Bois. 'You heard?'

'I got most of it. So she's here.'

La Croix nodded. 'She must be. She was on the N202. She was heading this way, after amusing herself with Maurice Baudouin.'

'What a young fool, allowing himself to be picked up by a strange woman in the middle of the night, on a deserted stretch of road in the mountains.'

'Some people never turn down what's handed to them on a plate. He thought he could cheat on his girlfriend and get away with it. He never expected to be killed for his pains. But we should be thankful. Baudouin's stupidity has helped us. We have an edge. She will never suspect we know about her.'

The next morning, La Croix felt the warmth of the sun as he lay in his bed at the hotel.

He opened his eyes and through the high glass panels of the French windows that opened on to his balcony, shot a golden shaft of a sunrise that gleamed upon the mirror-like waters of the bay on its way to him. The sky beyond the spine of the still dark silhouettes of the Alpes Maritimes was a blaze of morning fire. The motor yachts that had stayed the night looked like petrified markers on a giant board, as the rays of the ascending sun played light and shadow games with them.

La Croix remained where he was for long moments, looking upon the spectacle in wonder. He had seen more sunrises and sunsets around the globe than he cared to remember; but for some odd reason, he felt this one was special.

The rest of the previous day had passed without incident. None of the four men had seen anyone remotely like the person they had been warned about.

La Croix got out of bed. Solange, this time accompanied by Reze and Bertrand, would be going jet-skiing, following the coast to the beach at Plage de Passable on the Villefranche side of the peninsula, then back. The older men would make the few minutes' drive to the beach, to watch them come in.

But he would first have a leisurely breakfast at the café on Place Clemenceau, La Croix decided. He took his time having a shower and getting dressed, then made his unhurried way down to the port. He got to the café just as they were beginning to serve the first of the morning diners, and took a table on the terrace, under the extended awning. There were still few customers when his order was served. He enjoyed taking his time over his breakfast while watching the place come to life.

He saw no one that made him feel he was looking at the killer.

At the villa, Sharon Wilson was getting impatient.

'When the *fuck* are they going to give me the *fucking* go ahead?' she asked herself in the bathroom mirror.

She prepared herself for the day, and thought it would be a good idea to have breakfast at that café again, then go for another walk along the mole.

La Croix was about to finish his first cup of coffee.

A frumpish woman, carrying a copy of *Nice-Matin*, took a table some distance from him, at the far end of the terrace near the small newsagents, whose revolving newsstands were placed just on the edge of the terrace itself. The bespectacled woman sat down, facing the street.

La Croix took no notice of her.

Sharon Wilson frowned slightly when she noticed the man with the moustache, and wondered where she had seen him before. Then she remembered the fleeting glimpse of the man waiting for the traffic to pass, the day before. She thought no more of it, and concentrated on giving her order to the youngish waiter who had come to her table. She noted how the waiter barely looked at her, and had some quiet fun wondering how he would have reacted to seeing her in a bikini.

Having excellent French, she began to read her paper while she waited for her order.

She looked up from the paper when the order came, just in time to notice a man joining the other with the moustache. Again, a frown appeared briefly as she thanked the waiter who hurried away from her to serve two thin, loudly laughing blondes who had taken a middle table. Each immediately lit up as they sat down. The waiter beamed at them.

Sharon Wilson was deep in thought as she stirred her coffee. She had recognized the man who had joined the one with the moustache, from the target information. She had recognized Marcel du Bois, Solange's grandfather.

She buttered her croissant, then generously covered it with strawberry jam. Her movements were exactly as would have been expected of the character she was playing. During all this, she unobtrusively noted that a coffee had been brought to du Bois; which meant the two men would be at the table for some time yet.

She was on her second croissant, when she observed more movement at the far table. There were more customers now, and most tables were taken. The two men were leaving, but they had been joined by three younger people. Two young men . . . and a smiling Solange du Bois.

Sharon Wilson did not pause in what she was doing, kept on eating, apparently oblivious as all five walked past her along the street. She caught a snatch of their conversation.

'Don't go too fast, Solange,' she heard from du Bois.

191

'I'll be OK,' Solange replied in a "don't worry so much" tone of voice.

'See how long it takes us to make it to Plage de Passable,' one of the young men said, laughing.

The conversation faded as they crossed the street; but she had heard enough.

She remained where she was, and finished her breakfast, by which time she heard the first of the jet skis.

Only then, did she indicate to the waiter that she was ready to pay.

Nine

Sharon Wilson left the villa and walked down to the boat-house.

She was no longer frumpish. She now wore a thin, white dress that was buttoned at the front down to the waist, over a very minute bikini. The dress was itself little more than a long shirt. She wore sunglasses dark enough to appear mirrored, and backless sandals on her otherwise bare feet. She carried a waterproof backpack. In it were two large beach towels, body oil, a paperback, and a small plastic bottle of mineral water wrapped in an ice pack. Her hair was no longer dark.

It was red.

She put the backpack in the Superhawk, released its moorings, then climbed aboard. She started the triple 300 bhp, outdrive turbo diesels, and nosed the boat out. Once clear, she opened up the engines. The boat reared like a prancing horse and hurled itself forwards. It had a top speed of sixty knots and it seemed that Sharon Wilson intended to reach it in the shortest possible time.

But she did not. She held the power back, and the Superhawk skimmed towards Plage de Passable. It did not take long. She cut power abruptly as she approached the small bay on the Cap's western flank. The boat dropped its nose and grunted menacingly as it idled towards where she wanted to drop anchor. She handled the vessel with accomplished finesse. It was an astonishing display of boatcraft for someone who was prone to seasickness.

Plage de Passable had a pebbly beach backed by a high wall that dropped from the narrow, curving road. There were parking areas on either side; but further on past more secluded villas was a wide area with plenty more parking bays. From seawards, there was an open-air restaurant to the right, with its own beach area, and sun loungers beneath yellow parasols. There were showers and toilets in the restaurant area, while in the public section, tall standpipes were used for rinsing off the salt water. Both beaches were clean. A concrete pier seemed like a boundary between the two sections.

Sharon Wilson brought the boat within a few metres of the end of the pier, and dropped anchor. She then put her sunglasses, sandals, and the keys to the boat into a zipped pocket inside the pack. She removed her dress, and put that in too. She then put the backpack on. She lowered herself into the water, and swam powerfully for the shore, heading for the public section of the beach.

At that time of the day, there were not many people. One or two customers in the restaurant glanced from the boat to her and back again, but more in curiosity and a touch of friendly envy.

She found herself a spot to her liking, and smoothed out a small area; then she removed the backpack, and opened it. She placed one towel on the ground, rolled the other into a makeshift headrest, then took out the sunglasses and put them on. She got out the paperback, and lay down on the towel, leaving everything else in the backpack. She began to read.

It was a good half hour before she heard the jet skis approaching. She turned her head casually to look, watching idly as three riders circled the Superhawk clearly in admiration, but did not go close to it. They then headed for the beach in perfect line abreast formation. They beached a short distance from where she was.

She did not turn to look at them. Instead, she lay with her back towards them. She raised her right knee, leg propping the ball of the foot, heel raised slightly. Like an angler fish, she moved the knee barely perceptibly, to and fro, as if she were completely absorbed in what she was reading.

Etienne Bertrand could not help noticing as they peeled off their wetsuits to reveal their bathing gear.

'My God!' he whispered. 'Just look at that! She's a goddess!'

'Thanks, Etienne,' Solange said pointedly.

'You know what I mean, Solange.'

'Oh yes,' she said. She lay down on the sand at the water's edge. 'I do.'

'She'd eat you for breakfast,' Reze said to him. It was a good-natured leg-pull.

'Says who?'

'Me.'

Solange du Bois gave the unknown woman an appraising glance. 'She *is* sexy,' she admitted.

'Why don't I ask her if she'd like to join us?' Bertrand suggested.

'Why should she?' Reze asked. 'She looks like someone who enjoys being in her own space. Anyway, remember our little job.'

'Come on, Rez. This is just a woman sunbathing, like all the others here. She didn't come to us. *We* came here.'

'That's true enough,' Reze agreed.

'Let him go and humiliate himself if he wants,' Solange said. 'It should be fun to watch.' She gave him a smile that challenged.

'Watch me go to work,' he said, and began walking towards where Sharon Wilson lay.

'He's crazy!' Solange whispered to Reze.

'He's always been crazy . . . but a great colleague to have when you need him. He'll be OK. She'll slap him down, and he'll come back a wiser man.'

'I didn't know people still read Proust on the beach,' Bertrand began as an opening gambit. 'Sixties movies stuff.'

Sharon Wilson closed the book slowly, and looked over her shoulder and up at her visitor. Her sunglasses were perched just above her forehead. 'That's an original line,' she said in perfect French, 'if a bit rude.'

'You're French.'

'Paris. You're going to say something smart about that too?'

He grinned at her. 'Not me. I'm Etienne. Would you like to join us?'

She gave him the full benefit of her green eyes, noting how his own kept straying to her body. 'Marie,' she said. 'I'm a little too old . . .'

'Nonsense. Solange is still in her late teens, but we're in our twenties. You're certainly not older.'

'What an interesting man you are . . . rude *and* gallant. Thanks for the offer, but I'm afraid I can't accept. I have to be going soon.'

He looked disappointed.

'I'll be here tomorrow,' she said. 'Same time . . . if the offer is still open.'

Bertrand gave her a wide smile. 'It is!'

'Then I'll be here.' She gave him a sweet smile, and returned to her book.

They watched Bertrand return with the big grin pasted upon his face.

'I can't believe she actually *talked* to you,' Reze said when Bertrand had reached them.

'She's very nice. From Paris. Her name's Marie.'

'You even got her name!' Solange said. 'And could you keep your eyes off her . . . everything?'

Bertrand took no offence as he sat down next to them. 'I asked her to join us, but she can't. Got to be going soon.'

'What a shame,' Solange said. 'You didn't believe her, did you? That's the old "I'm washing my hair" thing.'

Bertrand brought back his silly grin. 'She'll be here tomorrow, same time. I get the prize.'

'Wait till tomorrow,' Solange said. 'See if she does come back. This is probably her last day down here. Her tan is real, so she didn't come down yesterday. She'll be on her way home to Paris, while you're waiting here for her like a lost dog.'

'It's worth coming back just to see,' Reze said, shaking his head pityingly at his friend.

'She'll come,' Bertrand said. 'I feel it.'

'I don't think I want to comment on that,' Reze said.

Over by the car park, La Croix and du Bois had watched the whole thing.

'What do you think?' La Croix asked.

'She's just a woman sunning herself. She did not go to them. Etienne saw something he fancied, and tried it on. She seems to have spoken pleasantly to him.'

La Croix glanced around. 'She could be anywhere . . .'

'Look,' du Bois interrupted. 'She seems to be leaving. If her car's up here . . .'

'She did not come by car.'

They watched in some surprise as the person they did not realize was Sharon Wilson put on a backpack, and went for a swim. They watched as she reached the Superhawk and climbed aboard. They watched as she raised the anchor. They stared as the engines roared and the boat raised its prow to skim off in the direction of Nice.

'Well, that takes care of that,' La Croix said. 'That's not someone who gets seasick. We might as well have suspected any of the other women here. Besides, she would not have known Solange was coming to this place.'

'This is not going to be easy,' du Bois said.

La Croix looked about him. 'No. It isn't.'

On the beach, Bertrand was still staring in the direction the Superhawk had gone. 'Did you *see* how she handled that boat? When she comes back tomorrow, I want to try it.'

'As if she'd let you,' Reze said.

'She might.'

'Probably her husband's boat.'

'Oh sure. He'd just let her take it to go lie around on any beach in a nothing bikini.'

'I think Etienne's falling in love,' Reze said to Solange with a grin.

'And I think we should come with you to see if she really does come tomorrow, Etienne. You'll need us, won't you . . . to help mend that broken heart?' Solange shot Reze an amused glance.

'You'll see,' Bertrand said. 'She'll come.'

'Well, loverboy,' Reze said, getting to his feet and putting on his wetsuit. 'Let's see who gets to the marina first.'

'I will, of course. Just as I am sure she'll be here tomorrow.'

Bertrand won the race back to the Cap Ferrat marina.

At the same moment in time, Müller and Carey Bloomfield were in the air, on their way back to Berlin. They would be landing in the morning, the next day.

*   *   *

197

Sharon Wilson had not gone all the way to Nice. She had waited close to shore, boat engines idling, near Mont Boron, until long after she'd seen the three jet skis round the point on their way back to the marina. She waited some more, then headed back to the boathouse.

She smiled. The fly had come into her parlour.

'Now if they can just give me the *fucking* OK,' she said, 'I can get the *fucking* job done and be out of here, before anyone knows what's *fucking* happened.'

If the men were still with Solange du Bois when the time came, she'd kill all three.

Back at du Bois' house, La Croix was quizzing Bertrand.

'You are certain she is Parisienne?'

'I know the Paris accent,' Bertrand said. 'I've spent time up there, and I have a cousin who's from Paris. You don't speak like that unless you were born there.'

'Educated?'

'She was reading Proust. She's not a dumbo, Monsieur.'

'Some people do that just for show, but don't take offence, Etienne. I am just being careful.'

'She did not approach us,' Reze reminded him. 'We . . . or more exactly, Etienne . . . made the approach. Besides, she was already there before us.'

La Croix nodded. 'We know. Wherever this woman is hiding and waiting, it's not at Plage de Passable. You're hoping to see her tomorrow?'

'*Is* he!' Reze said with meaning. 'He'll be a pain until then.'

'At least we'll know where you all are,' du Bois said. 'Whatever you do, don't leave Solange alone.'

'We won't,' Reze promised.

'And you,' du Bois said to Solange, 'don't go wandering off. Until all this is over, *listen* to them if anything happens. *Don't* stop to ask questions. If they say move, you *move*.'

'Yes, Grandpapa,' she said, expression serious.

'Should we take weapons?' Bertrand asked.

'If you carry guns on your wetsuits,' La Croix said, 'everyone will stare. This will draw more attention to you, including from the woman we're hoping to guard against.

This will warn her. She'll know we know. Your weapons are for when you're in normal dress, and can conceal them.'

Sharon Wilson awoke the next morning, feeling good.

She looked out upon the tranquil waters of Villefranche, and considered that all was right with the world.

'This could turn out to be a good day,' she said.

Naked, but carrying the white, front-buttoned dress she had worn the day before, she went downstairs to prepare a light breakfast. As she crossed the high-ceilinged hall on her way to the kitchen, she spotted something white peeping from beneath the main door: the corner of an envelope.

She remained where she was, staring at it for long moments, then continued on to the kitchen. She looked for, and found, a broom with a long handle. She went back, and reaching with the handle, very slowly manoeuvred the envelope from beneath the door.

'Someone who can get through the gate, eh? If it's a bomb . . .'

But it was no bomb.

She picked up the envelope and, still cautious, opened it. A small note, unfolded, was inside. She took it out.

'"TODAY",' she read. 'About *fucking* time too,' she said with satisfaction. 'I *knew* this was going to be a *fucking* good day.'

She took her time preparing her breakfast then putting on the dress, went out with her laden tray on to the terrace, to the spectacular view of Villefranche.

She enjoyed her leisurely breakfast. Finished, she took the tray back into the kitchen, then returned to her bedroom.

She took out an automatic, one of the guns that had been left in the safe for her to use, checked it, then attached a silencer to it. She knew exactly how she was going to do the job.

It was precisely ten o'clock.

In Berlin, the plane carrying Müller and Carey Bloomfield. landed.

Plage de Passable, 10.50 local.
'Well, Etienne . . .' Reze said, '. . . looks like she's not coming.'

They were sitting astride their partially beached jet skis, pointing seawards.

'She'll be here,' Bertrand insisted. 'I can feel it in my bones.'

Reze gave a short laugh. 'Politeness prevents me from telling you what I think you're feeling . . .'

'*Listen!*' Bertrand commanded.

'To what? Your excited heartbeat?'

'I can hear something,' Solange said.

'See?' Bertrand said to Reze. 'I told you.'

'Could be anything.' Reze was reluctant to admit it.

'Not *that* sound,' Bertrand said in triumph. 'Look! She's here! I told you she would come!'

The Superhawk, nose in the air, came charging from the direction of Mont Boron.

'Look at that!' Bertrand exclaimed. 'Isn't she beautiful?'

'The boat? Or Marie?'

'The boat, idiot. Can't see Marie properly yet.'

'Well,' Solange said. 'She came.'

'Don't sound so disappointed, Solange,' Bertrand said, shrewdly understanding what was behind the remark. 'There's enough room for two women.'

She responded with silence.

Bertrand exchanged secret smiles with Reze.

The Superhawk came charging on, until it seemed about to launch itself up the beach.

They stood their ground.

Then with a flourish, the speedboat swung away, engines throttling back and going into reverse. The nose dropped and the boat came to a virtual halt, almost dead in the water, directly in front of them.

'Now is that good . . . or is that good?' Bertrand enthused. 'And look at that bikini! Ooh God.'

The other two made no comment. There was little need to.

'See?' the woman they knew as Marie called. 'I kept my promise.'

'I'm glad you did,' Bertrand called in return. He grinned at her, and pushed the jet ski off the beach with his feet.

Trailed by the others, he moved slowly towards the boat.

'Morning,' Sharon Wilson said to them, smiling as they approached. The smile on the face of the tiger.

'Morning,' they responded together.

Bertrand glanced at Solange. 'This is, of course, Solange . . .'

Sharon Wilson gave Solange a slight nod. 'Pleased to meet you, Solange.' She turned to Reze.

'Marie,' Solange said, eyes watchful.

'And my very good friend, Antoine.'

'Hello, Antoine . . .'

'Marie,' Reze greeted.

Sharon Wilson glanced up at the cloudless sky. 'Going to be a great day, isn't it?'

'Normal stuff for us,' Bertrand said.

'Meaning not like Paris.'

Bertrand gave a shrug, and smiled his eager smile at her. 'Will you give me a chance to try her? I mean the boat, of course.'

Solange rolled her eyes heavenwards.

Sharon Wilson's green eyes seemed to dance at Bertrand. 'Of course . . . but on one condition.'

'Which is?'

'You've got to trap me. All three of you, try to prevent me from making it out to sea. Every time you block me, I'll have to turn away. Your job is to make me keep turning back towards the shore. My job is to try to sneak past you, to open sea. Are you game?'

They glanced at each other.

'You mean like hunting dogs cornering prey?' Reze asked.

'There's a man who knows about hunting,' Sharon Wilson said with approval. 'So? A little game on the water?'

'Let's do it,' Solange said with unexpected bite.

Sharon Wilson glanced at her with a tiny smile. 'And we have Diana. It can be dangerous,' she said to Bertrand. 'I will come close. Are you brave enough?'

'I can trap you,' he said.

Her smile widened. 'And a man who knows what he wants. I like that. All right then . . . form a patrol circle. I'll try to break it. And don't go smashing into any boats. Antoine, you give the call. Ready?'

'Ready.'

As they moved out to take up positions, Solange hissed at Reze, mimicking Sharon Wilson, 'There's a man who knows about hunting.'

'You're jealous,' he said, teasing her.

'Don't be ridiculous!' she said, and charged off to her position.

Sharon Wilson observed her departure with the tiniest of smiles.

Had either La Croix or du Bois been there to overhear the entire conversation from the arrival of the boat, they would have begun to feel unease. Without the knowledge of the older men, the three remained completely unaware of their impending danger.

They were now holding station some distance from the Superhawk. Reze lifted a hand, waiting until he was certain the others had seen it. Then he brought it down with a chopping motion.

Instantly, the jet skis rose out of the water and began to circle the speedboat. Sharon Wilson watched, biding her time, then, choosing a path, set off at speed for Solange.

The other two saw that, and raced to cut her off, leaving their positions open. She immediately put the boat into a tight turn, almost spinning it about on its stern, and headed for the cleared path.

Bertrand saw the trick and reversed direction.

This brought him fleetingly close to Reze who shouted as Bertrand flashed past, 'She tricked us! Watch out for that next time.'

Bertrand briefly raised a hand in acknowledgement, and set off after Sharon Wilson, who appeared to be getting away.

But Solange had reacted faster than either of the men, and was racing to cut off the Superhawk before it could gain sufficient speed to get away.

Sharon Wilson spotted the move. 'You've got guts, my little hunter,' she said quietly. 'But what you're doing is dangerous. Will you chicken out?'

Solange didn't. She kept racing on.

Reze saw what was happening. '*Solange!*' he yelled. '*Be careful!*'

Whether she heard or not, Solange did not falter. She held her course. Then at the last moment, it seemed, Sharon Wilson turned the boat, and saw that she was running straight into a pincer by Reze and Bertrand.

'Oh very good, my little hunter,' she said in a low, breathy voice. 'You three know your skis.' The game was exciting her, working her up to the moment when she would carry out the kill.

Moves and countermoves were performed, the jet skis looking for all the world like a waterborne pack of dogs, seeking to trap their prey. Everyone was whooping with the adrenalin rush of the chase, Sharon Wilson included.

She toyed with them for a full twenty minutes, while inexorably towing them out to sea. Her eyes were shining with the anticipation of what was to come.

At the airport in Berlin, Müller and Carey Bloomfield were surprised to find a welcoming committee in the shape of Pappenheim.

'Pappi!' she cried, embarrassing him with a quick hug. 'What a nice surprise.'

He made a noise that sounded like *hrmmph* to disguise the fact that he was actually quite pleased. 'Home are the hunters.'

'Well, my home's still an ocean away.'

'I'm sure you know you've got one here as well,' he said with an impish look in his eye. He held out a hand to Müller. 'Glad you're back, Jens. You don't look a day older.' He peered at Müller in the eye. 'And I can see you've got plenty to tell me.'

'Pappi,' Müller said as they shook hands. 'Australia was . . . very interesting, but it's good to be back. You've got a few surprises coming.'

'I can hardly wait. I like surprises.'

'And how are things in the madhouse?'

'The Great White's away.'

'I like good news. And the goth?'

'Stubborn, pretending she hasn't been shot, staying on station in the rogues' gallery if she gets half the chance, skirting the edges of insubordination, and trying to hide winces of pain when she thinks I'm not looking. Otherwise, in perfect health.'

'All normal then. Anything on Sharon Wilson?'

'Nothing so far. Too quiet.'

'I agree. Something is happening . . .'

'The question is what,' Pappenheim said as he picked up Carey Bloomfield's luggage.

'Hey,' she said. 'I can do that. I had to fight Müller off.'

'I'm bigger than he is. Car's over there.'

'Yep,' she said. 'I'm home.'

In du Bois' house, La Croix was sitting on the terrace, frowning.

'Why the frown?' du Bois enquired. 'At least we know she's safe out there on the water.'

'I'm thinking about Etienne's cousin.'

'Etienne's *cousin*?' du Bois was puzzled. 'What has his cousin got to do with this?'

'Not his cousin exactly. It's the word itself. It jogged a memory of another cousin.'

Wondering what La Croix was talking about, du Bois waited.

'Years and oh . . . years ago, I was in command of a small unit. A colleague's cousin had newly joined. It gave us a problem. He was really just a boy . . . relatively, and he got very carsick. I thought at the time, how can you have a *gendarme* who got carsick? Why did they send him to us? Why not leave him in an office somewhere? Then I realized he never got to *drive*. I decided to let him drive, just to see what would happen. Well, he turned out to be the best driver we ever had. Mad at the wheel, but brilliant. Give him a chase, and he was in heaven.'

Du Bois was staring at him. 'What are you saying?'

'I'm not saying it is . . . but what if . . . what if Sharon Wilson's seasickness *only* happens when she is a *passenger*?'

Du Bois' eyes widened in anxiety. 'Are you saying that this woman they met yesterday could be . . .'

'I'm not saying that . . . exactly. But it is known that a person who is sick as a passenger, changes completely when at the wheel. This happened with my young colleague. Why

204

not the same with seasickness? Even some pilots get airsick when they are passengers. It's something to do with not being in control of the situation. The woman they met is probably completely innocent. But what if she isn't? I know, I know. She did not approach them. They approached her. She was already on the beach when they got there. But this is a highly professional killer. What if she's playing a hunting game we cannot even begin to understand? She has all the cards. We don't know what she looks like, or where she is. No harm making certain. If she's not who we want, we can make some excuse. But if she is . . .'

Du Bois was looking like a fish gulping for air, making small movements with his mouth, clearly imagining Solange out on the water with someone whose specific purpose was to kill her.

Seeing the fear come into his old friend's eyes, La Croix said, 'I'm not saying she *is* the one, Marcel. Just that we should satisfy ourselves she *isn't*. Have you got a boat?'

'Do I have legs?'

'What about a gun. Do you have one?'

'Do I have legs?' du Bois repeated.

He stood up, and went to get the weapon.

When he returned, La Croix stared at it. 'What is *that*?'

'Colt .45, World War Two . . .'

'I know it's a Colt. It looks shiny, but does it still work?'

'As if it just came out of the factory. It was given to my father by one of the Americans who landed in this area. The American said at the time he was so happy that the landings were so bloodless, he felt he was on holiday. My father gave it to me. I've looked after it. It's as good as new. If that woman harms Solange, I swear I'll kill her with this.'

'If she doesn't kill you first. Come on, let's go . . . and hope I'm wrong.'

When they got to the marina, La Croix stared at the rakish speedboat that looked as if it belonged in the thirties. 'This is beautiful. It looks like a Colombo.'

'It does, but it isn't. It's all teak and mahogany. I found it on the island, lying on its side, abandoned. It was almost too far gone. It once belonged to a rich planter's son who died in the war. It was never used again. I got it for nothing, had it brought back here and worked on it for years. This is the result. It's got almost new engines . . . well, they were new years ago, but hardly used or stressed. It's not as fast as that boat she has, but it still moves well.'

'It's beautiful,' La Croix repeated.

As they headed out of the marina, they could not know they were already far too late.

The Superhawk had slowed right down, and the three jet skis were again close together.

Bertrand glanced back towards the shore. 'She won. She dragged us out to sea.'

'She's very good,' Reze admitted. 'Well, here she comes to give you your reward, Etienne.' He grinned. 'But as you didn't trap her, I don't see how.'

'You'll see,' Bertrand said, still hoping.

The boat was sliding towards them, almost stealthily it seemed, a predator about to pounce on easy prey.

When it was a few metres away, Sharon Wilson called, 'Looks like I won, after all.' She smiled at them.

'So I don't get the ride?' Bertrand said.

She shook her head. 'I'm afraid not.'

That was when they saw her raise the silenced gun.

Reze was quicker off the mark. '*It's her!*' he yelled. '*Solange! Go, go, go! Etienne, see to Solange! Go!*' Then he accelerated his jet ski in a sudden burst, rushing to place himself between the silenced gun and Solange.

Sharon Wilson was astonished by Reze's yell. The fact that he appeared to know who she was made her pause for an infinitesimal moment of time. Her finger was already squeezing the trigger, but by the time the gun fired, Reze was squarely in the path of the bullet.

It knocked him off the jet ski.

'*Antoine!*' Solange screamed, and tried to go to him.

But Bertrand was blocking her path. '*You heard him, Solange!*' he shouted. '*Let's go! Let's go! Come on! Don't let him do this in vain! Come on, come on!*'

Tears streaming down her cheeks, she obeyed.

'*She'll come after us!*' Bertrand continued. '*This time let's drag her towards the bloody rocks. Go, go, go!*'

'*Fuck* it!' Sharon Wilson raged on the boat. 'How the *fucking* hell did they know? Who the *fucking* hell talked?'

She shoved the throttles forwards and sent the Superhawk racing after the speeding jet skis. It ran over the dying Reze. She did not even look.

'Shit, shit, *fucking* shit!'

Bertrand glanced back. '*She's coming! Weave!*'

They were racing in the direction of Mont Boron, hoping to get so close to shore, she would think twice about chasing them and she would have to slow right down to take proper aim at the weaving, criss-crossing targets; it meant they had a chance.

They went as fast as they dared, which was certainly faster than they had done before. The need for survival was propelling them on.

Again, Bertrand glanced back. The boat had stopped. He said nothing to Solange. Their headlong rush continued, increasing the distance. Soon, no matter how fast the boat travelled, it would not reach them before they made it to the shore.

So what was she playing at? he wondered.

He glanced back a third time. The boat had still not moved.

'Solange!' he shouted.

She shot him a fearful glance, then saw he was perceptibly slowing down. She matched speed with him.

'*Why are you slowing down?*' she demanded, wondering if he were crazy.

'She's not moving! She hasn't moved for a while.'

'Can't she shoot us from there?'

'Not with a pistol, and certainly not with a silencer on. We're out of range.'

They slowed right down together, very close to shore now, and feeling safer, turned to face the speedboat, skis barely moving.

The speedboat was gone.

'Where . . . where did she go?' Solange asked, voice high with fear as she looked frantically around. Her face was streaked with tears and sea spray.

'I . . . I don't know,' Bertrand replied, puzzled. 'Maybe something's happened to the boat.'

'I think she's hiding out there somewhere, waiting for us to go back . . . then she will come speeding out to cut us off. I think we should stay along the shore, go into Villefranche, and call my grandfather from there.'

Bertrand nodded. 'OK.'

'But what do we do about poor Antoine? He's out there . . .' The tears again flowed down her cheeks.

'I . . . I'm sorry . . . but I think . . . he's dead, Solange,' Bertrand said with a heavy heart. 'He took that bullet right in the chest . . .'

'For me,' she said. 'He put himself between me and the gun! I can't believe he did that . . .'

Bertrand spared her further pain by not saying out loud what they both knew: that Reze's love for Solange had driven him to sacrifice himself for her.

It was du Bois who first spotted the drifting jet ski.

'Oh no!' he cried in anguish. 'Look!'

La Croix saw the ski, and feared the worst, then saw something else that told it all. 'What's that floating over there? Is that . . .'

'A body,' du Bois cut in as they drew closer. 'It's . . . it's not Solange. Oh my God. I think it's Antoine!' He brought the boat to a coasting halt. The body, face down, its wetsuit ripped open, was almost against the right side. 'He's been hit very hard by something. There are some cuts . . .' Then the gentle swell caused by the boat's arrival made Reze's body roll partially over. 'Ooh no . . .' du Bois said in a sad voice as he briefly spotted the wound. 'She shot him! Help me bring him in . . .'

Together, the two men dragged the body aboard.

Solange saw her grandfather's boat first.

'*Etienne!* It's Grandpapa! Look. Over there. Someone is with him. It must be Monsieur La Croix.'

He stared in the direction she had pointed. 'How . . . what are they doing here?'

'They've stopped for something . . . they're pulling it . . . Oh God, Etienne. I think they've found Antoine. Let's go.'

She turned her ski away from the shore and began to head towards the boat.

'*Solange!* What about . . .'

'She's not going to try anything now there are witnesses. I think she's gone for good.'

Solange was right.

Sharon Wilson had long given in to discretion. After the failed attempt, she knew that to hang around put her in great danger of discovery, and had decided to leave Cap Ferrat as fast as possible. She had raced back to the boathouse while Bertrand and Solange had been heading to the shore for dear life. They had therefore not seen her go, nor where she had bolted to.

She was now in the villa, already changed into an outwardly very different person. Her things were packed, and she was ready for immediate departure.

She hurried downstairs, out the door which she locked, then threw the keys back through an upper floor window that she had left slightly open for the purpose. She had left nothing in the building to betray she had ever been there. She had dropped the gun she had used overboard, into deep water. Barnacles would be the only things that would find it.

She got into the Mercedes, and drove unhurriedly away. She had already passed through Villefranche and was rounding the bend at Mont Boron, by the time La Croix and du Bois were fishing Antoine Reze's body out of the water.

Anyone taking even a passing interest in the black coupé would see that it was being driven by a frumpish woman in heavy rimmed glasses.

In her mind, was a burning question: how had they known about her?

'*Fuck, fuck, fuck!*' she hissed. 'I don't *fucking* fail!'

She continued driving unhurriedly.

Pappenheim had dropped Müller and Carey Bloomfield off at Müller's home in Wilmersdorf, and had returned to Friedrichstrasse.

Walking along the corridor to his office, he paused at the door to the rogues' gallery. He opened the door, but did not go right in. He put his head through. The goth was at the computer.

'Is he back?' she asked without turning round.

'He's back.'

'Is he coming here?' He knew she was smiling with pleasure.

'They will be,' he said.

'"They",' she said, voice descending several degrees.

'Yes. I dropped them off at his home. They'll be here once they've showered and changed. Anything come in?'

'Some more stuff from that computer out there,' she replied, still without turning round. 'I'd like to know how he's managed to have access to a machine that's active even when he's not there.'

'That makes two of us,' Pappenheim said. 'Later,' he added, and withdrew his head quickly before she could quiz him further about Müller.

He went on to his office as the door clicked shut behind him. Once there, he lit up even before he had taken his seat behind his desk.

'There's something in your eyes, Jens,' he said as he sat down. 'I hope you'll tell me what it is.'

He blew several smoke rings at the ceiling.

At that very moment, Sharon Wilson left Nice via the N202. On the longish straight towards Colomars, she pulled off the road to make a phone call.

'Why are you calling this number?' was the answer she received.

'Because,' she said in a sharp return, 'it's gone *fucking* wrong. Someone, somewhere, has talked, or passed information. They were *fucking* expecting me!'

'No one has talked . . .'

'Someone *fucking* has! You'd better *fucking* find out who! You've got *fucking* problems.'

'*I* have?'

'*All* of you!'

'Where are you now?'

'Not *fucking* there!'

She ended the call abruptly, and continued on her journey.

Pappenheim's phone rang.

'We must talk,' he heard La Croix say when he had picked it up.

'We can do so now,' he said. 'We've got five minutes before it becomes insecure to continue.'

La Croix did not waste time. Very quickly, he told Pappenheim what had happened. Pappenheim shut his eyes briefly in relief when he heard that Solange du Bois was all right, but was saddened by the death of Antoine Reze.

'Brave young man,' he said.

'Yes. She has taken it very badly.'

'And our killer?'

'Gone, of course. I would think she is out of the area by now.'

'I am certain she is. Thanks, Alphonse. You all did a great job.'

'Alas, we could not save Antoine . . .'

'That is the very sad part. Just in case you have problems with your active colleagues, I'll arrange something to keep them off your backs.'

'I appreciate that.'

'You did well, Alphonse. Your precautions saved the girl's life. Take comfort in that.'

'It has a price.'

'I know.'

'Something else you should know. There was a strange incident on the N202. Young man with a broken neck. I believe the same person is responsible.'

La Croix gave Pappenheim fast details of what had happened to Maurice Baudouin.

'I have no doubt whatsoever that you're correct. I am also certain she's taken that route back to wherever she's going.'

'Yes. It avoids the *péage*. She could be trapped at one of them.'

'We'll find her, Alphonse. Count on it.'

'Please do. I would like Antoine Reze to be avenged.'

211

'She has a long list of people waiting to hold her to account. We'll get her.'

'Thank you, my friend.'

After the call had ended, Pappenheim made another to one of his contacts.

'We're looking for someone,' he said when the person had answered. 'We don't want her stopped, or even alerted. We believe she may be on her way back to Germany. We want to be kept informed of her movements. We'll take her at the appropriate moment. I also want some French colleagues kept out of trouble.'

'You don't want much.'

'You know me. Why ask for a little when you need a lot?'

'Same old Pappi.'

'You'd hate me if I changed.'

A sigh came down the line. 'All right. Let's have the details.'

When Pappenheim had finished, the person at the other end said, 'You don't even know what car she's driving?'

'Who said it was going to be easy? I've given you a detailed description of her. Even if she has disguised herself, she might make a mistake. She has already made one, which is why she's running. She's driving a German-registered car. Whatever it is, it will be a fast car. She's on the N202 for now. My guess is she'll stay on that, and on the back roads, until she's forced to use the toll autoroutes, if she's coming this way. She might try to change cars. She won't hire one. Too risky. So she'll probably steal one. She won't call her people – at least not too often – in case the call gets traced, because she will assume we're looking for her. This is a person who likes to play things her way. That might, in this instance, leave her isolated. This might be a help to us.'

'All right.'

In Cap Ferrat, a senior policeman was in du Bois' house. He looked grim.

'One of the things that annoy me,' he was saying, 'is the fact that some people don't seem to know when they're retired. They want to keep playing *detective* . . .' he paused, and looked at Etienne Bertrand. 'Go for a walk, Bertrand. I want to talk to these senile deliquents alone.'

'Yes, sir.'

'But don't go far. I want to talk to you as well.'

'Yes, sir.'

'You are retired, aren't you, La Croix,' the policeman went on after Bertrand had gone.

'I am.'

The policeman, Jean Didier, did not look as if he believed it. He looked from one to the other. 'What did you two think you were playing at?'

'Trying to save my granddaughter's life,' du Bois said. 'What do you think?'

'So you didn't think of informing us she was in danger?'

'There are reasons.'

'I see. "Reasons". Why would anyone wish to send a professional assassin to shoot your granddaughter?'

Du Bois looked at La Croix, then at Didier. He said nothing.

Didier took a deep intake of breath and let it out slowly. 'Have either of you any idea what kind of heat I will get if I don't have answers? People respect you, Marcel. I know you did what you thought was best. I would probably do the same in your place . . . but even if you were still an active policeman, this would still get you into trouble. One of our officers is dead . . . whatever the reasons behind it. Explanations, *answers*, are required. You two are holding back. How can I help if you . . .'

His mobile rang. He took it out of a pouch on his belt. 'What is it? I'm busy . . . *what?*' His eyes widened slightly as he listened. He turned to look at both La Croix and du Bois. 'I . . . see.' He listened some more. 'I see,' he repeated. 'Yes. I've got that. Thank you.'

He ended the call and with great deliberation, put the phone back. He said nothing for several moments.

Then he looked at La Croix. 'Retired indeed. You two have powerful friends. That call I just got was – if you cut it down to essentials – telling me to mind my own business. It seems as if we have got instructions from somewhere very high up, that others are dealing with this case. I am to leave

213

you two alone. Wasn't there something years back, La Croix, that involved you?'

'I am not at liberty to tell you.'

'Of course not. Why did I expect otherwise? Can I not even talk to Bertrand?'

'I don't think there is more that he can tell you, Jean,' du Bois said, 'than he already has. He doesn't know any more.'

Didier nodded, a man who knew he had been outmanoeuvred. 'Who would be a policeman, eh? Thank you for your time, gentlemen.'

He went out.

Du Bois looked at La Croix. 'That was quick work. The people in Berlin?'

La Croix nodded.

'If only my daughter had never met that man,' du Bois sighed.

'You would not have had Solange. Another granddaughter, perhaps. But not Solange.'

'Of course you're right, old friend. Of course you're right.'

Berlin, Wilmersdorf.

Showered and changed, Müller and Carey Bloomfield were making their way down to the underground garage when his mobile rang.

'Where are you?' Pappenheim asked.

'On our way to the garage.'

'Good. We have movement.'

'On our way,' Müller said. As he put the phone away, he said to Carey Bloomfield, 'Pappi has news of Sharon Wilson.'

Her eyes grew cold. 'I'm looking forward to a return match with that redhead.'

'The queue keeps growing longer.'

As they entered the garage, the lights came on. The building belonged to Müller, an inheritance from his father. There were just three apartments, one to each vast floor, with Müller's the penthouse. The garage was itself spacious, with just nine wide parking bays, three to each apartment. BMWs predominated, but in Müller's bays were two Porsches – a seal grey Cayenne and a seal grey 911 turbo with large nineteen-inch wheels and the yellow calipers of the ceramic brakes.

'Last time I was here, Müller,' Carey Bloomfield said, 'this garage was so . . . *clean*. It still is. Do the cars float on air when they come in here?'

'Ho bloody ho,' he said, baring his teeth at her.

'So which one is it to be?' she asked. 'As if I didn't know. You're looking at it like a long-lost friend. You weren't away from it that long, Müller. I'll stroke it for you. Save you the trouble.' She went up to the car, and passed a hand over its roof. 'We're back,' she said to it. 'Not lonesome any more.'

Müller pressed the remote. 'Get in.'

'Yessir,' she said. 'At least you didn't say Miss Bloomfield. That's an improvement.'

He did not respond as he got in behind the wheel.

'I love the leather smell of this car.' She watched as he clipped on his seatbelt. 'When are you going to tell Pappi about Waldron, and the Hargreaves?'

'Time for that after we've got Sharon Wilson.'

Sharon Wilson had made good time, and was approaching the spot where she had killed Maurice Baudouin. She did not slacken pace.

'Killers are supposed to be drawn back to the scene of the crime,' she said. 'Not this killer. Hi, Maurice. Hope they found you by now.'

It was just as well that she did not stop. As she went by, she saw two motorcycle policemen, standing by their bikes.

She made no sudden movement, but continued to drive smoothly. She glanced in the mirrors. They made no move to follow.

'Well, well,' she said. 'Seems the *fucking* alarm's not on yet.'

She smiled to herself.

One of the motorcycle policemen said to his colleague, 'That was a German car, wasn't it?'

'A Mercedes is a German car. Yes.'

'Very funny. I meant the licence plate.'

'Yes. It was . . . with index letter B.'

'Better tell them. Middle-aged woman with glasses driving.'

His colleague reported the car and the full number.

'How many was that in the last hour?' the other asked.

'If you're just talking about German registered cars – three. This one, a red Porsche, and that funny little car . . .'

'Trabant. Sick yellow.'

'That's it. Imagine driving that all the way down here.'

'They're braver than me. The Mercedes and that Trabant were the ones with the B-plate, weren't they?'

'Yes.'

The first thing Müller did when he got to Friedrichstrasse was to call on the goth in the rogues' gallery.

'Miss Meyer,' he said. 'How's the wound?'

She spun her chair round, eyes shining with pleasure that he was back. 'Healing well,' she said, getting to her feet.

'Please. Don't get up on my account. You've got to look after yourself.'

'I'm fine. Really. Glad you're back.'

'Good to be back.' Müller approached her, to look closer at where she had been hit. 'You were very lucky.'

'I know.'

'Are you sure you're all right?'

'Yes, sir. I am.'

'You've been doing great work. Any time you feel unwell, do not hesitate. Get some rest. And make certain the doc knows.'

'You've only been here a few minutes and you're worrying already. I am fine.' But she was pleased that he cared. 'Is the colonel with you?'

'Yes. She's talking to the *Oberkommissar*. She'll be in to say hello.'

'She's here,' came Carey Bloomfield's voice as she entered, followed by Pappenheim. 'Hi, Hedi.' She looked at the goth's sling. 'Sorry to hear about Sharon Wilson's nasty present. You OK?'

The goth nodded, controlling her feeling of rivalry. 'I'm fine, thank you. I was lucky.'

'You won't believe how lucky,' Pappenheim said. 'The

first news about Sharon Wilson has come in,' he went on to Müller. 'She was in Cap Ferrat. She went for Solange du Bois, but got a policeman instead.'

'Is he . . . ?'

'Oh yes. One shot.'

Pappenheim gave the details of what had happened in Cap Ferrat, and about the killing of Maurice Baudouin.

'And now she's running.'

'I'd bet on it. I've spread a net. We should be getting something on that soon.'

At the listening post, not very distant from Friedrichstrasse, the man with the headphones said, 'She's running. I'm getting some police traffic.'

'Are they chasing her?'

'No. They have been instructed not to apprehend, and not to alert her.'

'Interesting.' The other picked up a phone, and called a number. He relayed what he had just been told.

'She gets no back-up,' the voice at the other end said. 'She is becoming a liability. If she makes it, good.'

'And if not?'

There was a long pause. 'If she is killed, the matter is closed. If she is taken . . . she must not be allowed to talk.'

The inference was clear.

'She is one of our very best.'

'That is fully appreciated. Her performance is exceptional. However, she is not indispensable.' There was another pause. 'She called this number to suggest that someone is passing highly sensitive information. What she said leads to that possibility. We shall investigate. But that does not change this situation. If she is taken, she will *not* talk.' The line went dead.

'Could not be clearer,' the man said as he put the phone down.

Ten

In the rogues' gallery, the computer made a pinging sound. 'We've got something,' the goth said. 'I'm collating everything that comes in about her on this map.'

She had a large-scale road map of France onscreen. Superimposed on the right was a transparent column, showing all the licence numbers that had been reported. All the non-German plates were filtered out, and of those, all non-Berlin plates.

'We have two Berlin plates about here,' she continued. A section of the N202 was highlighted. 'A big Mercedes coupé . . . black, and a Trabant.'

'I don't think she's driving a Trabi,' Pappenheim said with a straight face.

'Do you think the coupé could be hers?' the goth asked. 'It could be anybody's.'

'Let's see where it turns up next,' Müller said looking at the screen. 'We may also get more information on it which might help. People frequently see things without realizing they have. If she *is* on that road and heading back to Berlin, she'll be driving fast wherever she can. But she might not be heading for Berlin, nor be using the same car. We need an indication of her eventual destination.'

Pappenheim looked at him. 'What do you have in mind?'

'An intercept when she is in Germany. I want her alive.'

'If she'll let you. That kind go down shooting. Where would you intercept?'

'She's in a hurry. Depending on where she's headed, she *may* take the shortest route. She does not know that she's not going to be stopped for now, so she'll be expecting an intercept somewhere along the route. She will expect it in France, given she's killed a French policeman. Once she crosses into Germany, she'll relax. I don't expect her to go via Switzerland. But even if she does, she'll come out via Basel, and join the A5 autobahn.

'If she does not, she'll come through via the Europort at Mulhouse and still be on the A5, heading north. The only question then is whether she'll continue to the A8 to head for Bavaria and then on to Berlin; or whether she'll go further north first. I would suggest that we head southwest, via Bavaria, see if we can pick her up on the A5. Then we follow her to wherever she goes.'

'How many "we"s are we talking about?'

'Miss Bloomfield and I go in my car. You and Berger in your appropriated BMW . . .'

'And me,' the goth said.

They all stared at her.

'*Meisterin* Meyer,' Pappenheim said, 'did we hear you correctly?'

'And me,' she repeated. 'I'm not being left out. I have a score to settle.'

Müller glanced pointedly at her sling. 'Aren't you forgetting something?'

'I'm fine,' she insisted.

'You can't use a weapon, and you'll be . . .'

'I'm as good with my right, as my left.'

'You've got a bullet hole in you, Miss Meyer.'

'I *had* a bullet hole in me. It's healing.'

'Only because you are not stressing it. And we need you at the computer to tell us . . .'

'*Sir!* I need to do this. If . . . if I don't . . . I'll . . . remain scared . . .' She stopped.

There was a long silence, as they began to understand the magnitude of the fight the goth was having within herself.

It was Carey Bloomfield who broke it. 'I can understand that,' she said. 'I've been there.' She looked at Müller. 'Let her come.'

The goth's changeling eyes thanked her. 'I'll take a laptop,' the goth said quickly before Müller could recover. 'I can link it, *securely*, to this computer. We'll have all the tracking updates on it, just as on here.'

There was another silence as this time, all eyes were on Müller.

'All right,' he said at last. 'You go with the *Oberkommissar* and Berger. *And you keep out of trouble.*'

'Thank you, sir. I will. I could kiss you for that.'

'Don't. I might faint. Now you'd better get your gear set up. We'll be leaving soon. Can you even walk?'

'Of course I can. I wasn't hit in the legs.'

The small convoy was travelling at high speed. The hidden police lights beneath the headlights on Müller's Porsche were out and flashing. The headlights were themselves on. Behind the Porsche, Pappenheim's BMW coupé was keeping station, headlights also on, with a mobile flashing light placed on the roof. Berger was driving the BMW, and holding a steady 200 kph in Müller's wake. Cars parted like the Red Sea before them.

In the back, the goth was busy with her laptop.

'How can you do that without feeling sick?' Pappenheim glanced round to ask.

'I just can,' she replied, not looking up.

'What it is to be young,' he said.

It was an hour since they had left Berlin. The goth was frowning at the screen. 'I think we've got something,' she said.

Pappenheim looked round again. 'What is it?'

'The same car is now passing Sisteron. The Trabi is still on the same route, but far behind.'

'Can you pass that to Jens Müller's car?'

'Of course,' the goth said, as if that were the simplest thing in the world. She had rigged a connection with the Porsche's communication system. 'Done.'

In his car, Müller heard the ping and glanced at the map on the central console. A flashing dot was near Sisteron.

'Amazing what she can do with electronics,' Müller said to Carey Bloomfield.

'She's certainly got some skill there,' she agreed. 'Do you regret bringing her?'

'I am worried about whether she is fit enough,' he admitted. 'But her idea of the laptop is brilliant. I just hope she keeps out of the way if we have trouble.'

'So do I . . . but I understand where she's coming from. It's like my thing with snakes.'

He nodded. 'It was the way she admitted that she was frightened that swayed me. That must have cost her something.'

'Sometimes,' Carey Bloomfield said, 'letting your guard down is healthy.' She did not look at him as she said that.

'Perhaps,' he said.

'Let me know when you would like me to drive,' she said after a while.

'I remember the last time I turned you loose in this,' he said. 'You became a hooligan.'

'It's a fast car,' she said, unrepentant.

'You were on the same plane as I was. If I feel tired, I'll let you know. But right now, I'm perfectly all right.'

'Deal,' she said.

In Cap Ferrat, the phone rang in du Bois' house. He and La Croix were still on the terrace. Solange had remained in her room.

He got up and went to the phone. 'Du Bois.'

It was Didier. 'I don't know why I'm calling you, but do you or La Croix remember seeing a black Mercedes coupé, middle-aged woman with glasses driving?'

'Not me. But I'll ask La Croix.' Du Bois looked at La Croix and beckoned. 'It's Didier,' he said as La Croix joined him. 'Wants to know if we saw a black Mercedes coupé. Middle-aged woman in glasses driving.'

La Croix shook his head. 'No. I haven't . . .' He stopped. Du Bois looked at him questioningly.

'Black Mercedes, black Mercedes,' La Croix was saying to himself. 'Where, where, where . . .' He paused. 'Yes . . . *yes*. Up the road, when I first got here. I was standing on the grass divider, waiting for some traffic to pass. There was a Mercedes coupé with German plates, index B. But why would they . . .' He paused again. 'Woman in glasses? Spinsterish?'

'He says middle-aged . . . but I suppose a spinsterish woman could look older than she really is.'

'Yes. I saw her. Going in the direction of Beaulieu and Villefranche.'

'I heard that,' Didier said in du Bois' ear. 'Well, it looks as if the same car has been seen on the N202, and has just passed Sisteron. Anything you want to add?'

'Anything we want to add?' du Bois asked La Croix.

La Croix shook his head.

'That's it,' du Bois said to Didier.

'Ah well,' Didier said, sounding disappointed. 'Just thought you'd like to know.'

'Thanks for calling us.'

'Thanks for not telling me anything,' Didier said with caustic wit, and hung up.

As he put the phone down, du Bois said, 'You thought of something else, didn't you?'

'I've realized where I've seen that woman again,' La Croix said. 'I'm such a *fool!*'

Du Bois stared at him. 'What do you mean?'

'She was right with us, Marcel! She was sitting in the café when we were talking about the youngsters going to Plage de Passable. We walked right past her! She heard! I saw her, but didn't register it any more than I registered two yakking blondes who were sitting not far from her. But now that I remember the woman, I remember them as well.'

'So that's how she knew where to go,' du Bois said quietly. 'She heard, went back to wherever she was staying, changed, and was waiting by the time they came to the beach. But she never approached them.'

'She didn't have to. In reality, she's a very attractive woman, and she uses that as a weapon. All she had to do was lie on the beach and wait. She laid the trap, and Etienne Bertrand walked right into it. After that, it was easy. If she *is* the woman I saw, she's very, very smart. In her chosen profession, it means survival.'

'Well, she was seen on the N202, and has just passed Sisteron.'

'Heading north,' La Croix said. 'It's beginning to look like we actually saw the person who had come to kill your granddaughter, and who got Antoine Reze instead.'

'I hope they get her!' du Bois said with controlled savagery.

'They will,' La Croix said. 'They will.'

* * *

'*Sir!*' the goth said.

'You sound excited,' Pappenheim said, turning his head slightly in her direction.

'This might excite you,' she said. 'A black Mercedes coupé was seen in Cap Ferrat, middle-aged woman in glasses driving. It's the same licence plate as the one we're tracking. They say here it looks like a special. Same car, sir,' she finished in triumph.

'Send that to the Porsche.'

'Doing it.'

The ping made Carey Bloomfield look and Müller glance at the console display.

Müller returned his attention to the road. 'What's that about?'

'Well might you ask,' she said reading the message. 'The car we're tracking was seen in Cap Ferrat . . .'

'And here it is, right after the killing, heading fast for Germany . . . or at least, northwards. Coincidence?'

'I'll admit it's a stretch. No reason why a middle-aged woman in glasses should not be driving her souped-up coupé on the mountain roads, just after a killing in the place she had just come from . . . I think you've got your quarry, Müller.'

'I hope so.'

The next sighting had the Mercedes on the short A51 autoroute, heading for Grenoble.

'This is where we'll see which direction she'll choose. If she heads for Chambéry, we'll know she's going via Switzerland. If she goes via Lyon, then it's most likely she'll cross the border at Mulhouse . . .'

'Unless she's leading everyone a dance.'

'For that, she needs to suspect she's being tracked. So far, I don't believe she does know.'

Half an hour later, they had the route. The Mercedes was going towards Lyon.

'So it's Mulhouse, after all,' Müller said.

'It's a long way to Mulhouse,' Carey Bloomfield said, 'and a choice of a lot of directions.'

'True . . . but I believe she's heading our way. A hunch.'

'Hope you're right, Müller.'

'So do I.'

Müller was proven right. At 18.45, the Mercedes was tracked crossing into Germany, and on to the A5 autobahn.

'Damn, Müller!' Carey Bloomfield said. 'I hate guys like you. Let me drive.'

'Don't take it out on my car,' he said with a wary glance in her direction.

They were now also on the A5, approaching Baden-Baden, but heading south. They had stopped twice for fuel, for Pappenheim to grab a smoke, to eat on the run, and once for calls of nature.

'We should get off the autobahn to change direction,' he went on, 'and to get some fuel. I don't want to be forced to stop because we need to fuel, just when we're following her. It should take her about an hour to get to Baden-Baden. We should be waiting.'

He took the next exit off the autobahn, then went back on, heading north. Half an hour later, they stopped at the very next petrol station. When they had fuelled, they drove to the main car park, and waited.

That was when the goth received the next update.

'She's ten kilometres away!' she said.

She warned Müller, and the two cars moved to where they could see the passing traffic. They did not have long to wait. Just over three minutes later, the black Mercedes coupé shot past.

'She's doing two hundred K,' Berger said. 'At least.'

She followed Müller and Carey Bloomfield, in pursuit.

Müller had let Carey Bloomfield drive.

'I must be mad,' he grumbled, watching as the speed built in a rush. 'You've got to pass her. Pappi stays behind, completing the sandwich.'

The speed was now at 220. The flashing lights were no longer being used, but the headlights were kept on to warn traffic they were coming at speed.

'What if she recognizes me as we pass?'

'She won't be expecting to see you. She won't recognize this car. There are other Berlin licence plates around, so it should not alert her even if she does look at the plate. Pass her at speed, and she won't have time to look.'

Behind them, Berger watched her own speed mounting.

'Chief . . . is the boss crazy, letting her drive his car at this speed?'

'He must be feeling secure enough,' Pappenheim said, glancing at the speedometer.

'I saw that!' Berger accused. 'I can handle it.'

Pappenheim said nothing, and prayed silently.

Carey Bloomfield saw that they were catching up on the Mercedes.

'Don't slow down!' Müller ordered. He had sensed she was easing off the accelerator. 'Control the car, but don't fight it. You'll be fine. Don't slow down after you've passed. Put a few cars between you. Pappi will be doing the same behind her.'

They passed the Mercedes at very high speed, and kept going.

'Well done,' Müller said. 'All right. Start pulling into the centre lane, but don't slow down too obviously. We don't want her closer than a kilometre. We're still getting the updates, so we don't need to have her in sight. If she goes off, we'll know. If she gets ahead – which we should not allow her to – we would know. Pappi's watching the back door. Relax.'

In the Mercedes, Sharon Wilson wondered aloud about something that had been troubling her for some time.

'I've come all the *fucking* way,' she said, 'but nothing's been on the *fucking* news. A policeman dying out on the water should be worth a *fucking* mention. At least. Is it a news *fucking* blackout?'

She had watched, suspecting nothing, as the Porsche had rocketed past.

'Show *fucking* off!' was all she had said.

There was still plenty of daylight left when Sharon Wilson led them on to the A61, heading towards Koblenz.

They were nearing a motorway station some time later when Carey Bloomfield said, 'Unless her car's got unlimited gas, she's got to stop soon.'

'Or unless she took on fuel before Baden-Baden.'

But almost immediately after they had passed the stop, a message appeared on the console screen. The Mercedes was going in.

'We'll continue to the next lay-by, and wait there. She shouldn't take much notice, even if she sees the car. People stop for all sorts of reasons.'

As she took on fuel, Sharon Wilson watched as the BMW coupé with Berlin plates came off the autobahn, but did not approach the fuel pumps. Instead, it went right to pass behind the building where she would be going to pay. She did not see it go through to the main car park.

Some primeval instinct made her sense danger. She had no reason she could pinpoint, but the feeling was there. She decided to obey it.

'Time to dump this *fucking* car,' she said to herself.

It had to be something very different.

She stopped the pump, and went in to pay. She returned to the car, and drove to the main car park. She could not see the BMW, nor did she look for it. If it were an innocent car, it did not matter. If it were not, looking for it might well compromise her. She took all she needed out of the car, especially her guns, shut and locked it, then went into the service restaurant/shop near the car park.

She went down into the restaurant toilets to change. The female attendant was not there, which suited perfectly. When she came out again, she looked like a student. The glasses and the prim bunch of dark hair were gone. She was now a blonde with a nondescript haircut, T-shirt, jeans with open knees, and canvas boots. A backpack was slung from a shoulder.

The attendant had returned.

Sharon Wilson dropped a generous tip on to the waiting plate, and received a smile and a wish for a good journey in return.

She left the building, and began looking for a likely car.

From where Berger had parked the BMW, there was a clear view of the Mercedes. They were parked near the toilets of the service station building

'I need to go,' the goth said. 'Hope she doesn't come back soon.' She pointed at her sling. 'This will make it take a while.'

'Take your phone,' Pappenheim said. 'We'll warn you. But try to be as quick as you can.'

The goth nodded. Pappenheim got out to enable her to leave. But Hedi Meyer was not responding to a call of nature. Once inside a cubicle, she took her arm out of the sling, and moved it experimentally. She winced, but stuck with it.

'I can do it,' she said.

After a while, she put her arm back in the sling, and went out. She was about to leave the building when a towed caravan took her interest. She paused, frowning. It was not because of the caravan. It was because of the person standing next to the caravan, talking to the driver of the car. The caravan looked brand new, and had a licence plate with red letters and figures. She recognized them as Belgian plates. She also recognized the person talking to the driver. She hurried back to the BMW.

'Pull out until you can see a caravan!' she said to Berger in an urgent voice as she climbed in.

Berger turned to stare at her. '*What?*'

Pappehneim got back into his seat and shut the door. 'What are you talking about, Hedi?'

'Sir . . . she's leaving her car here! I just saw her talking to a man with a towed caravan. Belgian plates. She's changed, and is going to hitch a ride. I'll bet on it!'

'Ease the car out, Lene,' he said to Berger. 'Let's have a look.'

Sharon Wilson was still talking, and smiling at the man.

'Are you certain, Hedi?'

'Positive, sir. That is the woman who shot me.'

As the goth spoke, Sharon Wilson went round the car to get into the passenger seat.

'Works every time,' Pappenheim said in a dry voice. 'All right, Hedi. Warn Jens Müller.'

'Yes, sir.'

Carey Bloomfield stared at the console.

'She's *hitching*?' she exclaimed. 'So she made me, after all.'

'I don't think so,' Müller said. 'She's doing what someone who is good at her job would do. Changing the game, unexpectedly. If the goth had not gone to the toilet, we would still be watching that Mercedes. Sharon Wilson did not have to spot anyone. Isn't that what *you* would do?'

'She's not riding her luck.'

'Exactly.'

'I should have known that.'

'Yes. You should have.'

'Thanks, Müller.'

'Do you still want to drive?'

'You bet.'

'A towed caravan is not going to do two hundred.'

'You should have added, thank God.'

'I did not say that.'

'No. But you were thinking it.'

Then the caravan appeared, cruising on the inside lane.

'Follow that caravan,' Müller said, 'but not just yet.'

'Smartass,' she said.

When she pulled out, the BMW was right behind.

There was still just enough light in the day when Carey Bloomfield said, 'They're going off.'

They had just crossed a bridge over the Mosel, at a height of 935 metres. Once across, the caravan turned off to enter the Moseltal rest area. There was no fuel, but a shop-cum-café/restaurant on each side of the autobahn with plenty of parking, and toilets. Crossing to either side could be done on foot, by a walkway under the bridge. It gave a stunning, bird's-eye view over the Mosel valley.

'Perhaps he needs to go to the toilet,' Müller said. 'Pull in after him. This could be our best chance, and perhaps even save his life. I doubt if she will let him live when she no longer needs him. Keep some distance. She can't see through the mirrors of that thing, so we might be able to surprise her.'

The BMW followed.

They stopped behind a tourist coach, which hid both cars from the caravan.

'Hedi,' Pappenheim said as he got out, 'you stay here.'

'But sir I . . .'

'No "but sir I". You've done a great job. Now let us do this one without having to worry about you. OK?'

228

'OK,' she agreed with reluctance.

'Do you have your gun?'

She nodded.

'If she somehow comes to this car, you have my permission to empty it into her. Better get into the front to give you better freedom of movement if you need to. Otherwise . . .'

'Stay put.'

'That's it. All right, Lene,' he said to Berger, 'let's see what Jens has to say.'

Müller and Carey Bloomfield were already outside the Porsche.

'Where's the goth?' Müller asked.

'Told her to stay put,' Pappenheim answered.

'She agreed?'

Pappenheim nodded. 'I hope she means it. So how do we do this?'

'You and Lene take the underpass to the other side, to block her if she tries to run that way. Try not to frighten the citizenry. We'll start the ball from here.'

Pappenheim and Berger, weapons out, made their way in the twilight towards the steps that would lead to the underpass.

As they left, Müller said to Carey Bloomfield, 'Ready?'

'No. But what the hell. I have a date with that bitch.'

'Let's hope we survive it.'

They set off, making for the caravan from different points. They closed in on it from opposite sides, keeping as far as was possible from being spotted in the mirrors. They worked in a casual way, seeming to stroll towards the caravan so as not to excite interest from the other people around.

When they finally got to the tow car, there was no one inside.

'What the hell?' Carey Bloomfield said. 'Another switch?'

'I doubt it. Not enough time. They are probably both in the toilets. She's not superhuman. Calls of nature affect her too.'

'Now what?'

'We wait till she comes out. I don't want her near anyone. She might take a hostage.'

'What about the driver?'

'We must make certain she can't take him.'

Several minutes passed.

'This is taking too long,' Müller said. 'Wait here. I'll check the toilets.'

'OK.'

Müller had been gone for about two minutes, when the caravan door burst open, and Sharon Wilson was standing before Carey Bloomfield.

'Hi, Miss *fucking* America,' she said in a soft voice, in English. 'Nice conversation you just had with *Hauptfuckingkommissar* Müller. What a *fucking* surprise you two are. But now, *I'm* the *fucking* surprise. Want to know what I was doing? Come have a look. The driver wanted to stop for a fuck in his little caravan. I gave him one . . . and a broken neck. Don't . . . try to be a *fucking* hero. I can bring this gun up faster than you could use yours. Don't want to look? Then come with me. A little walk before your boyfriend gets back.'

Carey Bloomfield glared at her.

'Oh, oh, oh,' Sharon Wilson said. 'If looks could only *fucking* kill. Now come on, don't try to attract the sheep. I'd kill them. You wouldn't want that, would you? Come on. Let's go. That's a good girl.'

Carey Bloomfield allowed herself to be led towards the very steps that Pappenheim and Berger had taken to cross under the bridge.

'Come on now!' Sharon Wilson urged. 'Faster!'

At that moment, Müller came out of the building and saw what was happening. He did not shout. Instead, he moved quickly, using vehicles as cover until he was close enough.

The two women were on the first flight of steps that led down to the walkway, when he arrived behind them.

'Far enough, Sharon,' he said.

She stopped. The gun was now at Carey Bloomfield's back.

'Hello, loverboy. You have a choice. Drop your gun and come join your girlfriend, or watch me shoot her *fucking* spine away. There is no *fucking* room for negotiation, so don't waste your *fucking* time, and mine.'

Müller said nothing.

She turned slightly, to look up at him. The gun remained firmly against Carey Bloomfield's spine.

'I am not joking, Müller.'

Müller waited some more, until certain she would believe his reluctance. He put down the gun.

'Not *fucking* good enough,' she said. 'Safety on, then bring it down to me.'

Müller obeyed.

'There,' she said as she took the Beretta. 'Not so *fucking* bad was it? Nice gun. Killed a few with that, eh?' She swapped guns. Now Müller's Beretta was at Carey Bloomfield's spine. '*Fucking* poetic, that, I'd say. Now join the lady.'

As they went down the steps, the traffic above boomed across the bridge with a regular, thunderous double beat.

The steps turned right to lead down to the walkway itself. Beyond its railing, the ground dropped steeply, all the way down to the river.

'Quite a fall isn't it?' Sharon Wilson said, as if in conversation. 'Wouldn't be *fucking* much left of anyone taking that exit. How did you manage to track me, Müller?'

'Good police work.'

'*Fucking* bollocks.'

'Suit yourself.'

'It was more than that. Who talked?'

Müller countered. 'Sharon . . . you know they've abandoned you, don't you? They are ruthless . . .'

'Müller, you don't know what you're up against. They're all around you. And do you know you speak English like a Brit?'

'So people keep telling me.'

'And if you're going to tell me I've been left to make it out on my own . . . I *fucking* know that. When I'm finished with you, I'll *fucking* attend to them . . .'

'For how long do you think you will last?'

'Long enough.'

'So you get one, perhaps two. As you've said, they're all around. Wouldn't it be better to do some real damage . . .'

'What's this? A *fucking* deal? Then you'll let me go? Don't appeal to my better nature, Müller. There isn't one. And don't think – oh, she had a deprived childhood, look what it did to her. Forget it. I was born into a comfortable family. My dad really loved me and no, he didn't abuse me. Well I did go to a good Catholic girls' school – does that *fucking* count? And I had a good university education. Sorry. No meat to feed on there.'

'I have a picture of you, Sharon . . .'

'Is it *fucking* sexy?'

'. . . on a horse, no saddle, shorts, barefoot, in Guatemala.' She stopped. 'You *what*?'

'I also know about . . . oh let me see . . . Henry Tollerton in Hong Kong . . . Anuncio Arres in Paraguay . . . the Jameson family . . . and many more . . .'

'*Fucking* Jee . . .' Sharon Wilson stopped, genuinely astonished by the revelation. 'I was right! I was *fucking* right. I warned them!'

'Help us bring them down, Sharon . . .'

'And you'll forgive all my sins? Bless me father . . .'

'Sharon . . .'

'Sorry, Müller. Wrong person. Now move on down.'

'Stop right there!' Sharon Wilson heard in German.

'I believe I know that voice,' she responded in the same language. 'The little mouse in the Beetle. So I didn't kill you, after all. What a *fucking* strong little thing you are. You don't really think you can stop me, do you? How's that wound? Hurting? Badly? For how long can you hold that big gun?'

The goth had got out of the BMW, and had seen Carey Bloomfield being led away. Then she had spotted Müller. Feeling that something had gone badly wrong, she had followed until, in the increasing gloom, she had heard voices.

Now she stood on the steps, arm out of the sling, holding the gun two-handedly, and trying not to wince in pain.

'Don't . . . don't even turn round,' the goth said.

'Do you think you can *fucking* shoot me before I kill your pals?'

'I'll shoot you in the head.'

Sharon Wilson gave a soft laugh. 'Have you any *fucking* idea how hard it is to shoot at the head, even in good light? In this light, you haven't got a *fucking* chance.'

'*Fucking try me, bitch!*' the goth yelled above the boom of the traffic. The pain fired her.

'Oooh! The little mouse is getting *fucking* mad. Let me do the job properly this *fucking* time . . .'

Sharon Wilson spun with astonishing speed, guns coming up.

The goth fired. Twice. Both shots hit Sharon Wilson in the chest as Müller and Carey Bloomfield threw themselves flat.

Sharon Wilson staggered, and stared at the sudden red blooms in her chest. 'You . . . you . . . said the . . . the . . . head . . .'

The goth had gone closer. 'I lied. *This* is the head shot, *bitch*.' She fired again.

The shot tore through Sharon Wilson's skull. The force of the blow tipped her over the railing. Her body pinwheeled down the steep slope, gathering speed. It thudded on to the road far below, bounced across the railtrack that bordered the river, and into the river itself.

The goth, breathing hard, sat down suddenly on the steps. She gave a low moan.

Müller and Carey Bloomfield rushed to her.

'*Hedi!*' Müller said. Then he saw the tiny dark bloom in her side. 'She's been shot! But how . . .'

'No, no . . .' the goth said weakly. 'Not shot, just the old wound bleeding a little. I'll . . . I'll be OK . . .'

Berger and Pappenheim came running, and drew to a halt when they saw the goth.

'What happened?' Pappenheim asked.

'You're looking at the person who just took on Sharon Wilson, and won.'

Pappenheim stared at the goth. 'You're joking.'

'I don't think Sharon Wilson got the joke,' Müller said.

'Where is she?'

Müller pointed at the river. 'Gone for a last swim. Goth,' Müller went on to Hedi Meyer, 'thank God you're insubordinate. Here. Let's get you home.'

Very gently, he and Pappenheim picked her up, and took her back up the steps.

Berlin-Wilmersdorf, the next day.
Müller and Carey Bloomfield were in his study, dancing to Tom Petty's 'Into the Great Wide Open'.

233

When the chorus came, Carey Bloomfield sang to the chord progression just before the end of the line, 'Ching-ching, chang-chang . . . ching-ching, chang-chang . . . I kind of like those singing guitar chords.'

'So I see.'

'Are you a rebel, Müller? And do you have a clue?'

'Rebel? I do not see myself as one. As for clues, I have many now . . . as you know.'

She held her head back slightly, to look into his eyes. 'Müller?'

'Yes?'

'What do you think possessed the goth to do something as dangerous as that?'

'Payback?'

'I think it's more than that.'

'Oh?'

'Never come between a woman and the man she loves.'

'How many hidden meanings in that statement?'

'More than you can count. Müller?'

'Ye-es . . .'

'When do you tell Pappi about the Hargreaves, and Waldron?'

'That's the next task. Then we can really start taking down the Semper. Now aren't we supposed to be dancing to Tom Petty?'

'We are. Time you kissed me, Müller.'

As he was about to do so, the phone began to ring.

'*Leave* it, damn it! Even if it is Pappi.'

The phone kept ringing.

'Tell you what,' Müller said. 'I'll switch on the machine.' They danced towards the phone, and Müller pressed the button to turn on the answering machine. 'It could be Pappi, or Aunt Isolde. Not many people have this number.'

'I have.'

'I know you have.'

The song came to an end, just as the caller began to speak into the machine.

'Mr Müller,' an American voice began. 'I knew your parents . . . the Hargreaves.'